D0854034

WATSON'S APOLOGY

WATSON'S APOLOGY

Beryl Bainbridge

Duckworth

For JSW, Miss White and CBH

First published in 1984 by
Gerald Duckworth & Co. Ltd.
The Old Piano Factory
43 Gloucester Crescent, London NW1

ISBN 0 7156 1935 7

British Library cataloguing in Publication Data

Bainbridge, Beryl
 Watson's apology
 I. Title
 823'.914 [F]   PR6052.A3195

 ISBN 0-7156-1935-7

Photoset in North Wales by
Derek Doyle & Associates, Mold, Clwyd
Printed and bound in Great Britain by
Unwin Brothers Limited, Old Woking

Contents

Author's Note

This novel is based on a true story. The documents presented have been edited here and there to fit the needs of the narrative, but are otherwise authentic. Almost all the characters are drawn from life, as are the details of the plot. Even the house in St Martin's Road, Stockwell is still standing (though the number has been changed). What has defeated historical inquiry has been the motives of the characters, their conversations and their feelings. These it has been the task of the novelist to supply.

12, New Park Road,
Stockwell,
Surrey.
Wed. December 4th, 1844.

Madam,

I must entreat you to pardon the liberty which I take in addressing you this note. You have known me only from seeing me some years ago at Mrs Curran's in Marlborough Street, when I was attending the College. You may, perhaps, have forgotten me, but I still recollect you. I am now in orders, and head master of the Proprietary School here. When I know that you have received this I should wish to say something more, if you will allow me to write to you a second time. I need not beg of you to favour me with an immediate reply, for I am sure that you will have the kindness and politeness to do so.

I have the honour to be, Madam, with the highest esteem and respect, your very obedient servant, J.S. Watson.

12, New Park Road,
Stockwell.
December 9th.

Madam,

I have to thank you for your obliging letter, which I received this morning. I knew nothing of you when I saw you at Mrs Curran's, but that you were a lady who had lost her fortune. That you have since been doing what you mention I was aware. You were always regarded by me as a lady of great excellence. Had I been able soon after leaving college to establish myself as I wished, I had it in mind to make you a proposal of marriage. It may now be too late. Nor should I, however you may receive this intimation, wish you to consider that I have done so until we have again met. In the meantime, I may give you some little notion how I am situated here. Though I have the title of head master, I cannot say that I have all the emolument which I could desire attendant on it. My income is something more than 300L. a year, but without a house. I may perhaps in time find means of increasing it a little. Boarders, by the condition of my appointment, I am not allowed at present to take; but that is a restriction which I may possibly get removed at length. The neighbourhood of London I like, and there are greater facilities for adding to income near town than in the country. I am of very humble birth, and have been obliged to make my way in the world by my own efforts. I have a few relatives living in an humble station, but none that would interfere with my domestic affairs. This is sufficient for me to say at present. I have to beg your indulgence for having said so much. Whatever you think of this, you will, I am sure, oblige me at once with the straightforward answer of a woman of sense. Believe me to be, Madam, with the most perfect esteem, your very obedient servant, J.S. Watson.

12, New Park Road,
Stockwell.
Dec. 13th.

Madam,

I had the pleasure of receiving your very sensible letter just now. I have only time to write a few lines in reply. As you do not discourage me, I will say that I think it possible that I may cross over to Dublin about Christmas for a few days. I shall have but a fortnight at my disposal, and should not be able to leave this place before tomorrow week. Will you have the kindness to reply on the receipt of this, and say whether, in the event of my coming, I might be allowed to see you where you are now residing? I am certain that I can have but little personal attraction in your eyes, and perhaps you will think that any alteration that may have taken place in my appearance since you last saw me has not been for the better. You do not appear displeased with my prospects, but when I reflect that there is nothing – or very little – but prospect (for I have not been settled here long enough to lay by anything, having received my appointment only last July) I am almost afraid to venture. I am living in apartments, because I cannot afford to take a house, but I cannot but think that, with a person of your (as I judge) staid, quiet and domestic habits, there would be no fear. Believe me to be, Madam, very faithfully and obediently yours, J.S. Watson.

Madam,

I have just received your second (that is, third) letter. Pray write to me as often as you please, without entreating my pardon for doing so. To what I said yesterday I would just add that I write to you as if you were pretty much your own mistress, as at your age and with the travels which you have experienced through the world, it may be expected that you are. I believe that you are residing with a relation, but whether you have any relations in England, especially in London, with whom it would be to any purpose for me to communicate, I have not the least notion. I think it well to say that my mother is alive, and (with a sister) will probably for some time look to me for a little assistance. I have also two brothers in the 'valleys of life', but, having been early separated from my parents and brought up by a grandfather, and put into quite a different track in the world, I maintain but little connection with my relatives except by occasional letters. All that I should deduct from my own income would not be more than 50L. a year, which would still leave, if the school continues to flourish, more than 300L. for a consort and myself. It is a very populous and increasing neighbourhood, and a school of this kind is much needed in it, so that I trust all will go well. They are all at present day boys. My hours of work are from nine till twelve, and from two till five, with one or two half-holidays in the week, and a month of freedom at Midsummer. This Christmas I hoped to get three weeks, but I can get only a fortnight. I do not know whether you have any conception what a proprietary school is, but the management of the funds and so on is in the hands of a committee of proprietors, who have a control over me so far as to see that I do not break the rules. I should conceive that your parents are both dead and that you have no brothers and sisters, or that, if you have any, they are at a distance from you. I have not forgotten the game of draughts, in which you did me the honour of beating me. Believe me to be, very faithfully and obediently yours, John Selby Watson.

Stockwell.
Wednesday.

Dear Madam,

I have just had the pleasure of receiving your letter of Monday. I have written so much in the last note which I sent, but which you had probably not received when you wrote, that I need only, I think, be brief at present. I do not know Dr Connor, nor would it, perhaps, be of any use for me to say anything to him until we have met, after which I may be happy to make his acquaintance. Do not think that you need say much about your family to me, who am of no family. I hope to be in Dublin by Sunday or Monday next, but a fortnight's absence from home is the utmost that I can command. What you say concerning your lodgings makes me believe that you must have much of that independence of spirit which I always supposed you to possess. You have told me that your hand shook, but not why. Trusting that I shall find you well when I have the pleasure of seeing you, I remain most sincerely yours, John Selby Watson.

Friday.

Dear Madam,

As to being angry with you, as your humour is to express it, that, I trust, can never happen. I am very glad that you have written so often. I do not see what purpose it would serve to write to your Aunt, as I said before, with respect to your cousins, until we have seen each other. You say that you have something to communicate to me, personally, more fully than you think proper to write, and it had struck me that in your last letter – to say nothing of what you have expressed before – you speak with much emphasis of having had much to annoy you, and of being of great anxiety of mind. Now I earnestly beg of you, that if you have had anything more particularly than mere labour for a subsistence to trouble you – if anything has happened to you to lie heavy on your mind – if anything has been either done by yourself, or said or done by others, to cause you vexation or throw you into despondency, you will when we meet tell me honestly and fully what it is. It is long since I saw you, certainly more than seven years, and I know not, at least know but imperfectly, how, during that period, your time has been passed. It will be difficult to make me believe that it has been spent other than honourably to yourself, and I should have hoped that the result would have been self-satisfaction and cheerfulness of mind. Forgive me, dear Miss Armstrong, that I write this: you have only to burn it, and give me an answer when I have the happiness of meeting you, for it will be a happiness to me, whatever you say to me, to see once more that dear face which I once so much admired, and which I thought – and think now – far above anything I had or have any personal pretensions to aspire. I have no right, in the present stage of our acquaintance, to write thus freely to you, but you must pardon me. I know something of the world, and I know what unpleasant things you, as you have been living, may have been exposed to, but I again say to you that I entreat you not to conceal anything from me, but to tell me anything which you have to tell as freely and as fully as you would tell the friend in whom you most trust either of your own sex or the opposite. Of anything which you may have to tell you will find me a most lenient judge, for I have too many faults of my own not to be an easy censor of those of others. I said that I admired you, yet I have been unfaithful to your image in my memory. I will tell you when we see each other. This will be another thing which you will have to forgive. 'From the sublime to the ridiculous there is but one step.' A fool of a hairdresser has cut my hair too short. You must guess why I care about this. Believe me that all the liberties which I have taken in writing thus to you have been taken with the warmest regard to yourself, a regard which, I hope, will never be diminished, but that I shall still be always yours sincerely, J.S.W. 'Will you accept my second offer, dearest? With love. This riband in exchange for the other. J.

Fraser produced them, although what he hoped to gain by it was difficult to understand. The letters had been posted almost thirty years before, and the sentiments expressed in them were couched in such stilted prose, that, if the circumstances had been different they would surely have provoked laughter. When they were handed up, a length of threadbare ribbon, no thicker than a bootlace, dropped unnoticed to the floor and was trodden underfoot. Fraser said the letters had been found wrapped in a satin gown much attacked by the mildew.

11

PART 1

Mrs Cronin was about to enter the area door of Mrs Gallagher's boarding house in Great Britain Street when she stepped back, alarmed at the smell of smoke. Recently widowed and the absentee mother of a twelve-month-old boy, she had a nose for disaster. 'Is the house on fire?' she asked.

Mrs Gallagher assured her that it was in her imagination and coaxed her into the kitchen.

'Don't you sniff it?' persisted Mrs Cronin.

Mrs Gallagher held a candle in a jam pot. Before the arrival of her visitor she had been about to go upstairs with another letter for Miss Armstrong. 'It's probably the wax,' she said, 'or the lamp. Maybe it's the chimney. It needs sweeping but I'm not up to the bother.' She hesitated, holding the candle in one hand and the letter in the other. It was no use asking her friend to sit down. Mrs Cronin's state of mind kept her perambulating round and round the room like a dog who had lost his place at the hearth. 'I'm away to the first floor,' she said. 'I won't be a moment.'

'Don't leave me,' cried Mrs Cronin.

Death had snatched her husband from her so abruptly that it was not surprising she still quivered from the shock. Mr Cronin had been sitting in his chair by the door, pulling on his boots. Only minutes before he had taken his watch from his vest pocket to place to the ear of his infant son. The ticking of the watch had sent the baby into a peaceful sleep. Between Mrs Cronin's turning round to stab the coals into a blaze and young Henry's drawing his next breath, the life had gone out of the man. She had thought at first he was codding her – because of his stooping position, thighs pressed against his corpulent stomach, he had not toppled forward on to the floor but had remained stuck in his chair, forever pulling on an old boot. His watch was still ticking but his heart was not. Mrs Cronin had sent the child to lodge with his maternal grandmother in Connemara. She missed him sorely but she wouldn't have known a second's peace if he had stayed in the city.

Death could have returned at a change in the wind and lifted him while her back was turned.

'You'd best come upstairs with me,' said Mrs Gallagher. Even now, Mrs Cronin's eyelids were fluttering to stop the tears from falling.

In the hallway the smell of smoke was more pronounced than ever.

'Am I going out of my mind?' appealed Mrs Cronin. 'There's something charred in the house.'

Reluctantly Mrs Gallagher told her that it was probably on account of her new turkey runner, or her new blinds in the dining-room. 'Well, almost new,' she conceded. 'I've Mr O'Connell to thank for them'

All over Dublin there were windows open to let out the smell of salvaged goods. The delight of O'Connell's supporters on hearing of his release from prison had led to an excess of zeal in the lighting of bonfires. Mrs Gallagher's blinds and her carpet runner, greatly reduced in cost, had come from a house in Fermoy inadvertently burnt down during the celebrations. 'The blinds is only scorched in the creases,' she said. 'And the carpet hardly singed.'

She took her visitor into the dining-room to see for herself. Being the third Saturday in the month it was the servant girl's afternoon off and the fire was not laid. The room, lit by that solitary candle, was as mysterious as a cathedral.

'Mrs McElroy from further down the street,' said Mrs Gallagher, 'purchased a sofa from the very same house. It came on a barge to the Quays. Don't you admire my blinds?'

Mrs Cronin held the edge of her black shawl to her nose and nodded. She was distracted by other voices, other murmurings. Time will heal me, she thought, pressing herself against the sideboard and staring fixedly at the open door.

'Her man trundled it home on a cart,' Mrs Gallagher said. 'When he fetched it inside, its back was snapped from the unloading.' She was disconcerted by her friend's expression and by the dilapidated tilt of her bonnet. The brim was buckled, as if Mrs Cronin had sat on it before wearing it.

Mrs Cronin was studying a spot midway between the floor and the table. Someone or something engaged her attention. Mrs Gallagher was not an imaginative woman but she too looked at that black shadow in the angle of the dining-room door, half expecting to see the departed Mr Cronin in his chair, his head bent down and his foot perked up, his two hands pulling, pulling.

'Don't you hear it,' whispered Mrs Cronin, for now she listened to the unmistakable sound of sobbing. She started forward in terror, convinced it was her child far away in Connemara. That instant there came a muffled thud from overhead. The lamp above the table leapt on its chain.

'It's only Miss Olivia,' said Mrs Gallagher. 'She's always pitching over the poor furniture.'

'Is it a fight?' asked Mrs Cronin, as a second bump followed the first and the lamp swung back and forth.

'She's not a married woman,' Mrs Gallagher said. 'She lives with her sister.' She stared upward and murmured, 'They've both come down in the world.'

Mrs Cronin thought it might not be long, judging from the commotion, before they came down even further. It was too dark to tell whether the plaster was flaking off the ceiling.

'They were born into wealth,' said Mrs Gallagher. 'Then they were reduced. A butcher in Dawson Street told me as much. They continue to dwindle. Only last month they gave up the back room which they had for sleeping in. While they had the use of it Miss Olivia did nothing but complain. She said the window frames were rotten and the walls was damp. Life, she told me, was nothing but chilblains and bronchitis and the room would be the death of her.'

'I have to get out,' Mrs Cronin admitted. 'Left indoors I'd go mad.' Mrs Gallagher agreed, though for days on end she never felt the need of stepping further than the back yard. She confided that last Sunday Miss Anne hadn't gone to church and that Miss Olivia had made out it was because of her health.

'Is she delicate then?' asked Mrs Cronin.

'Her boots is worn through,' said Mrs Gallagher. From the same butcher in Dawson Street she had learnt that Miss Olivia, some years previously, had been dismissed from a situation in Blackrock, but her informant hadn't been able to get his mind to the details. She herself knew only that Miss Anne was the more forthcoming of the two and that the older woman had a stingey disposition. When the boy carried the coals up of a morning didn't she make him stand there while she counted the lumps in the scuttle?

'That'll be Miss Anne crying,' she told her visitor. 'She's the sensitive one.' She had once had an extraordinary conversation with the younger Miss Armstrong. They had met in the hall when Miss Anne was coming out of the dining-room after her tea. 'Mrs Gallagher,' Miss Anne had asked, 'did you know that in winter in Upper Sackville Street, in the extreme depths of winter, the trees appear to be in leaf?' 'Well now, I did not,' Mrs Gallagher replied. 'The trees appear to be in bloom,' Miss Anne had explained, 'because the wag tails perch so thickly on the branches.' Just then Miss Olivia had come out of the dining-room and Miss Anne had hurried off up the stairs.

'Is the other one blind?' Mrs Cronin demanded, wondering at the continuing thuds and bumps.

'She's a clumsy woman,' said Mrs Gallagher. 'Miss Anne has all the lightness. Once she wrote to a solicitor on my behalf, on account of some monies that my brother was holding back from me.'

'I have two brothers surviving,' Mrs Cronin told her. 'They are both good to me. But for them I'd be taking in washing.'

'I didn't receive any reply,' Mrs Gallagher said. 'But it was civil of her to go to the trouble.' Remembering the letter she still held, she went out into the hall.

'It might be best not to disturb them,' said Mrs Cronin anxiously, climbing the narrow stairs in pursuit. 'Could it not wait?'

Mrs Gallagher was inclined to agree, but she was in a quandary. If she left the letter on the landing table it could be stolen. She suspected the Customs clerk of being light-fingered, yet she couldn't prove it. Things had gone missing before now. Equally it would be unpleasant if Miss Olivia answered the door, especially if she was in the middle of a tantrum. She'd be bound to ask why the letter hadn't been delivered earlier.

'You take it,' she said, turning round to give the letter to Mrs Cronin.

But her visitor, distressed by that muffled weeping, had fled back to the head of the stairs and now crouched there in the dark, her hand trembling as she clutched the banister rail. Somebody's heart was breaking. It's not my heart, she thought, for that is already broke.

Mrs Gallagher was forced to knock half a dozen times before the door opened. Mrs Cronin heard a voice ask 'Who is it?', and then, as though the speaker had been expecting someone else, 'Oh, it's only Mrs Gallagher.' Mrs Cronin pushed back her ruined bonnet and peeked through the rails. For an instant she glimpsed the head and shoulders of a woman who wore a mob-cap and whose false front of curls had in some fashion come unstuck and now hung at an angle over one eye. On her cheek was a small patch of colour, vivid enough to be noticeable in the candle light, like a dab of rouge or a birth mark.

*   *   *

When the lamp was lit and the coals had caught, the letter could be seen propped on the mantelpiece. Olivia, hearing that first knock at the door, had run to the recess in the corner and flung herself across the double bed once used by Henry Boxer in Upper Sackville Street. She had continued to cry while Anne attended to the fire, gulping and sobbing in time to the pumping of the bellows. She was now quiet, apparently exhausted.

Anne sat at the table and waited. She wanted to be quite sure that her sister slept. She wouldn't give Olivia the satisfaction of seeing her open the letter. Nor would she tidy the room; Mother's chair had been pitched over at the window and the carpet was scuffed up round the leg of the sofa. As to that old blue dress which had caused such trouble and which lay in a bedraggled heap on the linoleum, its torn hem shifting in the ferocious draught from the window, for all she cared it could stay there until Kingdom Come.

It was a shabby room. The carpet was so worn that its pattern had faded altogether; there was nothing of any decorative value in sight save for a china cup and saucer displayed on the mantel-shelf, and a large oyster shell encrusted with coral which leant against it. The cup had been filled to the brim with rose petals plucked long ago in the gardens of Inchicore, until, in a gloomy fit Anne had scattered them across the floor, where they had drifted for some days, splintering underfoot, before being swept beneath the carpet. Later, restored to a more cheerful state of mind, she had assured Olivia that it was not everyone who could boast of walking on a bed of roses. Olivia had looked as severe as ever. Often she too seemed so desiccated by age that a smile might have broken her into little pieces.

There was nowhere to hide. If Anne wanted to avoid her sister she sat at the table with her back to her, or else padded up and down the landing, fearful of encountering the emaciated clerk

17

from the Customs Office. A balcony, fronted with ornamental railings, ran the length of the double windows, but it was condemned as unsafe. Olivia had dryly remarked that this was a blessing, for had it been otherwise, Anne, in one of her moods, might have struggled out on to it and hurled herself into the street below. Escape, for either of them, was out of the question. Even in sleep they were flung together; their mattress sagged in the middle and the slightest shift in balance sent them rolling downhill like logs to the river. Existing as they did in such dreary proximity, Anne thought it hardly surprising that they were perpetually at war.

Their most recent quarrel had started because earlier she had asked Olivia if she might light the lamp – she had been trying to read – and Olivia had said she couldn't. It wasn't Olivia's refusal that had enraged her, but her own cowardice in seeking permission. She had told herself that if she was not careful she would soon become one of those people who had served their purpose. After all, it had been her wages that had kept the wolf from the door when Olivia had limped home, apparently consumptive, from the Knoxes in Dungannon, and again, three years later, when she had been sent packing, this time with a mysterious inflammation of the joints, from the Magee household at Blackrock. As to the frugal allowance sent to them each quarter by their brother Edwin, why that was intended for them both and Olivia had no God-given right to decide on how it should be used. And then to make matters worse, she had suddenly noticed exactly what dress it was that Olivia clumsily sewed as she crouched on Mother's chair at the window. It was a dress Anne had worn eight years before, in summer-time, when in the habit of visiting Mrs Curran. She had told Olivia that she was wasting her energies, mending a dress that would never be used again. In the darkening room the silk had shimmered like water. Olivia had retorted that it was her energies that were being dissipated and that, unlike Anne, she couldn't bear to be idle.

If the day had been brighter or the fire banked more cheerfully in the grate, Anne might have let the matter rest there – the satisfaction to be gained from upsetting Olivia's feelings wasn't often worth the injury to her own. But she had found herself trembling, both from the cold and from the consequences of those lost afternoons at Mrs Curran's. She drew Olivia's attention to the weather, the threat of snow in the air, the unsuitability of the mildewed garment upon which so much time was being uselessly squandered. She debated whether Olivia's notoriously weak constitution could stand such frenzied activity with a needle and thread, and had implied that it would be less expensive, all things considered, if Olivia lay flat and conserved herself. More than once she spat out the word 'stupid'.

'It may be,' she had said cruelly, 'that I shall go to England. We have never got on.' Going even further she suggested that, left alone, Olivia might have to seek cheaper accommodation on the second floor. Olivia had a dread, architecturally speaking, of moving up in the world. She feared she would end her days in some attic, listening to the sound of rainwater dripping into buckets as the life drained out of her.

For a time, addressing the pattern of leaves and flowers above the picture rail, Anne had felt justified in ranting as she did. If Olivia hadn't interfered with the lighting of the lamp she would have been harmlessly immersed in her book. Then, in the middle of stressing that only the previous month various malfunctions of Olivia's ailing body had cost them several shillings in patent medicines, she became uneasy. Olivia, save for a firmer set to her naturally determined jaw, gave no outward indication that she listened. And yet Anne had known her indifference was a sham. Inwardly Olivia was weeping.

Anne had sat imprisoned in her chair, hardly able to breathe. She felt it was disgusting to live in such a way, neither intimidated nor wholly in control. At last, she had defiantly shouted her intention of lighting the lamp. Still, she remained at the table for quite five minutes until the room grew completely dark. The fire appeared to have gone out. Finally she stood, and approaching Olivia, tapped her on the shoulder. 'Please,' she had said.

'Don't touch me,' Olivia moaned.

'Please,' Anne said again, but she hadn't been able to think of the right words.

'I will not be bullied,' Olivia had cried. Then, of course, she had dragged up Blackrock and County Cork, as though there was some similarity in what had happened in either place. The injustice of it had struck Anne like a blow. The incident concerning the Ferguson child had been an isolated one, and she detested being reminded of it. When she had hit him he had heaved that small involuntary sigh, his lashes already beaded with tears, his mouth foolishly grinning. There were those in her profession who regarded brutality as commonplace. At Miss Pyke's Academy she had seen a young girl boxed about the ears until she fell down in a faint, and another time she had seen a child punched so savagely in the face that her nose had burst like a plum. Both occasions had sickened her, not least because she had kept silent. It wasn't as if she had disliked the boy in Cork. She had never told his father that it was he who had cracked the glass in the summer-house, or that he had let the pig out of its pen and into the vegetable garden. They had gone fishing together on the lake, sitting at opposite ends of a little, motionless boat.

Was it any wonder that she had lost her temper with Olivia? How dare her sister mention Cork in the same breath as Blackrock. Just thinking of it incensed her so much that she rose from the table and went to the recess, half inclined to start up the argument all over again. For two pins she would shake Olivia until an apology rattled in her throat. But Olivia was lying on her back with her mouth open, a pathetic sight and dead to the world. When Anne pulled the coverlet over her she grasped at it with both fists and muttered incoherently, but she didn't waken.

Anne returned to the table and looked at the envelope on the mantelpiece. She was afraid to open it. When she had received Mr Watson's first letter she had told herself that she must be on her guard. The present was so drab and the future so bleak that it would be natural for her to confuse gratitude with love. At all costs she would keep her imagination in check. She knew it was useless to try to stop love except in its very early stages – if she had stepped back from Mr Roche in time she would have avoided unhappiness. Even so, it was already too late. It wasn't in her nature to be guarded and her imagination had always run away with her. Mr Watson's melancholy allusion to Marlborough Street had brought the past about her ears, and instantly she had been affected. In those far-off, sunny days how simple it had been to deceive, to seem remote and unaffected in public. Through that crowded drawing room in Marlborough Street she had walked as though there were nobody in the world but herself. She had always gone there on foot and the hem of her gown had trailed brick dust up the stairs.

How ridiculous it was, how sad, that while she had eyes only for Mr Roche, some unknown boy, standing at the perimeter of that sun-filled room, had been gazing in her direction, willing her to look at him.

Olivia had thought the conversation too free at Mrs Curran's, and the company too mixed. She had spoken, as usual, out of ignorance, for she had never gone there, which was just as well because otherwise she might have noticed Anne's moonstruck expression when looking at Mr Roche, and would have lost no time in pointing out that he was barely eighteen whereas Anne herself was galloping towards thirty. She would have approached Anne's feelings for the young man with the subtlety of a ferret entering a rabbit hole and, having flushed them to the surface, ripped them to pieces.

Mr Watson had not referred to Mr Roche in his correspondence, nor to Mrs Strafford or to those pushy Hannahan girls with their salmon-pink cheeks. Neither had he explained how he had come to be at Mrs Curran's. To be truthful, save for that first introductory note, his letters had proved something of a disappointment. Though frank about prospects and income, and touchingly quaint in describing members of his family as dwelling in the *valleys of life* (she had replied that she had once held a situation in Switzerland and henceforth thought of his brothers as labouring in the fields at the foot of snow-capped mountains), he had failed to bring himself to life. She had no clear picture of the man behind the words; and it wasn't surprising, for she was convinced that most of his words had been borrowed from a handbook on an approved method of letter writing. No matter – she would use him to free herself. She had nothing to lose – the roof had fallen in on her and it was unlikely that anyone, after him, would come along to sift the wreckage and see if she still lived. If she had to cheat, she would do so. She had never been to Switzerland, but in inventing her past she was constructing her future. A single blunder, she warned herself, could ruin her chances. And yet, perversely, when it actually came to putting her thoughts on paper, she had thrown caution out of the window. She had written to him as if she had known him for years, telling him of the poverty of her existence and the vexations she endured, day after dreadful day, through being forced to live, cheek by jowl, among people who were inferior to her in intellect and imagination. She had hinted at humiliations and spoke of the immense gulf that separated her from the other occupants of the lodging house. *Do not think that I am merely vain. I am what I am, and if I am clever, which I judge myself to be, it is because I have had an education – though there are some who would consider that a disadvantage in a woman.*

She was not a fool. Reading between the lines it was obvious that a wife, or 'consort' as he chose to put it, was a necessity to a man in his position. Three-hundred-a-year was hardly a fortune but with careful management should be sufficient to live comfortably on, and afford the rental of a good-sized house, large enough to accommodate boarders and so increase income. Perhaps space could be found for a schoolroom of sorts. She herself might advertise for pupils: she could teach a little French and geography. At the back, in the small garden, she would plant lobelias, hyacinths and foxgloves – it was a pity roses were the wrong colour – and she would supervise the laying of a path made out of stepping stones, just wide enough for two, down which they would hop in summertime, as if leaping from one ice-floe to another, when the tea things had been cleared away. Some people thought of foxgloves as weeds, but she had a fondness for them. Country folk called them Virgin's Finger. What harm did it do to daydream? In that dappled hour between late afternoon and dusk, the head master would thrust his hand in hers and marvel at the sky-blue flowers grown entirely by her own efforts. *I am one of those few who think it a torment to be idle. I am well used to making provision for myself and am capable of much energy.*

The more freely she wrote, though she was sensible enough to omit any reference to either houses or gardens, the more cautiously Mr Watson replied. Then, on Wednesday, without comment, he had enclosed a snowdrop in the fold of his letter. The following day she sent him a snippet of scarlet ribbon filched from Olivia's work-box.

Sometimes she wondered whether she hadn't conjured him up out of thin air, out of that fatal imagination of which she so often boasted. Mr Watson had twice written that he intended coming to Dublin expressly to visit her, yet she hardly believed him. Surely it was impossible. Where would they meet? In the Botanic Garden – it was shut at this time of the year. In the Phoenix Park – in the snow, in her darned stockings and her boots that let in the wet? She couldn't bear to receive him here, in one room at the wrong end of Great Britain Street, with a gale whipping through the windows, and Olivia, whom she had never mentioned, simpering on the sofa, a duster tied about her head because of earache, gabbling of torch-lit suppers and six horses with long tails in the stables of Inchicore House.

Besides, if they met out of doors, how would they know each

other? She would be forced to act like a low woman, eyeing each man as he approached, and he could pass her by without a glance. He might take her for somebody's mother. The average age of a student of the College was nineteen years or thereabouts, and a woman aged faster than a man, particularly if life had been cruel to her. J.S. Watson would stride impatiently round and round the oblong of the artificial lake, waiting hopelessly for a young woman who had once worn a blue silk dress, while she, unrecognised, the deer bounding ahead of her through the white park, would flee in her sodden boots towards the bustle of the Chapelizod Road. *I have an independence of mind and a sensitivity of temperament that have not always worked in my favour. The lift of an eyebrow, the droop of a mouth, plainly indicating lack of imagination, can plunge me into the depths of despair.*

If he did come to Dublin and she was forced to meet him, what would she wear? She had two pairs of stockings, one top coat patched on the shoulder, a grey dress that had seen brighter days and a bonnet with frayed ribbons. She wondered for the umpteenth time whether she should risk going to see her Aunt Lawson. Surely, it was her aunt's duty to advise her. But then, there had been those other occasions on which advice had been sought, and ignored. And if she unburdened herself prematurely and it all came to nothing, she would look a fool.

At that moment Olivia whimpered and sat upright in the bed. Her hair was mussed up and her cap hung askew. It seemed to Anne that she looked no different from the way she had looked as a girl, when, seated on a straw-plaited stool she had tugged the curling rags from her hair and wept with self-inflicted pain. The simplest of tasks had always been beyond her. As she watched, Olivia closed her eyes and fell back again. Already asleep, she plucked at the neck band of her dress as though she was choking.

What will become of her, thought Anne. She is incapable of looking after herself. Then, almost immediately, she thought, whatever will become of me? She took the letter from the mantelpiece and tore open the envelope. A length of dark blue ribbon spilled on to the tablecloth.

The letter was long and the handwriting cramped and difficult to read. Mr Watson had a habit of underlining certain words as if they were significant. He asked her to conceal nothing from him and spoke of that dear face which he had once so admired. He was worried because some dolt of a barber had snipped his hair too short. Jealousy pierced her when she read that he had been unfaithful to her image in his memory. She studied his post-script and grew calmer. *Dearest ... with love ... dearest ... dearest.* She fingered the scrap of dark ribbon and tears came into her eyes. How sweet it was to be loved! At the same time, she knew that the happiness she felt was against all the rules of common-sense – she hadn't the least notion who J.S. Watson was. For a week now, she had struggled to remember each and every one of the young gentlemen of the College who had called on Mrs Curran. Except for a medical student with a complexion scarred from the small-pox, and a Frenchman who had sent her an impudent note, none of them came to mind. They were all lost, forgotten, and though she had positioned herself at the table in front of an imaginary draughts board and stared at the empty chair opposite, it was always Mr Roche she saw, always eighteen years old, his cuffs childishly stained with ink and a little burst blood vessel showing at the corner of his eye.

* * *

John Selby Watson disembarked at Kingstown Harbour on the 23rd December. He would have called on Anne Armstrong the following day if Quin hadn't talked him out of it.

'At this time of the year,' Quin advised, 'she'll have family obligations to consider. It would be best to wait a few days.'

'She has no family,' said Watson.

Quin reminded him that there had been some mention of an aunt residing in Dublin who had daughters living in England. Watson reluctantly agreed that it was possible they had crossed over for the holiday and that Miss Armstrong was visiting them. Perhaps they were discussing him. He sent her a note instead, informing her of his arrival, and begging to be allowed to call on her at her earliest convenience. At this moment he didn't think he was in love with her, but then neither did he love anybody else.

He heard nothing from her for four days, during which time he became so uneasy that he imagined he was hopelessly in love with her and could not believe, would not believe, that he would ever hear from her again.

'From what you have told me,' Quin said, 'it hardly seems likely.' Only ten days before, Watson had written to him expressing alarm at the speed with which Anne Armstrong had replied to his initial enquiry. Letters were arriving by every post. She had hinted that he should make himself known to a Dr Connor, a past acquaintance of her dead mother, presumably to lash him to the mast in regard to his future intentions. Quin had urged him to parry the request: he had said he would be unwise to commit himself either on paper or by word of mouth.

'Probably Miss Armstrong has gone into the country,' he said. His own wife, recovering from a bout of the shingles, was staying with an uncle in Tuam.

'There would be no point in it,' said Watson. 'She is alone in the world.'

Quin thought this an exaggerated statement, on all counts. Wasn't everyone in Ireland related to someone else? Instructed by Watson and helped by the curate of St Thomas's Church, it was he who had discovered Miss Armstrong's address. He happened to know that an agent for guano manure, by the name of Edward Armstrong, lived in the very same street in which she lodged. There was also a John Armstrong Esq. settled in a fine big house in Dawson Street. Doubtless there was some connection. As it was obvious that Watson was determined to think of Anne Armstrong as an orphan, in spite of the fact that the lady was approaching forty years of age, he kept his thoughts to himself. 'A letter will come soon enough,' he said. 'Depend upon it.' He suggested that Watson should visit old friends while he had the opportunity.

'I have few friends,' said Watson. 'And none that I wish to see at this crucial time.'

He was speaking the truth. He hardly thought of anyone as his friend, although he was aware that several people, Mandell for one, considered him as *their* friend. In England, there was the Revd Mr Harcourt of Eltham, and Mr and Mrs Crawley of Maidstone who had looked after him when he had been attacked and robbed on the common by marines, but all three were elderly and more like relations than agreeable companions. He had known them for years, ever since he had been taken on as an assistant teacher at Charles Burney's school in Greenwich. Mrs Crawley had fed him and washed his shirts and done the things he supposed a mother did for a son. The Revd Mr Harcourt had lent him books and warned him not to gesture so flamboyantly when he talked.

At Trinity College he had been too busy studying to bother whether he was popular or not. He was determined to make something of himself, to get on in the world. He was already thirty years old and he hadn't the time to waste on fooling about under the trees in Phoenix Park arguing politics, or to run round St Stephen's Green after midnight in nothing but his shirt. He was as poor as a man from Connaught and he wasn't going to squander his money on excursions into the mountains or afternoons at the theatre – he hadn't the slightest idea who had persuaded him to call at Mrs Curran's in Marlborough Street. He did remember that Quin had taken him to visit Isaac Butt, editor of the Dublin University Magazine, at his rented house in Eccles Street, but that was stimulating and the right sort of people frequented the place. Ferguson went there, and Connor, and Lever had been known to sleep on the sofa when he was in town. In the back room was an organ said to have belonged to Handel. Butt was always in debt and the instrument was hidden under an old curtain lest the bailiffs suddenly arrive. Butt was a great man for parlour tricks – Quin said he had attempted to levitate Connor and had actually raised him as high as the mantel-shelf, only it necessitated the rest of the company singing hymns and they had been too drunk to keep it up. Connor had fallen and hit his head on a footstool. Once, Watson had gone there without Quin. Butt was out, and Mangan, the poet, was sitting there with an old woman who did nothing but belch. Mangan wore a flax-coloured wig and green spectacles. His false teeth were said to be borrowed from his sister. Caught between the clacking and the belching, Watson had found himself unable to utter a word.

Deep down, he did not even think of Quin as his friend. Last August Quin had been there to cheer him on when he had come over to receive his Master's degree, and that was friendly of him, as was the hospitality he unfailingly showed, but if feelings entered into such an arrangement then they were all on Quin's side. For his own part, years passed and he never gave Quin a thought.

'Do you suppose,' he asked Quin worriedly, 'that Miss Armstrong is ill, or that she's been advised against me?' Days were passing and nothing was settled. Soon he would have to return to England for the start of the Easter Term. He couldn't bear the waiting, the inactivity. Quin said he supposed neither. He tried to persuade Watson to go out with him, but he wouldn't budge, even when told that Duffy, the bookseller at the Quays, had come into possession of some rare editions previously in Lord Allen's library at Stillorgan.

26

'A letter might come when I was out,' he said. 'I have to be here.'

Nor did he perk up when Quin, hoping to divert him, attempted to repeat the anecdote concerning the legal wit, John Philpot Curran, who, pleading before his friend Yelverton to a jury of illiterate shopkeepers, had quoted two lines in Latin purporting to have come from the *Phantasmagoria* of Hesiod, a non-existent work. 'Yes, yes,' said Watson wearily. 'It was all Greek to the jury.'

It was true that he had heard the story many times before, but then never before had he failed to be amused by it. Perhaps, thought Quin, he was unpleasantly reminded of the reception of his own work, *Geology – A Poem in Seven Books*, recently published by Pickering. The *Athenaeum* had given it a scathing review. 'A didactic poem in blank verse, written as we learn from the dedication to Lyell, on the geological principles which he has so ably established and illustrated. The idea is absurd – as there is no poetry, and scarcely an attempt at poetic diction in the whole work.' The book had been printed at Watson's own expense, and Lyell, the recipient of a free copy, had so far ignored it.

There was no further talk of Miss Armstrong between the two men. When Watson was not at the dinner table – Quin noted that his appetite was unimpaired – he sat by the fire in the front room, occasionally jumping up when he fancied he heard a knock at the hall door, and now and then poking the coals so absent-mindedly that his host was afraid he would scatter them across the hearthrug and set the house ablaze.

In repose, Watson's expression was serious, even severe, but when animated by argument or enthusiasm his features reflected his thoughts to a startling degree. The most private of men, he made an exhibition of himself. Quin had never forgotten seeing him on the steps of Trinity Library, thrashing out some theological point with his tutor. His grimaces – the exaggerated lifting of his eyebrows, the rolling of his prominent eyes, above all the peculiar way in which he stood on one leg like a stork in a swamp – had caused a crowd to gather. Conversely, when depressed, as he now was, his face was stamped with such savage gloom and his whole demeanour so expressive of despair that those who didn't know him could be excused for thinking he was mad. Fortunately Quin was used to him. They had met during the Hilary Term of '36 when both had contributed some verses to the Dublin University Magazine. He was neither amazed nor offended by the behaviour of his guest.

None the less he was relieved when a letter finally arrived from

Miss Armstrong. She wrote that she was unable to receive Mr Watson at her lodgings, *for reasons which I do not have to put into words*, and inquired whether there was a Mrs Quin residing at Clare Street. If this was indeed the case, as she was led to believe it might be, was it possible that Mrs Quin might allow them to renew their acquaintance *in the surroundings of a more peaceful establishment?* She would not dream of making such a request, she wrote, if circumstances were not against her. Tomorrow would be a suitable time, morning or afternoon.

No sooner had the note been delivered than Mrs Quin, senior, happened to call on her son with a gift of preserved fruit. Urged on by Watson, who was in a state of excitement, Quin told her of the dilemma in which they found themselves. Mrs Quin was intrigued and said she would come the following day to assist in welcoming Miss Armstrong. 'Cissie's children are dear little things,' she said, 'but they climb over me as if I were a boulder. I shall be glad to be out of the house.'

Watson thanked her so profusely and shook her hand so often, that later, when he had gone to his room to read over his letter in privacy, she told her son she felt exhausted. 'Is his leg damaged?' she asked.

'Both legs are sound,' said Quin. 'It's a mannerism he has. Having made his own way in the world he is not always easy in company. But he is a good man.'

'I feel it,' said Mrs Quin and added, 'He doesn't seem to have learnt to hold anything back.'

'He is certainly very emphatic,' Quin agreed.

His mother secretly thought that 'strange' might be a more descriptive word; yet, in spite of Mr Watson's disconcerting habit of cracking his knuckles during conversation, she couldn't help knowing there was something compelling about him. Through no fault of his own, as she afterwards confided to her daughter-in-law, he inspired affection.

Watson went to bed early that evening. He had meant to scribble a few lines to Mandell and Hardy, but he couldn't settle to it.

Before he had left for Euston Square, Mandell, accompanied by the School Secretary, Henry Grey, had knocked at his door to wish him well. 'If it wasn't for the holidays,' Mandell had said, 'Hardy would be here too. I'm sure of it.' Watson had felt bemused by the evident good will flowing in his direction. He had even allowed Grey to shake him by the hand, though he didn't care for the man and disliked the idea of his being party to the more private details of his life. Apart from Quin, whose help had been essential in locating Anne Armstrong, he hadn't intended anyone to know of his future plans. Once too often, over breakfast, he had brought up the question of marriage, in a roundabout way, and then, of course, the letters had begun to arrive almost daily from Ireland. Mandell had put two and two together, and next Hardy had been consulted, and soon every master at the school was giving his opinion on the subject, asked or not. He was surprised at how little he minded.

Mandell had offered to go with him to the station. 'It would give me pleasure,' he said, 'to see you safely aboard the train.' He had fluttered his fingers in the air as though waving a handkerchief. Watson had refused his offer, perhaps churlishly, but it was not yet five in the morning, and bitterly cold, and he was sure that Mandell, who took the Modern class, didn't possess an overcoat. When they left he had shut the door so firmly on them that the fox terrier in the cellar had woken and set up a howl.

Why, he asked himself, as he undressed for bed, did he concern himself with Mandell at such a time. No doubt Tulley, the drill sergeant, disturbed by the barking of the dog, had come roaring out in his nightshirt to complain of the noise, but it was of little importance. He would write to both Mandell and young Hardy when he was in a less nervous frame of mind. Curiously, though he spoke her name out loud, several times, he could not think of Anne Armstrong.

Once in bed he found it difficult to sleep. It wasn't unusual for him, and he took up a volume of Bishop Warburton's letters to his lackey Hurd which lay on the bedside table. No sooner had he begun to read than his mind wandered. At first he was thinking about his hair – he was still able to pick out various words on the page – and the dismay he had felt at the barber's shop when he saw what quantities of it lay sheared on the towel about his shoulders, and then he fell to worrying about his teeth. Since childhood he had suffered from toothache: it would be a catastrophe if they played up when he saw Miss Armstrong. Pain in the mouth could be guaranteed to swamp every noble feeling known to man.

He was lying there, tugging at a lock of his hair to make sure it concealed the scar on his temple, one thought following another, when quite suddenly a memory which he had believed buried forever bobbed abruptly to the surface.

29

He was in a wood, in Dartford, with boys older than himself. One of them led him by the hand. He had a stalk of wheat between his teeth. There were midges spiralling above his head and the trees were so thickly in leaf that the sky was blotted out. He was afraid and dragged behind, and every few steps the boy jerked at his hand, forcing him to trot. A spider's web broke against his face. He clawed the strands from his cheek and felt something scuttle through the roots of his hair. If he had not been gripped so tightly he would have screamed and pulled away. As if in a nightmare, he jolted beneath the sticky trees, torn at by brambles. Presently they came to a clearing in which a solitary pheasant strutted in sunshine; its legs were the colour of marigolds and there was a little tuft of moss caught in its beak. The boys halted and he stopped too, though he was no longer held, his fist pressed to the stitch in his side. The bird continued to strut and peck. Reared by the gamekeeper, it was as tame as a house cat. The biggest boy – he had a bald patch on his scalp from the ringworm – threw a handful of peas on to the ground. Against the grass they were scarcely visible. Each pea was threaded onto a short length of coarse hair docked from the tail of a pony and coated with wax to make it stiff. The pheasant dipped its neck and gobbled at the undergrowth. All at once it flew straight up in the air, wings beating, and then plummetted downwards, and rose, and flopped again like a bundle of rags, until, spent and earthbound, it began to stagger round and round the clearing, neck stretched out as if drawn on a string, feathers flashing emerald-green in the sunlight, tail raking the grass. A man's voice was heard calling in the distance. Closer, a second voice replied. As if blown apart by the wind, the boys scattered and ran.

Watson sat upright in the bed. He could hear the hiss of the gas as it flared in the mantel on the wall behind him. For the life of him he couldn't turn his head. The recollection of that August day was so vivid – the sense of place, the sense of fright – that he actually felt an obstruction in his throat.

* * *

Watson had ordered a carriage to be sent for Miss Armstrong. There was some muddle over the time and she was fetched an hour earlier than expected – Mrs Quin had not yet come and Quin was upstairs. It was just as well perhaps, for otherwise Anne might have mistaken Quin for Watson.

He was standing with his back to her, looking down at the fire, when she was shown into the room. The width of his shoulders made him appear shorter than he was. Above his head hung a painting of a ship going down in mountainous seas. When he turned round from the fire she thought he was a shade pompous, a shade dandified. He was also a complete stranger.

She knew that her first impression of him was important. Soon, feeling and familiarity would alter her perception of him. Never again, after today, would she see him as he was.

He was older, stouter than she had imagined, and he had a snub nose. His hair was a gingery colour. For such a powerfully built man he had surprisingly small hands and feet. Though he was clothed entirely in black, save for the white stock at his neck, he looked more like a prize fighter than a schoolmaster.

She herself had dressed deliberately in dark grey. It was in fact her only dress, but if a whole wardrobe had been at her disposal she would have chosen no other. She had felt instinctively that Watson wouldn't be the sort of man to notice what she wore, unless it was garish enough to be intrusive and then he would think it vulgar.

Watson, for one brief moment, saw an insignificant little woman standing there with a handbag dangling from her wrist. Then he moved forward to greet her and took her hand in his, and she looked at him without smiling. Perhaps she was fuller in the face than he remembered, and bulkier in figure, but her eyes were unchanged and when she spoke he recognised that same husky intonation of voice which he had picked out above all others in that crowded drawing-room in Marlborough Street.

She said, 'I hope I am punctual, Mr Watson.'

'It has been a long time,' he replied.

She withdrew her hand and began to pull off her gloves. Though he himself never wore anything but black – he believed it made him look thinner than he was – he thought it an unbecoming colour on a woman. When last he had seen her she had worn a bright dress of some shade of pink or lilac. He wondered if she was in mourning for someone. It would explain why she had taken so long to reply to his note.

'It isn't snowing yet,' she said.

'Such a very long time,' he repeated.

She had rehearsed how she would put him at his ease and draw him out in conversation. She would use Mrs Quin as a go-between, discussing people they might know in common and then proceed to more weighty topics, such as Mr Peel's Commission of Enquiry into Land Tenure, and the lamentable fact that men of merit had to go to England to be appreciated. Her dialogue would be informed but lively. Somewhere she would bring in one of Dean Swift's witty rejoinders. She would seem at first womanly, and then better than a woman. On no account would she fall back on the weather. However, there was no sign of Mrs Quin, or Mr Quin for that matter, and alone with J.S. Watson, who was so much older than expected – he was actually older than herself, or appeared so – it was she who felt awkward. He had not asked her to sit down and they remained standing in the middle of the room. 'We are fortunate it isn't snowing,' she heard herself saying, as though they were on a hillside and in danger of dying from exposure.

He didn't reply. They had never had a conversation before. When he had played draughts with her she had spent her time looking out of the window. After she had beaten him – he was hardly concentrating – he had thanked her and she had merely nodded. He had known her for a short while in life, and for a longer time in dreams, and now that she was here, in Quin's front room, he could see no difference in her.

'Perhaps it will hold off for a few more days –' she began.

'If I had written to you years ago,' he interrupted, 'would you have replied then?'

'Ah,' she sighed, and she backed away from him and, finding the sofa behind her, sank down heavily upon it and mindlessly arranged her gloves on her lap.

'I imagine,' he persisted, 'that your existence then was such that you wouldn't have replied. At least not favourably.' He paused, and when she didn't immediately answer, concluded, 'I have always supposed it to be the case.'

Still she could not speak. She felt he wanted to hear that her life in the past had been full of promise, that but for adverse circumstances she would be unobtainable. He needed to believe she was a catch. Already he doubted it – she was not what he had expected. How apt had been his use of the word *existence*. When he had written that he was of humble birth, implying that he was above conceit, he hadn't been telling the truth. He was like everybody else, herself included: he pretended one thing and desired another. Humble his birth may have been, but in all other respects he was arrogant and ambitious. She did not dare look up lest the dislike she felt for him might show on her face. She couldn't remember ever having seen him before and yet she found him unbearably changed.

'Five years ago,' she said at last, 'I was with the Devany family at Rathmines. Are you acquainted with them?'

'No,' he said.

'They are not just people of means,' she said. 'Mr Devany is a collector of paintings. The conversation at table was both instructive and amusing.'

'I knew it,' she thought she heard him say.

'Sometimes as many as thirty people sat down to supper,' she said. 'Afterwards we played charades. In Ireland, being an inferior is no bar to mixing in society, on one level at least. The Thwaites and the Guinnesses began as brewers. The Gardiners started in the building trade. Miss Ambrose married a baronet.'

How dreadful it was, she thought, to be of the same flesh and blood as Olivia. Soon she would begin boasting of her father's connections, of the number of rooms in the house in Upper Sackville Street, of the size of the gardens at Inchicore.

'I was never excluded from the company,' she said. 'And never more dejected or miserable.'

'I, too, have not felt at ease with people,' he said. 'When I first began to make my way in the world and became classical master at St Elizabeth's College in Guernsey, I hadn't the knack of sparkling in company. Invited to the house of a colleague for supper, I was either so uninterested in what was being said that I went to the bookshelves and read all evening, or else so carried away by the topic under discussion that I monopolised the conversation entirely.'

'I have often sparkled in company,' Anne said.

'Either way,' he continued, 'I was afterwards convinced that I had made a spectacle of myself, and shrank from visiting the house ever again.'

'I was also governess to a child in Cork,' she said. 'I did not get on with my employer.'

'It's often the case,' Watson cried out. He felt he could tell her anything. He wanted to confide in her all the tribulations and longings he had known in the life he had endured since his separation from her. 'I never got on with the Revd Mr Davies in Guernsey,' he admitted. 'Not for an instant. He was a one-time fellow of St John's College, Oxford, and so used to comfort and power that he had quite forgotten there was another kind of world. Once, when taking the Upper Class ferociously through Horace of a Monday morning, a pupil –' He broke off abruptly. He had been about to tell her that a boy of seventeen had urinated out of fright and that Davies had made him sit in his pissed breeches until nightfall. He was suddenly fearful that he was casting himself in the role of an isolated man, a man unable to achieve intimacy. He said, 'I was friendly with the French master. He came from the same lowly background as myself. We understood each other.' It was far from the truth. Le Courtois and he had shared a sort of friendship, but it was one formed from necessity rather than compulsion, and had only lasted for the duration of the winter months. When summer came, Le Courtois had spent all his spare time down at the beach, tumbling about like a porpoise in the icy water and expecting *him* to be ready with a towel. 'I cannot believe,' he said, 'that you have ever lacked friends. When I knew you at Mrs Curran's you were always the centre of attention.'

She was careful not to look at him. 'Do you remember Mrs Strafford?' she asked.

'No,' he said. 'I do not.'

'Mrs Strafford and the Miss Hannahans were almost inseparable. Sometimes they came with Dr Ormonde and Mr Roche.'

'The names mean nothing to me,' he said.

'Dr Ormonde wore green slippers in the drawing-room.'

'I remember no one but you,' said Watson.

At that moment Quin came downstairs, and shortly afterwards his mother arrived. Mrs Quin couldn't tell whether things were going well or not. Watson was standing behind the sofa, staring at the back of Miss Armstrong's bonnet. It was difficult to interpret his expression – he was either engaged by her or infuriated with her. Miss Armstrong was perched on the edge of her cushion like an overfed sparrow. In many respects both she and Mr Watson looked as if they had just returned from a funeral.

Miss Armstrong seemed at first shy, and then less so. She ate most of the bread and butter the girl brought in at tea-time. Mrs Quin began by thinking she was plain, and later thought she was handsome. When spoken to she had a way of inclining her head as though she was listening to music. Mrs Quin didn't quite catch the drift of the story she told about Dean Swift, but her son was so

34

amused by it that he shook with laughter.

Mr Watson hardly opened his mouth, except to drink his tea. How opposite they are, thought Mrs Quin. They will never mix.

Then, in answer to her inquiry, Quin told Miss Armstrong that his wife was at present staying with a relation in Tuam.

'Tuam,' she cried, pressing her hand to her heart in a spectacular manner, as though she had been stabbed. Recovering, she said that it was in Tuam that intimations of her father's ruin had been confirmed. 'I was but a child,' she said. 'Yet it distresses me to talk of it.' In spite of this, she proceeded to do so in some detail.

'In the summer of 1814,' she told them, 'the Banking House of Ffrench and company failed. The news first broke in Dublin. At a quarter to three on the afternoon of the 27th June the Bank closed its doors to business. Rumours of impending collapse had already circulated and a crowd had gathered. A small window with iron bars was opened for the admission of notes, and a notice was posted up on the wall outside – "Bills accepted, but none paid". Would you believe they could do such an inflammatory thing? It was like trying to prevent people travelling up a private path by writing a sign saying, "No way, this way". Stones were thrown and the police had to be called. Two of the partners in the firm left by a back door and hid in the bedroom of a nephew who was simple-minded.' She paused dramatically. Far from being distressed, she appeared elated. Her dark eyes were luminous with excitement.

'What a calamity,' said Mrs Quin, though she was finding it difficult to follow the point of the story.

'My father,' said Miss Armstrong, 'was land agent to Lord Strahan, among others. He stood to lose his entire fortune. At that time we lived in Sackville Street, and at Inchicore House in the Phoenix Park –' Her voice faltered momentarily.

'I know it,' said Mrs Quin. 'It's much run down.'

'There was another branch of the Bank in Tuam,' Miss Armstrong continued – she seemed determined to hold nothing back – 'and a Discount Office in Galway. My father, poor soul, unable to receive any satisfaction in Dublin and out of his mind with anxiety, went immediately to Tuam. There the manager, Mr Keary, scrambled out of a window at the rear of the premises, spraining his ankle in the process, and escaped on horseback. He was pursued on foot by creditors, and later gave himself up to the Sheriff, preferring to be locked away rather than torn limb from limb. My father lost all his money. Every penny. He never got back even a farthing in the pound.' All the while she spoke she was looking over her shoulder at Mr Watson. 'For a time we stayed on in the house,' she told him, 'but it was never the same. How could it be? You cannot imagine the way it was, the parties, the excursions, the company at supper. Often as a child I was woken in the small hours by the noise of laughter. Such excitement in the house, such sounds of life. Sometimes I crept to the head of the stairs and watched them tumbling from the dining-room: Henry Boxer in his nightcap, bringing out the coats and the scarves and my father running backwards to the door, finger held to his lips for silence for fear my mother should wake. There was a plaster eagle in the alcove. In the lamplight its wings seemed to quiver. I used to think it would fly.' She was still talking directly to Watson, as though there was no one in the room but themselves. 'And then out would come Mr Cooley,' she cried, 'the old militia man from Ballyraheen who had piped a tune of death up the slopes of Vinegar Hill, supported at either elbow, hands clutching the waistband of his breeches as tilted like a lance he was skimmed across the polished floor.' For a moment she continued to gaze at Watson animatedly, and then, as though she heard a door close on those departing guests, her face grew melancholy. Turning to Mrs Quin, she said, 'The bailiffs came in their bowler hats and their leather aprons. They took away the furniture and the plate. All that was left was Mother's chair, and the bed on which Henry Boxer had slept.'

Mrs Quin could think of nothing adequate to say. It was most unusual, she thought, even in Ireland, to lay one's past on the rug for strangers to walk over.

'Lord Ffrench,' Anne said, 'later took his own life.'

'And so he should have,' said Watson. He came and stood in front of her, kicking over the cup and saucer which she had put down on the carpet.

Mrs Quin felt it was an extraordinary pronouncement, coming from a man in holy orders.

'He would certainly never have been able to sleep easy in his bed,' said Quin. 'Not after such a disaster.'

'I sleep in a second-hand bed,' Anne told him. 'It belonged to a servant.'

'What lives we lead,' murmured Mr Watson. 'There seems little order or pattern to our existence.'

How alike they are, thought Mrs Quin. They are made for each other.

Mr Watson, without explanation, began to tell them about some children who had gone poaching in Kent. He said that if they had been caught they would have been sent to the hulks. When they had heard the gamekeeper coming they had run away. As they ran the twigs snapped beneath their feet and the noise echoed through the trees like the sound of musket fire.

Mrs Quin noticed he was standing on the handle of Miss Armstrong's teaspoon. As he swayed backwards and forwards, the spoon jerked up and down.

'One of the boys,' Mr Watson said, 'was calling for his mother. When they broke from the copse into the mustard field, smoke from the papermill was drifting across the sky.' He raised his hand and waved it languidly in the air, imitating that floating cloud, and looked down at Miss Armstrong's upturned face. 'The boy continued to call for his mother,' he said. 'Over and over as he ran across the field.'

After a moment, Anne said, 'Poor little boy.'

'Was he a pupil of yours?' asked Mrs Quin.

But Watson didn't reply. As far as he was concerned there was no one there save Anne Armstrong and himself. It had grown dark and he could see the firelight reflected in her eyes.

Ever since last night, when he had first remembered that August afternoon so long ago, he had been bothered by the feeling that he had forgotten something, something of significance. Now he understood what it was. It wasn't the bully boy running ahead of him, blubbing for his mother, or the bird choking to death in the undergrowth that had caused the incident to rise from the layers of his mind, but an old, unaltered sense of loss. The fat child he had once been, who had run behind those others, the tears coursing down his cheeks, had wept not from terror but from grief. There was no one called Mother waiting for him beyond the five-barred gate. He had told his schoolfriends that she was dead, but it wasn't true. She lived in Crayford, in a cottage by the church. She had given him away.

Anne Armstrong's words, the juxtaposition of poor and little, affected him so deeply that it was only an act of will that prevented him from sinking on to his knees at her feet and resting his head on her lap.

The following morning, at breakfast, Watson asked Quin his opinion of Miss Armstrong. The question was a formality – he had already come to a decision.

'She is very lively,' said Quin. 'You will not be bored. Nor is she secretive.'

'She is used to hardship,' Watson said. 'She will not shrink from adversity.

'No,' said Quin. 'I suppose not.'

'And her eyes,' cried Watson. 'Did you ever see such eyes? How they shone! Her whole nature is contained in the brightness of her eyes.'

'They are certainly very fine,' said Quin thoughtfully. It was his experience that a sparkling eye couldn't be relied upon. Far too often it was extinguished in the darkness of day-to-day living. Still, he was pleased that Watson was showing signs of happiness. He had never before seen him moved by anything that did not come from inside a book.

That afternoon Watson called on Anne in Great Britain Street. He proposed to her in Mrs Gallagher's back parlour and she accepted him without hesitation. She had always behaved impulsively, and in any case it was plain that he intended to return to England within the week. This was not the time to shilly-shally.

He asked her whether there was someone he ought to speak to, in regard to the marriage arrangements.

'There is no one,' she said. 'That is, no one whom I respect. I live with an elder sister, but she hardly needs consulting.'

He looked surprised. 'I knew of an aunt,' he said. 'I didn't know you had a sister.'

'If I've not spoken of her before,' said Anne, 'it's because I've never felt she counted.'

'I understand,' he said.

'By that I mean she isn't dependent on me.'

'You don't have to explain,' he assured her. 'My own experience, in that field, has been unsatisfactory.' He told her he had been taken from his mother as an infant, tucked Moses-fashion into a wicker basket. His grandfather's assistant had fetched him away in a pony and trap along the road which led to Dartford. On the journey he had apparently screamed with fright; the assistant had lent him his knuckle to suck on. At this moment, looking at Anne Armstrong and observing the concern in her eyes, it occurred to him that all his life he had been searching for the road back. He spoke of the paternal grandfather who had brought him up – he had been a bookseller in Dartford. 'When he died,' he said, 'he left me three hundred guineas.'

'Hardly a fortune,' she said, and he was a little irritated, because he had always felt that it was a substantial sum of money.

'No,' he agreed, 'but without it I shouldn't have attended Trinity College.'

'I received nothing,' said Anne.

'He also left me some books,' Watson said. 'A few of them were of more than general interest.'

'There was nothing to leave,' she said. 'Apart from the chair.'

'And a collection of horse pistols,' said Watson. 'I have a curious affection for them. He bought them as a young man.'

'I have an oyster shell,' she said. 'My sister persists in thinking it was given to her, but she's mistaken. My father picked it up off a beach and gave it to me one Easter Sunday. I remember because I had been ill with bronchitis and was temporarily deaf, and he told me to hold it to my ear and listen to the sound of the sea.'

'An oyster shell is flat,' said Watson.

'All the same,' Anne said, 'I heard the sea.'

He told her that he had no recollection of his father at all, and that he had seen his mother but once in his entire life. He began to kick at Mrs Gallagher's fender as if it had done him an injury.

'If you had stayed with your mother,' Anne said, 'you would not be here today.'

'If the Bank had prospered,' he replied, 'you too might be somewhere else.'

'It's an ill wind,' she murmured.

In referring to the Bank, he had fully intended it as a romantic statement. He was shaken at the thought that they might have missed each other on the road of life. He would have gone on to hold her hand if she hadn't butted in about ill winds. He was so disconcerted by her remark that for a moment he misconstrued the meaning of it and thought she implied that it was a misfortune for her to have been blown into Mrs Curran's drawing-room in Marlborough Street. He found it difficult to show his feelings for her. He was like a barometer which was unable to give a correct reading. All that was needed, he told himself, was an adjustment, an altering of position, and nature, abhorring a vacuum, would cause the mercury to rise and the instrument to function. Courtship, being a social phenomenon, was surely a matter of display. There had to be witnesses to the event, observers, relations constantly commenting on the activities of the courting couple. Anne Armstrong and himself were too solitary. They had only themselves to fall back on. He was inhibited by a lack of numbers. How peculiar he felt, miserable and happy by turns. The embarrassment of being with her was almost as painful as the thought of living life without her.

He began to describe the school at Stockwell, in particular the newly planted poplars by the railings.

'I like poplars,' she said. 'Especially if the wind is blowing.'

He told her that Stockwell, for the moment, was a pleasant suburb, although unfortunately it was beginning to be built up. It lay between Clapham and Brixton, neither of which were fashionable districts. As he had mentioned in his letters his salary was as yet small, but that would be remedied by time. The reputation of the school grew term by term.

She thought of spacious parsonages set in gardens full of fruit trees and wondered out loud whether he wouldn't be happier earning his living as the Rector of some quiet and prosperous country parish.

'I would rather be head master of a good school than Archbishop of Canterbury,' he protested. He knew he was unsuited to the clerical life, but then he was unsuited to so many things.

'When I was ordained priest,' he said, 'by Dr Law, Bishop of Bath and Wells, I was appointed curate at St Mary's, Huish Episcopi, in Langport, Somerset. It was my first and last curacy and I got it through influence. One of Law's sons had been a pupil with me at Burney's school in Greenwich. I was nothing but a dog's-body in Langport.'

'I have never been to Somerset,' Anne said.

'When I was not riding about the countryside in all weathers,' said Watson, 'or examining those poor workhouse wretches in the Catechism, I was endeavouring to coach the Rector's four, equally stupid, sons.'

'I understand,' she said, with feeling.

'I had formed a friendship with a man called George Stukeley. But for him I would have been utterly miserable.'

'How fortunate,' she said. Already she hated George Stukeley.

40

'But when it came to it,' said Watson, 'Stukeley failed to understand me.'

Instantly she felt more cheerful. She said brightly, 'It isn't wise to rely on anybody.'

'One night,' Watson said, 'I was coming home on foot, after baptising an infant who was dying of the croup, when I thought I heard an animal bleating in the darkness. But it was a young woman, crouched by the wall of her father's cottage, half crazed from a beating she had received. I wrapped my coat round her and carried her to the vicarage.'

'How dreadful,' Anne murmured, and now she hated the young woman more than George Stukeley.

'She was a hefty girl,' said Watson, 'and I felt as if I was carrying the burdens of the world.' He did not tell Anne that the girl had been almost naked and that when he had lifted her in his arms her bare breast had bounced against his wrist and it was as though his skin had been seared by fire. 'I had not a thought in my head,' he said, 'but that I was doing God's work. At last I was gathering a sheep to the fold. I carried her up the vicarage path, past the winter cabbages, and kicked at the door. Unfortunately the Reverend Henslow was away for the night. Mrs Henslow came down in her nightgown. She looked at me as if she had never seen me before. I was dripping wet and the girl in my arms was uttering shrill little cries. Mrs Henslow reminded me of the girl's reputation and of the four innocent souls asleep in the room above. She told me to go away.'

'How uncharitable,' Anne said, though inwardly she approved of the Rector's wife. Watson had surely gone too far, taking that beaten girl in his arms.

'There being nowhere else to go,' said Watson, 'I crossed over the road to the church. As I picked my way between the tombstones I shouted to the dead that here was someone alive and suffering. It was after midnight, you understand, and the elm trees by the boundary wall rattled as the rain swept down. I laid the girl beside the christening font with a purple cushion beneath her head. All night I stayed with her, cradling her feet in my hands and chafing them lest the blood freeze in her veins. I hadn't had my supper and I offered my hunger up to the Lord, but my stomach continued to rumble.'

'What a business!' said Anne. If she had to listen to this Good Samaritan nonsense much longer she knew she would lose her temper.

41

'The next morning, her father, informed by every Tom, Dick and Harry in the parish, came for her. The villagers were waiting for us in the lane, gawping as we came out. She was still wearing my coat, and she had a black eye. Both her lips were split and bloody. She ducked through a gap in the churchyard wall and jogged away down the stubble field without a backward glance. When the Rector came home, he accused me of naiveté. He said the girl should have been left where she was. Her father would have fetched her in before day-break. I mentioned the weather, the deluge. He said the climate had nothing to do with it.'

The Rector, thought Anne, was a sensible fellow. She forced herself to look sympathetically at Watson, but it was a terrible effort.

'George Stukeley,' said Watson, 'went even further. He said I had acted out of self-importance. It was obvious he had never understood me. Since then I have come to believe that true friendship, compounded as it must be of imagination and tenderness, can only be found with a woman.'

'Yes,' she said eagerly, 'yes, I think you are right.'

Now that he had found his ideal, he knew he could lay bare his heart. 'My real interest,' he admitted, 'is in a literary career. It is, of course, a precarious occupation. These days, critics deal in destruction. If they could, they would burn the author at the stake.'

'They will not burn you,' she assured him. There was something very dramatic about her. He couldn't help noticing the demure set of her bloodless mouth and the contradiction in the bold, almost insolent gaze of her glittering eyes. It seemed to him that when she looked at him directly the melancholy little room with its dusty curtains and dark linoleum was swept by flame. He could have sworn there was actually a smell of charred wood in the air.

'It's not just a question of ability,' he said, 'but of getting on with people. Some men can charm the birds off the trees. I'm not one of them. I suffer from too much independence of spirit. I'm not tolerant of people.'

'We are very alike,' she cried enthusiastically. 'I have always been my own worst enemy. Everyone has always told me so.'

He was alarmed at her words. He didn't need her to be like him. 'I don't expect much financial return from my writing,' he said. 'However, what little I may earn I shall share with you.'

She stared into the fire and felt chilled – she had always had so little of everything. He didn't attempt to kiss her, or even to hold her hand, and she was disappointed. At first she thought it was because he lacked ardour, and then because he didn't think it necessary, not at this moment. She found him very masculine and overbearing – he crossed his legs and swung his foot up and down in a casual manner. During their conversation there was an occasion when she didn't instantly grasp what he meant, and immediately he grew impatient with her, as if he had known her for a long time. Already she believed she loved him. At this moment she was not concerned whether he loved her or not. He admired her, she could tell, and that was sufficient; she had always considered admiration as important as love. She would soon cure him of standing on one leg.

* * *

They were married four days later, by special licence, at St Mark's Church. Anne wore the same grey dress she had worn to Quin's house. Her aunt, visited by an hysterical Olivia, had sent round a more suitable gown of brown merino, only slightly stained at collar and cuffs. Anne had promptly returned it. She wanted no hand-me-down favours from that quarter.

She was given away by Quin, who was also the best man. Her brother, Edwin, was ill and it was thought unwise for him to make the journey from Tyrone. An elderly acquaintance of Quin's, a teacher of the pianoforte, was to have escorted her up the aisle, but when it came to it he was found to be drunk and unable to walk in a straight line. He was left outside the church, slumped against the railings.

Olivia, quite alone, sat in a middle pew, her sobs rolling round the empty church.

'She is moved at the happiness that awaits you,' explained Mrs Quin, when signing the register in the vestibule. She is appalled at the prospect before her, thought Anne, nodding in agreement.

After the ceremony was over, two hackney cabs waited to take them to an hotel near the harbour. By some mischance Anne went ahead with Quin and his mother, and Watson found himself left behind in charge of the music teacher and Olivia. Both had to be assisted into the remaining cab. The music teacher, scooped up off the railings, was in danger of vomiting over his boots and had to be persuaded to travel with his head stuck out of the window.

At the hotel Watson had booked a room for the wedding party. Cuts of cold meat and a cold apple pie were laid out on a side table decorated with artificial flowers. No expense is being spared, thought Anne, as the champagne was brought in. She was irritated that Olivia was too distressed to take advantage of the food. Perhaps when no one was looking some of the meat could be hidden in a napkin and given her to take home.

Mrs Quin was disappointed that there wasn't a bride's cake. She had offered to provide the couple with a small reception at her own house but Watson had refused. There was a steamer leaving for Liverpool at seven o'clock and he wanted to be as close to the dock as possible.

Toasts were drunk, and Quin made a speech in which he spoke affectionately of his friend. He said that Watson had already made his mark in literary and academic circles, and now that he had taken a wife he could not fail to further his reputation. She would watch over him as he laboured at his desk, ensuring that atmosphere of tranquillity and order which was essential to a man of letters.

Watson seemed indifferent to what was being said about him. During Quin's optimistic portrayal of his future he occupied himself with scratching the ears of a black-and-white dog which had run in from the street. His grandfather had given him a dog when he was a child. It had followed him everywhere. If he was in the schoolroom it had waited in the lane, sprawled out in the mud like a dead thing. When he had run his hand down its spine, its hindquarters had shivered uncontrollably. He felt curiously empty and could not look at Anne Armstrong. Her sister was pulling the petals off an artificial rose. She was sitting with her back to the window and he could see behind her the branch of a tree jerking against a patch of grey sky. He too was at the mercy of the elements: if he did not bend with the storm he would snap in half.

Anne told Mrs Quin she would write to her. Mrs Quin, in return, promised to visit Olivia whenever possible.

'She is a difficult woman,' said Anne. 'We have never got on.'

'You must not worry about her,' advised Mrs Quin. 'We are none of us as indispensable as we imagine.'

Anne believed she had stopped worrying about Olivia. She told herself that her sister was no longer her responsibility. From now on Edwin would have to contend with her. She was far more concerned about the imminent farewell – she doubted whether she

44

could muster up the tears expected at such a moment.

But, when the time came for Watson to settle his bill and she was required at last to look Olivia in the eye, her sister's face was so blank with grief – the lines of discontent and petulance quite smoothed away – and her nose so pathetically flushed from crying, that instantly she broke down and took Olivia into her arms. She could not bear anyone else to see the stains on the bodice of her sister's dress. 'You must sponge your dress with warm water,' she whispered. 'If the marks are too stubborn you must try vinegar.' Her own tears dripped down her cheeks and leaked into her mouth.

They walked the short distance to the pier. The gutters were filled with refuse. It had gone five o'clock and land and sky had merged into darkness. The gas lights blazed along the edge of the quay. There was so much noise, so many pockets of light and dark, so many people hurrying in the same direction that Olivia grew confused and more childlike than ever. Just then the train connection from Dublin drew into the station: a cloud of steam, sulphurous yellow and stitched with sparks, rolled across the black sky. Olivia lagged behind, holding tightly to Anne's hand as they struggled against the wind towards the landing stage.

'I'll send for you very soon,' cried Anne. 'I will, I will.'

'I want –' cried Olivia, but what she wanted was torn away by the wind.

Watson strode ahead, keeping pace with the porter who carried Anne's trunk on his shoulder. He had refused to hand over his own bag because his books were tied to it. He said he couldn't trust them to be transported by anyone but himself. The black-and-white dog trotted at his heels. There was nothing in Anne's trunk but old clothes, a miniature of her father and the oyster shell which had gathered dust on the mantel-shelf in Great Britain Street. When she had taken it down, Olivia had said, 'That is mine. You're a thief.' 'Be quiet,' Anne had shouted. 'I will take what I want.' It was too late to give it back.

They reached the departure point. Olivia was not permitted to go any further. The sisters clung together as though drowning. They could hear the slap of the river as it heaved against the granite slabs of the harbour wall. We are surrounded by strangers, thought Anne, looking over her sister's shoulder at Watson and his friends.

'Make sure they take you home in a cab,' she whispered to

Olivia. 'Mind you insist. They can afford it.' The dog ran round them in a circle, snapping at their ankles.

'It's time,' said Mrs Quin. 'Your husband is waiting.'

How absurd, thought Anne. Then she straightened Olivia's bonnet and draped the shawl more securely about her shoulders, and backed away from her, her arm stretched out and her fingers clawing the air as if she was sliding into an abyss.

'Goodbye, goodbye,' called Quin and his mother.

'*Bon voyage*,' shouted the pianoforte teacher, waving his hat from side to side like a flag.

Watson assisted Anne up the gangway – she stopped and looked back. Below her, she saw Olivia's upturned face, white as chalk under the artificial light, her black lips mouthing a farewell. The world slithered up and down. In the desolate streets the houses climbed, lamps blooming in the windows, towards the windswept sky. Watson pulled at her elbow. Almost before Anne had set foot on the deck the tears had dried in her eyes and she was thinking of the future.

They had supper on board an hour later. Both were hungry and neither of them felt queasy.

'I have never been seasick in my life,' said Anne with satisfaction.

Watching her husband devouring his grilled chops, she remarked, 'There is plenty of time. No one is going to remove the plate before you have finished.'

He was taken aback at her criticism. He pushed his elbows closer to his sides and held his knife and fork as if they would burst into flames.

When the boat had left the harbour they went below. The cabin was small and airless and the floor vibrated with the noise of the engines.

'I am afraid you will not be very comfortable,' he said, ducking his head to avoid the swing of the safety lamp which hung from the ceiling. They were scarcely beyond the Bar, and already the boat was bucking and pitching as it fought the wind.

'I don't mind,' she said. 'I think of it as an adventure.'

He was not sure what he should do next. Women were so fragile. He imagined she should rest, and yet he felt it would be heartless to leave her alone when so recently wrenched from both country and sister – even a sister she disliked.

There was nowhere to sit. Her trunk and his bag stood side by side at the foot of the narrow bed. His books, tied with string, were attached to the handle of his portmanteau . Squatting, he untied the string and selected a volume bound in green cloth. 'It is mine,' he said, standing up and showing her the cover. 'That is to say, I wrote it.'

She was impressed and asked him to read her something from it. Still wearing her bonnet, and clutching the ends of her shawl, she looked at him expectantly.

After a decent display of reticence, he began, ' "He whose dead soul seeks not to be enlarged",' and frowned. 'I have read it wrongly.' he said. 'I'm too nervous.'

'Please,' she said. 'Pretend I am not here.'

Clearing his throat, he started again.

> He whose dead soul swells not to be enlarged
> From sensual bondage, and to be relieved
> From mists of ignorance and direful stench
> Of the world's common sewer, is but fit
> To worship Plutus, hug vile yellow dirt
> And wrap himself in filth. Let such a thing
> Go quench the little feeling nature gave –

He stopped abruptly, and muttered, 'Perhaps I have chosen the wrong extract. It is after all not very good.'

'Let me judge for myself,' she insisted.

He gave her a brief lecture on the premise behind the work. He didn't seem to have hit on a very poetical subject. She understood it was about rocks and electrical currents and the formation of the earth. Still, she urged him to continue.

> What if this earth (he read) which ours we lordlings call,
> Lordlings of all things on it, we boast,
> Be but one mighty animal, and we
> But parasitic animalcules, made
> To add to his enjoyment? What if, when
> We furrow deep into the soil, delve mines profound,
> Level tall forests –

Breaking off in mid verse he slammed the pages of his book together as if he hoped it would fall to pieces. 'I was trying to write a scientific poem in the manner of Lucretius. Perhaps I was too ambitious,' he said.

'There is nothing wrong in asking questions,' she told him.

The boat rolled suddenly and she clutched at his arm to steady herself. Watson suggested she should lie down. He would go for a walk on deck to clear his head. He said he was not used to drinking champagne.

He got no further than the flight of steps which led to the deck. Already he could see a burst of spray above him and hear the roar of the sea as it broke over the bows. He didn't dare contemplate his clothing being ruined by sea water. It was alarming enough to think of the money he had spent during the last two weeks. 'I have nothing to bring you but myself,' Anne Armstrong had told him when he had proposed to her. At the time he had not realised how truthful she was.

He peered through the glass partition of the second-class saloon. Several figures lay full-length upon the wooden benches, their baggage heaped about them. Somewhere in the semi-darkness an infant was crying. He would have liked to go inside into the warmth, but he hated the idea of being spoken to, of being asked his opinion of the weather. Huddled against the glass, he thrust his hands into his pockets. He was annoyed with himself for having picked the wrong moment to read his verses aloud – she would only remember how many times he had stopped and started. He should have waited till they were sitting by the fire in a comfortable room, not shifting up and down on the deep.

The saloon door opened. The child's wailing grew louder. A man, hatless and pale as death, stumbled out into the passageway and, clutching at the brass rail of the stairs, hauled himself towards the deck. Before he reached the top he fell onto his knees and retched.

A man's life, thought Watson, was a coarse affair, compared with a woman's. Was it possible, he wondered, to be one of those sons of strength, a hero even, and yet retain qualities of gentleness? If a man wanted to remain on his feet, wasn't it advisable for him to stand alone? When Quin had spoken of the future, he had felt in his heart that he was unsuited to be a companion to anyone. When it came to it, wouldn't he find it an unbearable distraction to have someone sitting in the same room as himself when he worked at his desk? Only an hour before Anne Armstrong had said there was nothing wrong with asking questions. He could have replied, 'Provided one doesn't already know the answers'. What bothered him – he was watching a half-eaten orange, which had been flung down in the passage, rolling backwards and forwards in a slick of oily water – was his conviction that feelings, of any kind, were as repetitious and as conditioned as the movements of the tides. He had no more control over his own feelings than a migratory bird had of choosing the direction in which it should fly. I am an angry man, he thought, and damaged. My table manners are at fault. Depressed, he retraced his steps to the cabin.

Anne Armstrong was lying on the bed, as if in a coffin, her hands clasped together on her stomach. She had taken off her bonnet and her boots which lay several yards apart, one pointing towards the door, the other at the bulkhead. She appeared to be asleep. He had never seen her hair before. Picking up her boots he stowed them tidily under the valance of the bed.

'Poor Olivia,' she said. 'She is destitute.'

'Would you like her to live with us?' he asked. 'I would be agreeable, if it would make you happy.' Hardy had two of his wife's sisters living with him. He said it was pleasant to have more than one woman dependent on him.

'No,' Anne said. 'I wouldn't like that.'

'Perhaps I could make her an allowance,' he said. 'Would ten pounds be sufficient?'

'She would be very grateful,' Anne said, but she herself sounded less so.

'Fifteen,' he offered, as if he was bidding at an auction.

'It is quite a large amount,' she said, 'considering the cost of living.'

In the end he agreed to seventeen guineas a year, paid quarterly. In some way the transaction rattled him, though it had been he who had instigated it. He sank down on to the edge of the bed and stared at the wash-stand.

Anne was cold, but now that he was sitting beside her she was too nervous to disturb him and burrow under the covers. It would look as if she were settling down for the night. She comforted herself with the thought that it would be far colder on deck. When last she had made the crossing to England she had sat up all night under a tarpaulin, surrounded by wailing babies and vomiting boys. A man with two fingers missing had played on a mouth organ. What should she do if J.S. Watson turned round and took her into his arms? What was expected of her? She was exhausted and yet she was sure she wouldn't be able to sleep a wink. By now

Olivia would be climbing into Henry Boxer's bed with her stockings on for warmth.

After a time, when he could tell by her breathing that she slept, Watson eased himself further on to the bed and lay flat. There was something rather soothing in the wallowing motion of the boat. He could hear Anne's boots sliding across the floor. Through half-closed eyes he saw the blood-red glow of the swaying lamp, and it seemed to him that it grew smaller, like the rear light of a train receding into the darkness. He rolled on to his side and drifting into sleep flung his arm across Anne Armstrong's waist to anchor himself.

He dreamt he was at the hotel, caressing the ears of the mongrel dog. The coarse hairs on its neck dragged against his wrist. For some reason, though he knew it was a dog squatting there, he thought its mouth was a purse and he was curious to know how much money it contained. He stroked the closed muzzle, searching for an opening. The dog squirmed under his touch but he persisted. At last his fingers penetrated the fiery warmth of its jaws, and he looked into its pumpkin-coloured eyes and slid his thumb across the moist and silken lining of its gums. He was sure the brute would never bite him.

The next moment he was wide awake and leaning over Anne Armstrong. Her eyes were open and she was shuddering. He uttered little broken sentences ... 'Forgive me ... dearest ... I need ... my love ...', though afterwards he couldn't remember whether he shouted the words aloud or if they stammered unspoken through his mind. She cried out. He pushed himself against the crushed folds of her dress and groaned. The sweat dripped down his face and touched his lips, and the taste reminded him of tears though he hadn't wept in thirty years. Spent, he slumped sideways, his head resting on her shoulder.

She could feel his fingertips on her neck. She had only to move a fraction and the palm of his hand would cradle her cheek. She had thought there would be embarrassment and pain – she was so grateful that she smiled. My dear, my dear, she said to herself. She felt she was now as precious and as bound to him as the parcel of books tied to the handle of his luggage. They would never be parted. Soon her arm ached from his weight, and he smelled like an invalid, but she would have died rather than shift him.

When she woke, Watson was combing his hair in the looking-glass above the wash-stand. The noise of the engines had stopped.

'Is it morning?' she asked, staring at his broad back and waiting for him to turn round.

'Yes,' he said. 'We came up the Mersey three hours ago.' He didn't dare look at her – he was afraid he should see, in the curve of her mouth or the widening of her eyes, some vestige of that expression of pure delight, of impure joy which had ravaged her face the night before. He still heard, ringing in his ears, her long-drawn-out howl of abandonment.

Her dress crackled as she rose from the bed. She was putting her arms about his waist as if he was an accomplice. No longer modest, she thought she could be as intimate with him as she liked.

'It's a calm morning,' he said, 'though it rained in the night.' He drew away from her and began to smooth the covers of the bed.

'You're wasting your time,' she said. 'Any minute the steward will be in to fetch the linen.' She was dipping the edge of her handkerchief into the pitcher of water on the wash-stand. There was a crusted stain in the folds of her dress. He went out of the door and almost ran down the passageway.

Left alone, Anne rubbed at the white mess on her wedding gown. During the reception at the hotel she had resigned herself to living for her husband. Now, having expected so little and received so much, and altogether convinced that she had made that rare thing, a love match, she was willing to die for him.

The Secretary, Henry Grey, questioned by Mr Denman, said that the head master was known to be a man of considerable attainments and learning. His habits were methodical and regular, and his general manner and way of doing things rather formal. He had a minimum salary of 300L. a year, with a capitation of 4/4s per annum for each boy in the school above the seventieth. For the five or six years preceding 1869 the number of boys was between 90 and 100, and, in consequence, the head master's income had often touched 400L. a year. In 1866 the pupils had presented him with a silver salver. The list of Distinctions gained by the boys at the school, and those who had gone on to the Universities or taken the competitive examinations for the Civil, Military and East India Services, was very satisfactory.

PART 2

Summer 1853

Dr Munford had an appointment with the head master for a quarter to three. By rights, Hinchley, the timber merchant, seeing he was chairman of the School Committee, should have gone instead, but he'd flatly refused to do so. Hinchley said that an hour spent with J.S. Watson would bring him down for a week.

Dr Munford arrived on foot; he lived round the corner from the school in Lansdowne Road. Sometimes he thought he was too close for comfort. The slightest emergency and Tulley felt free to send for him.

The school, made of grey brick with facings of Portland stone, was set well back from the road in a quarter of an acre of dirt playground. It was built in the Gothic style with turrets and a tower, and a loggia which extended the full length of the front, under whose stuccoed arches the drill sergeant stood of a morning, wielding his hand bell. Attached to the side was a School House with a slate roof, in which, until last year, the head master had lodged with his wife. Mrs Watson had put flower boxes on the window ledges. The boxes were still there but the plants had long since withered through lack of attention. Behind the school was a brick wall and a few struggling beech trees. Though he admitted it was impressive, Dr Munford thought the building looked too much like a church.

When he came through the ornamental gates the Revd Mr Williams was parading up and down in front of the railings. Mr Williams was vicar of St Andrews and a member of the Examining Board.

Dr Munford nodded at him and hurried past. They had met numerous times, both at the school and at meetings of the society for the Promotion of Christian Knowledge; recently they had attended the same series of scientific lectures held at the Town Hall. In the middle of the final lecture – which had taken place the previous Saturday – during a discussion on the uses of the electro-magnetic chronoscope, some sort of rumpus had broken out at the doors and two ladies had fainted. Mr Williams's hat had been pitched from his head. Dr Munford had saved it from being trampled underfoot. Even so, they had spoken but once, some years back at a reception given for the head master and his bride. Hardy, the junior mathematics master, had goaded the committee into holding the party. Dr Munford, introduced to the Revd Mr Williams by the head master, had remarked that he disliked functions. Mr Williams had replied that they were useful since they allowed one to observe human nature. The head master had laughed.

Dr Munford was ten minutes late for his appointment owing to an extended afternoon surgery, and was kept waiting in the entrance hall for a further five minutes. It was a warm day and the main doors were pushed back; a cloud of flies buzzed above the steps. There was not an atom of shade in the playground. The poplars, of which the committee had been so hopeful, had never flourished. Tulley said it had something to do with the soot from the railway.

From somewhere within the building Dr Munford could hear the stamp of feet and the noise of a piano. As it was a half holiday he supposed it was the dancing class. Dancing was an extra subject and one which had been inaugurated at the start of the summer term. Right from the beginning the head master had been against it, and Dr Munford had taken his side. Both had agreed that it would never catch on and both had been astonished at the response. Every Thursday afternoon at least a dozen boys from the Lower School could be found circling energetically about the gymnasium under the tuition of a dancing master fetched from Soho.

Dr Munford was tapping his foot on the dusty floorboards when the head master's door opened and the Secretary, Henry Grey, appeared, laden with books and papers. He was carrying several documents in his mouth. Unable to speak, he indicated with a jerk of his head that Dr Munford might go in, and after holding the door ajar with his foot trotted off up the corridor like a gun dog.

The head master was seated at his desk, dressed in black and wearing spectacles. On the window ledge behind him stood a scarlet geranium in a china pot. There was nothing to be seen outside the window save a cinder path leading across a strip of yard to a small gate set in a brick wall.

The head master stood and came to shake hands with his visitor. In doing so he swept a pile of text books from desk to floor. 'The delay was unavoidable,' he said. 'I hope you weren't kept waiting too long.'

'Not too long,' Dr Munford said.

'The demands of the summer term,' continued the head master. 'The midsummer examinations. And then, of course, there are the recitations to be prepared for prize-giving.' When he spoke he hardly moved his lips: Dr Munford suspected he had trouble with his teeth. 'Smithson will give part of the oration of Cicero *pro Milone*. It all takes time.'

'I arrived late,' admitted Dr Munford.

'This year they will be examined in the *Birds* of Aristophanes, in the third book of Thucydides, in parts of Herodotus, Sophocles, Euripides –'

'I'll be brief,' Dr Munford promised. He sensed that there was something wrong with Watson. Conducting a conversation with him was normally a strenuous business – Hinchley said it was like dragging a loaded cart up a steep hill.

'And in Latin, in parts of Livy, Tacitus, Horace and Juvenal.' The head master squatted on his haunches and began to gather up the fallen books.

'Good. Excellent,' said Dr Munford.

'Bruane, son of the civil engineer, will give the French recitation. As you know, his people hail from Bordeaux.'

'Excellent,' repeated Dr Munford, remembering that Bruane suffered from adenoids. He waited until Watson stood upright. 'My own business,' he said, 'is rather more mundane. The committee are concerned about health. There's a quantity of dust in the hall and far too many horseflies in the playground. It promises to be a very warm summer –'

'Dust!' said Watson.

'Twelve deaths were registered in Wandsworth last week,' Dr Munford told him. 'Twenty in Camberwell. There were sixty-two in Lambeth.'

The head master appeared not to have heard. It was a trick he pulled. Another man in his position might have cried out that such matters as dust and death were the concern of the drill sergeant and the coroner. Still, Dr Munford couldn't help thinking that today there was something genuine about his air of indifference. Perhaps he was unwell. He had flung the books carelessly on to the desk and was standing with his hands clasped beneath his coat tails, staring at the floor. His boots were quite grey from walking along the cinder path.

'The facts speak for themselves,' murmured Dr Munford, and waited.

After a moment Watson returned to his desk. He said irritably, 'I myself haven't noticed any more flies than usual.'

'It's the weather,' said Dr Munford. 'It's warmer than usual.' He too would have liked to sit down but the only other chair was set against the wall by the door and it would have looked as if he were retreating. He felt uncomfortable. He should have insisted on Hinchley's accompanying him, or else they should have mentioned the flies to the Secretary, who could have passed on the complaint to Tulley. But then, as everyone knew, neither Grey nor Tulley had an ounce of initiative between them. Grey would probably write a lengthy report, and charge for it.

'It's an administrative problem,' he began apologetically. 'And I hesitate –'

'It's what I have become,' said the head master. 'More and more I am thrust into the role of administrator. I do not submit cheerfully.' In the circumstances his tone was mild, even melancholy. Dr Munford had the feeling he was talking about something else. Poor fellow, he thought. Whatever is the matter with him?

All at once the head master started to rail against the short-sightedness of the Committee. It was an old grievance of his. Rather than make an investment they had allowed the school to be encircled by bricks and mortar.

Dr Munford argued that he had done his best. 'It was not up to me.' he said.

'If the speculators had been stopped –'

'I was out-voted,' Dr Munford protested.

'If the Committee had bought up the land when I recommended –'

'It's no use going over the past,' interrupted Dr Munford. He was relieved that they were now on familiar ground. All the same he detected a note of self-pity in Watson's voice. 'If I might sit down,' he said, and without waiting for a reply he fetched the chair from beside the door and brought it to the desk.

'Where there are houses there are stables,' said Watson. 'Where there are stables there are horseflies. That too speaks for itself.' He began to draw winged insects on a sheet of paper.

Dr Munford remained silent. He was one of those few members of the Committee who had been impressed by Watson when he'd been interviewed for the post at the school. In a sense he had fought for him. For various reasons, Mortimer, Daley and the President had all opposed him.

Daley, the son of a butcher from Stamford Hill, had asserted that a man of lowly origins could go one of two ways: either lapse into complacency, or else, tipsy with power, behave like a despot. Leaving aside his mannerisms, which were off-putting to say the least, and his surly approach to questioning, why had he left Langport so soon? The Revd Mr Henslow's second paragraph was plain sailing ... *his appearance and little oddities of manner rendered him liable to caricature* ... but what was one to make of the sentence ... *though Mr Watson was in no way to blame, there were one or two small incidents of a nature too delicate to disclose* ...

The President had been bothered by what he called the 'guarded wording' of the testimonial supplied by the Revd Mr Davies, Principal of St Elizabeth's College, Guernsey. There was something he couldn't quite put his finger on. Fortunately Dalton was known to be swayed by intuition rather than good sense, and as no one else could find anything wrong with the letter his opinion was discounted.

Mortimer had objected to Watson for being too liberal in his outlook. When asked about discipline the applicant had bluntly rejected the notion that flogging was either desirable or necessary. He went further – he said that in his view the use of force demoralised the master quite as much as the pupil.

Hinchley, for his part, had come up with no reasoned argument against the large, uncommunicative man who sat there, heavy jowls quivering, his blue and curiously innocent eyes fixed on some point above their heads. Hinchley simply didn't take to him, and never had.

Though he couldn't find the precise words of persuasion, beyond mentioning that he was a Gold Medallist in Classics and built like a bull, Dr Munford had stubbornly reiterated his belief in Watson's fitness for the job. Being a medical practitioner, he was more aware than most of the physical effect a man could have on his fellows, and though he hadn't listened to the beating of Watson's heart or to the workings of his lungs, he would have staked his reputation on the soundness of both, and, if it came to it, of those other, less easily located parts of a man, his will and his soul. 'He's too dour,' Daley had protested. 'Too uppity.' 'He's an honest man,' Dr Munford had replied. 'An honest man knows his own value.'

Now even Hinchley recognised the worth of the head master. The University results, the scholarships gained to King's College, went beyond anything they could have envisaged ten years before. And in marked contrast to the last head of the school, whose constitution had been so feeble that he had spent more time on his back than at his desk, Watson had never had a day off sick. Even those exaggerated gestures which, in the beginning, had caused such hilarity among the younger boys had become modified with the years. Sometimes, when he was tired, he developed a small facial tick which gave a contemptuous curl to his lip, but the calming and beneficial influence of Mrs Watson was obvious.

It was a pity that Watson had thought fit to leave the School House. It was true that householders in the vicinity of Stockwell Crescent had complained indignantly of the nuisance caused by beggars swarming about the railings at night, but against that should be set Mrs Watson's success as a second mother to the boarders. There had been one or two other complaints of a gossipy and domestic nature – doubtless drummed up by the widow woman the drill sergeant had married – which had come to the ears of Mrs Munford. Dr Munford had refused to listen to her. Their own home, he reminded her, could often be described as seething with discord.

'What is to become of Langley?' asked the head master suddenly.

Dr Munford hesitated. He understood that he was being tested. Langley was a Lower School boy whose father had gone down on the steamer *Adelaide* off Margate Sands at the beginning of the year. There had been some concern over whether his fees would continue to be met. He said cautiously, 'No decision as yet.'

'I see,' said Watson cryptically.

'Is he a clever boy?' asked Dr Munford.

'No,' the head master said. 'But without an education he will be even less so.'

After a pause, Dr Munford said, 'I shall do my best.' He stood and put on his hat. Before going out of the door he mentioned that Mr Williams was waiting in the playground.

'Indeed,' said Watson, and asked abruptly, 'What happened to the straw in the yard?'

Dr Munford told him that in the long run it had been found uneconomical. 'It blows about,' he said.

He went up the corridor and passed Mr Williams loitering in the hall. The thudding of the dancing boys had ceased. He was pleased to have settled the matter of the flies – Watson was sure to come up with a sensible solution. As to Langley, some relation of the boy's mother had already written pledging payment of fees for the next three years.

Dr Munford had just turned the corner into Lansdowne Road when he saw Mrs Watson coming towards him. As soon as he saw her his heart beat more rapidly: he hadn't forgotten his first meeting with her, when Watson, newly-wed, had brought her back from Ireland. The reception, given for them in the gymnasium, a room so lofty and so full of draughts as to put the damper on any occasion, and attended by the Committee, the masters and a selection of the more influential parents, had turned out to be extremely lively. Mrs Watson had exerted a magnetic pull. She wasn't particularly handsome and her dress, according to Mrs Munford, had definitely seen better days, but it was hard not to look at her, both directly and over one's shoulder. Quite apart from the incident with the handkerchief, the Revd Mr Dalton, late Rector of Lambeth and President of the school, had stayed at her elbow for two hours. When Mrs Watson said to him that she hadn't expected to find such an imposing building outside of the City, for a moment even Dr Munford had felt gratified. There was no way of proving it, but in her presence it did seem that more than one person grew peculiarly confidential. The drawing master, a young man from Aberdeen who was naturally incoherent, spoke lucidly for five minutes, not on watercolours but on the distressing relationship he had with his father. Mrs Hinchley maintained that he used the word 'detestable'. Mr Clissold M.A., who was so secretive that only the school board knew his age, his Christian name and where he had come from, was heard telling Mrs Watson that, if circumstances and a cowardly disposition hadn't propelled him into the church, he would have signed on for a life at sea. Mrs Watson herself had said little. She listened with her head tilted to

59

one side, as if to catch undertones. Mrs Hinchley thought she had the air of a lady, which was surprising, as Mrs Munford pointed out, when one considered the state of her clothes. Somehow Mrs Watson had managed to give the impression that it was she, not the Committee, who had organised the party. On leaving, one or two ladies had actually thanked her for her hospitality. Among the men the head master's stock had risen – he was referred to as a 'dark horse'. Afterwards, though she had come to live on the premises, Mrs Watson had been rarely seen except at church or on speech days. Then her husband generally brought her along at the last moment, deposited her on a bench at the side of the gymnasium and hurried her away the instant the ceremony was over. Nevertheless, the memory of that one winter evening when fog had rolled along the corridors and the President had been spotted,by several reliable witnesses, picking up Mrs Watson's handkerchief and holding it to his nose, still lingered.

Mrs Watson was carrying a green parasol with a cobweb border. Dr Munford asked her if she and Mr Watson were comfortable in their new lodgings.

'We are very quiet,' she said. She told him she was on her way to see the head master. It was a surprise visit.

'Mr Williams is with him,' said Dr Munford. He noticed she was perspiring slightly. Under the parasol her face had assumed a greenish tinge. They agreed that the weather was very warm and that a good downpour of rain would be appreciated.

'The poor flowers,' wailed Mrs Watson, gazing with compassion at a rose bush wilting in a nearby garden.

Dr Munford said he was sure she had a sympathy for plants – the geranium in Mr Watson's room was a credit to her.

'Thank you,' she said. 'You are very kind.'

When Dr Munford had walked on, Mrs Watson lingered at the fence of the parched garden. It seemed she was overcome with the heat; she dabbed at her eyes and her cheeks with a little white handkerchief. Then, after several minutes had elapsed and still holding the handkerchief to her face, she retraced her steps and began to walk in the direction of the Clapham Road.

* * *

As soon as Dr Munford had gone, Watson went out to look for Williams. But Williams was no longer there. He went back into his room, and when Henry Grey came in with some query about exercise books he spoke to him quite sharply, demanding to be left in peace. A moment later he felt ashamed, and finding the Secretary in the small room off the main hall, apologised to him. 'I have a headache,' he said, and returning to his desk immersed himself in work.

An hour passed and he'd accomplished nothing. He simply couldn't concentrate; all his thoughts were of his wife, and in particular of the ominous statement she had made that morning. The night before she had seemed listless and depressed. He hadn't known how to comfort her. Often she suffered from stomachache, and he believed pain in the stomach caused depression. When he had offered to go downstairs and ask Mrs Chapman for a hot brick, Anne had retorted that she hadn't an ache in her body. Yet in her sleep she had cried out; twice she had turned to him and put her hand on his shoulder. She had muttered her sister's name. He had tried to take her in his arms but each time she had flung herself away from him and lain on the extreme edge of the mattress.

In the beginning he had been astonished at how easily he adapted to marriage. They had settled in two rooms in Park Road, a stone's throw from the school. He'd feared she would allow him less space for his books, but beyond her propping her father's miniature on the dressing table and putting the oyster shell on the mantel-shelf he would hardly have known she was there. After only a month he got used to seeing her clothes in the wardrobe and to sharing his bed with her. She made things very pleasant for him. Whenever he came into the house she never failed to look at him as if he was important to her. During the bad weather she always had his slippers waiting by the fire; if he had not stopped her she would have knelt at his feet and removed his boots for him. Apart from her welcoming smile and the warmth of his bed, his way of life remained unaltered. He was at his desk by half past eight of a morning, took his dinner at home at twenty past twelve, returned to the school at half past one, and he stayed there until six o'clock at night, sometimes later if the Secretary required his signature at the last minute or one of junior masters needed advice.

In the evenings, as usual, he dealt with school business, read educational reports or added to the list of books he was compiling for a school library and which he intended to surprise the

Committee with at the end of the year. Dale of Blackheath had built up a collection of four thousand volumes, mostly privately donated, and he had been determined that Stockwell should not be left behind. Anne had sat by the fire and read. Once, thinking he was neglecting her, he had asked her opinion on whether it would be better for the sixth form to spend more time on Edwards' *Latin Lyrics*, and less on Keightley's *History of Rome*, or vice versa, but she said she had little knowledge of either textbook and was equally in the dark as to the principles involved. Nor would she interfere, as she put it, in the choosing of the liturgical prayers or the Bible passage to be read the following morning at Assembly. It was a selection he had to make every night and he could have done with her taking the task from his shoulders.

Occasionally he was asked to contribute some article of a scholarly nature to *The School Master* or *The Mirror*, and then he worked at the table with his back to her. He had made no attempt to embark on any serious literary work of his own because he knew that for the time being his energies must be directed towards establishing his position at the school. Often he was dozing over his books by half past nine, and he was always in his bed by ten.

A year later, the Committee having obtained a licence to board three pupils, he and Anne had moved into School House, along with Mandell and Henry Grey. Tulley, who had just then married a widow woman from Connemara, had lived at the back of the premises.

There too they had been content, in Anne's case even more so, if that was possible. She had the boys to look after, and her windowboxes to plant, and the dubious benefit of Mrs Tulley's company. If there had seemed any difference in her attitude towards him – rather too many outbursts of temper, or a new note of sarcasm in her voice – he had put it down to the fact that they were growing used to each other. There was a passage connecting the house to the school and she had only to push open the green baize door in the kitchen wall to be within a hundred yards of him. It gave him pleasure, coming out of the Sixth Form room, or going into his study, to see her gliding along the corridor, though several times she had burst into his study without knocking and interrupted meetings with parents.

One such time she had surprised him with Mrs Peterson, the bereaved wife of a curate from a parish in Norfolk, who had children to support. He had got funds for her out of the

Clergymen's Dependents' Charity, and brought two sons into the school at reduced rates. Afterwards Anne had accused him of making sheep's eyes at Mrs Peterson. Though he despised himself for it, it both bewildered and excited him that he had aroused her jealousy. He had thought himself fortunate. For the first time in his life he had come to recognise one particular step on the stair. If he had been blindfolded and placed with his face to the wall and a dozen people had trooped past, he would have known instantly whether she was among them or not. There had been moments, moments of sentiment, when he couldn't help feeling that something had been denied him, some dimension of returned emotion which he had been led to believe, through hope, through literature perhaps, was his due. On these occasions, he had sought to hold her closer and, like Odysseus attempting to clasp the ghostly shade of Anticleia, thrice like a dream or shadow she fled, and his hands closed on unsubstantial air. He blamed himself entirely.

Now and then, brushing his hair of a morning, he was so moved by the sight of her hairpins scattered across the dressing-table that he slipped them into his pocket and carried them about with him for the whole day.

What she had said to him at breakfast had shaken him dreadfully. If only he had held his tongue. He had felt amused rather than perturbed by the sullen expression on her face. She hadn't opened her mouth, until, provokingly perhaps, he had remarked that he hoped she would soon feel more cheerful. She had replied, 'To submit cheerfully to an existence that is unpleasing is only possible if one feels it to be temporary.' He knew those were her exact words because he had gone over them a dozen times in his head, and even if he had remembered them incorrectly he hadn't mistaken the look which had accompanied them. He had begged her to reflect, and she had mockingly reminded him of the dangers of reflection, bringing up the facetious story of Counsellor Connaghty, who, spotting himself in a mirror unawares, fell down in an apoplectic fit, went off his head and in three weeks died of constipation. As he was due to take prayers at twenty to nine, and as it was already twenty-five minutes to the hour, he had left the house as quickly as possible. All day he had been struggling to think what he should say to her on his return home.

An existence that is unpleasing, he thought; and consumed with guilt he rose from his desk and, putting his papers into some form of order, rushed from the room. As he entered the corridor he narrowly missed colliding with a Lower School boy who was leaning in an attitude of despair against the wall. He had swept past him before he realised that the child was snivelling. Turning, he was in time to glimpse the boy rubbing at his eyes with his fist. He recognised Fraser, the son of a local solicitor, who only recently had begun to attend the school. Though not especially able, the child was considered to be generally cheerful and diligent.

'Why are you in the corridor?' he asked.

The boy mumbled something and looked down at the floor.

'Speak up, sir,' said Watson.

'Mr Hutton sent me out,' replied the boy. He was trembling either from fear or misery, and yet when he looked up Watson saw in his eyes that same expression of defiance which he had encountered earlier that morning across the breakfast table.

'Send Mr Hutton to me,' Watson told him, and he too leaned against the wall, his chin sunk on his breast.

When he heard footsteps approaching he remained in the same position, as if deep in thought.

The junior master, who had stepped jauntily enough along the corridor, walked the last few paces on tip-toe. He waited for the head master to speak and, when he kept silent, stammered, 'I am here, sir,' and, still met with silence, blurted out that he was in charge of the detention class.

'And what of Fraser?' said Watson.

'Inattentive, sir,' explained Hutton. 'I had occasion to speak to him twice.'

'The boy is obviously labouring under a sense of injustice,' Watson said. 'A delusion, no doubt, but one cannot be too careful.' Reaching up his hand he flicked at Hutton's shoulder, as though smoothing away chalk dust.

The junior master took a step backwards.

Watson told him he had observed a red mark on Fraser's cheekbone. 'Did you notice it?' he asked.

'No, no, I'm afraid not,' said Hutton, discomfited.

'Possibly,' suggested Watson, 'he brought the lid of his desk up too smartly.' Staring thoughtfully at the junior master, he began to stress the inadvisability of driving young boys too hard. 'From the earliest time,' he cautioned, 'the schoolmaster has been the natural enemy of his pupil. Plato never lost an opportunity to attack the profession, and Horace, referring to the only schoolmaster he mentions by name, dubs him Flogging Orbilius. Remember Shakespeare's Holofernes, a name of outrage cribbed from Rabelais. Remember the pedant in *The Taming of the Shrew* –' He broke off and looked blankly at Hutton; he was thinking of Anne again. Without another word he turned on his heel, and ignoring Fraser, who was loitering in the front hall scraping with a pocket knife at the panel of the door, he went out into the playground. He had an idea that he would go straight home, but even as he came out of the school gates his footsteps faltered. He had intended to turn left; instead he kept straight on in the direction of the South Lambeth Road.

As he walked he spoke to himself out loud. 'To submit cheerfully,' he muttered, waving his fist despairingly in the air. How could he have been so deluded as to think that Anne was happy? Her bitter remark, which, as far as he could judge, stemmed from expectations not realised, was only a natural reaction to the depressing reality of her life. He didn't believe it mattered to her that they had never had children, though they hadn't discussed the subject. He himself was glad to have missed fatherhood. In his experience a man's relations with his offspring were often unsatisfactory, once the dandling days had gone. Anne was affectionate towards young boys between the ages of ten and fourteen, but he had never caught her looking tenderly at an infant. Though the issue of the boarders still rankled, perhaps he should never have agreed to leave the School House. Given time, Anne's unfortunate quarrel with Mandell and Grey might surely have blown over.

He was so preoccupied crossing Stockwell Lane that he was almost run down by a brewer's cart. It was only when he branched into South Lambeth Road and the noise of traffic broke into his thoughts that he realised where he was. And then a peculiar disturbance attracted his attention.

Opposite him on the other side of the road an old man and a boy were circling each other with fists held up. They had already come to blows; the old man's shirt was flecked with blood and he was wiping his mouth with his sleeve. The next moment he bent down and scooping up a length of wood from the gutter began to hit the boy about the legs. The boy's boots, unlaced, flapped against his naked ankles. Suddenly a brown dog trotted from the doorway of the pie shop and came to sniff at the old man's heels. He whirled round, the stick raised above his head.

At that instant two passing cabs, one following behind the other and both travelling in the direction of Vauxhall Bridge, blocked Watson's view. When they had gone by, the men and the dog had disappeared. In their place stood a woman in a red dress biting on an apple. Watson peered across the street; in the heat haze the woman's skirt seemed to quiver.

He walked on, certain in his mind that the dog's back had been broken. Then he thought of the two men and felt ashamed for considering the brute rather than them. What harm people did to one another! How cruel they were, he thought. How they beat and struck and thrust at one another!

A few minutes later he found himself on the steps of Montpelier House. He hesitated before ringing the bell; he hadn't meant to visit Williams.

The Revd Mr Williams had been lying on the sofa enjoying a nap. He was older than Watson and he suffered from pains in the legs. Watson couldn't help comparing his own dingy quarters in Park Road with the large sitting-room at Williams's disposal. The previous occupants had used it as a billiard parlour. The slate-topped table, covered with a damask cloth, still stood in the middle of the room.

Mr Williams was surprised at Watson's bothering to return his call so quickly. 'I remembered an appointment,' he said. 'Otherwise I would have waited.'

'I thought it might be urgent,' Watson said. He refused to sit down and stood instead at the bay window, looking out at the garden. The lupins drooped over the uncut grass; there were more weeds than flowers.

'Old Clissold goes out of an evening,' said Williams, 'and snips the heads off things. There isn't a gardener among us.'

'I have been a disappointment to Mrs Watson,' said Watson suddenly.

'Surely not,' protested Williams, but he believed it to be true. From discussions he'd had with Mandell and from observations of his own, Mrs Watson was a neglected wife. He had always found her very much on edge. Once he had visited Watson at the School House and admired an oddly shaped shell on the mantel-shelf. Mrs Watson had flown at him and snatched it out of his hand. Later she had excused her behaviour by saying she feared it might fall into the hearth and shatter. She was sentimentally attached to it, she said; her uncle had brought it back one Christmas from the South Seas.

'I have always intended to rent a house,' said Watson, 'and buy furniture. Mrs Watson would like a piano. I'm not often at home, as you know, and since quitting the School House she's alone most of the time.'

'Perhaps you should consider moving here,' suggested Williams, remembering that Mrs Watson loved flowers. 'Now that Hardy's gone there are rooms vacant on the second floor.'

'The traffic,' objected Watson. He left the window and paced up and down beside the billiard table.

'The rooms are at the back,' Williams said.

Watson thought it over. When he had returned to Park Road, the boarders – there being no one suitable to take care of them – had been put into lodgings and the School House partly given over to the mathematics department. Mandell and Grey had moved in with the Revd Mr Williams and Hardy. How could he inflict his wife on them, after that evening when Mandell had bled on to the carpet?

He himself had been dining at King's College when it happened. It appeared that Anne's stomach disorder had flared up again; she had obviously become distraught. She had charged both Mandell and Grey with aiding and abetting *him* in his pursuit of Miss Lancing. She had accused Grey of letting Miss Lancing in at the side door of the school as late as five-thirty in the evening. Naturally Grey had denied it – the story was a fabrication of the wretchedly ignorant Mrs Tulley.

Miss Lancing was the daughter of the late Colonel of a foot regiment in India. On returning to England she discovered that certain share certificates in the Stockton and Darlington Railway Company, for want of a stamp, were worthless. She was destitute. Williams had put her in touch with the school, thinking that one of the parents with female children might be persuaded to take her on as a governess. Watson had successfully placed her with a chemist's family on the Brixton Road, and she had shown her appreciation by knitting him mittens and bringing him pot plants; she was a lover of geraniums. Exceedingly thin, she had a sallow complexion left over from her days in Bengal. Anne's delusion – which scarcely a year before would have gratified him – that he found Miss Lancing to be anything more than a lonely and mildly irritating woman had exasperated him. According to Mandell, who was the soul of tact, Anne had accidentally knocked two glasses into the grate and he had cut his hand picking up the pieces.

'Miss Cockshott and Mrs Brewer live here,' said Williams. 'Mrs Watson would have plenty of female company, though Miss Cockshott keeps school hours.'

Turning from the window, Watson asked, 'Do you go on holidays?'

Williams was taken aback and admitted that he did. Every year he went to Hastings.

'Alone?' said Watson.

Williams replied that usually he met up with one or two friends. There was a Mr Bush and his son Fred who were often in the town at the same time.

'And Hastings is pleasant, is it?'

'Very pleasant,' said Williams. He took an envelope from his pocket. 'I received a letter this morning from Professor Browne of King's College.'

'There are boarding houses, I suppose?' persisted Watson.

Williams told him he believed so; he himself stayed with his sister. He tried again. 'I thought this letter might be of interest to you,' he said. 'Professor Browne has recently completed a translation of Aristotle's *Ethics* for Bohn's library. He wants to know whether I would be prepared to write for the series.'

'And are you?' asked Watson.

'He is referring to the classical series, rather than the theological. I'm not up to it. I was thinking more of yourself. You would find it child's play.'

Watson shook his head. His duties at the school filled all his hours. At this moment his only concern was for Anne's happiness. He must give her more time, not less. 'It's because you're not up to it,' he told Williams, 'that you dismiss it so lightly. Literary endeavour of any kind, even hack work, is always laborious.'

'My dear fellow,' objected Williams. 'Apart from the translation it's just a question of a preface and a few footnotes. And it pays well.' He was convinced that the Standard Library, started by Bohn out of pique – his rival, Bogue, had made a success of the European Library – would jump at employing Watson. His prodigious energy, his attention to detail, the pace at which he drove himself, would make him an asset to any publisher. Should he, he wondered, mention that Dale of Blackheath was translating Thucydides for the same series?

'I work nine hours a day,' Watson reminded him. 'I don't think I could give of my best.' All the same, by the time he had walked twice round the billiard table he had already composed a letter in his head to Bohn. He noticed that the grass was fading as the sun left the garden. A black cat was picking its way across the darkening wall; poised for a moment on a loose brick, it arched its back. Suddenly sensing that the surface of the wall was unsteady, the cat leapt sideways and streaked away through the nettles.

The platform of my own life is shifting, thought Watson. I must save myself. Abruptly he began to tell Williams the story of the dog in South Lambeth Road.

When he had finished Williams said, 'Poor brute. I suppose it has crept into a dark corner to die.'

'But what is it thinking?' asked Watson.

'Thinking!' said Williams. 'Why, it is incapable of thought.' He was baffled by the discussion. Such a fuss over the death of a dog! He hadn't known that Watson was so fond of animals. Last year the head master had accompanied him on the St Andrew's Sunday school treat – they had picnicked in a wood beside a cornfield. In the afternoon a farm dog had come racing along the boundary of the field in pursuit of a rabbit. Unless his memory deceived him, Watson had fairly danced on the spot and hollered as loudly as anyone. He was now rambling on about his belief in the reasoning power of animals. He had read Leibniz and Livy on the subject and was persuaded by them. He himself had first-hand experience of such reasoning. Riding along a country lane in Maidstone he had come across two mongrel bitches lying in the dust. One of them had a broken leg, and the other had crawled under the injured limb to support its weight.

'Possibly for warmth,' said Williams.

'It was a summer day,' cried Watson, 'a day like today.'

Shortly afterwards he said he must go home. In a blundering sort of way he apologised for the random and rather personal nature of the conversation. Williams imagined he was thinking of his earlier reference to Mrs Watson.

Hurrying along South Lambeth Road Watson took no notice of the spot where the two men had fought; he had already forgotten the incident.

'Hastings,' he said aloud, 'Hastings', and ran full tilt into Henry Rogers, manager of the Beulah Laundry. Rogers apologised to him, and Watson said the fault was his; he had been preoccupied.

Afterwards he was annoyed with himself for being so fulsome.

* * *

As she let herself into the hall Anne heard her husband come out
of the top room; he'd obviously been listening for her. He
appeared on the first landing, and though, as usual, the gas was
turned economically low, she could see that his face was pale. He
had never before arrived home and found her absent, not even
when the school had caught fire and smoke had seeped through the
green baize door. He was frowning; a stranger might have thought
he was angry.

'I was anxious,' Watson said. 'Where have you been?'

'Mrs Iselin asked me to tea,' Anne said. 'Didn't I tell you?' She
climbed slowly towards him and, having reached the landing, fled
past him and up the stairs as if she had left a pot on the boil. When
he had followed her into the sitting-room she was standing with
her back to him at the grate, both hands clutching the
mantel-shelf.

'It's gone eight o'clock,' he said.

'It's so warm out,' she murmured, and went through into the
bedroom to take off her cape and bonnet. 'I left you a note,' she
called.

'There was no note,' he said.

'It's on the mantelpiece,' she told him. And sure enough, now
that he knew where to look he saw a scrap of paper tucked under
the oyster shell.

He wanted to know whether he should go downstairs and tell
Mrs Chapman to bring up the supper. He had eaten an hour
before, standing at the window with his plate in his hand,
watching the corner for a sight of her.

Anne didn't answer. She came and sat in the armchair by the
fireplace and shut her eyes. He stood behind the chair, putting his
hand on her shoulder. Immediately she shrugged him away,
though it was possible she was settling into a more comfortable
position.

He asked her again whether she wanted anything to eat.

'No,' she said. 'I'm not hungry.'

She had taken off her skirt and was in her petticoats. It was
something she had always done. She said that in Ireland no one in
their right mind would loll about indoors in their best things. He

had protested that he had never found it to be the case, but then, as she had quickly pointed out, he had not mixed in society; his time in Dublin had been spent in the company of tradespeople and students. 'There is no one to see me,' she had pronounced carelessly. It dismayed him. He fretted lest Mrs Chapman, bringing up hot water or coals, would think her slovenly.

A moment later he too went into the bedroom. It was separated from the main room by double doors. On winter nights he liked to push back the doors and fall asleep watching the firelight playing on the ceiling. Anne herself preferred to lie in total darkness.

She heard him opening the wardrobe; he had got into the habit of picking up her clothes after her. Sometimes, if she forgot to place her hair pins tidily in the dish on the dressing-table, she found in the morning that he had swept them away altogether. Soon he would start brushing the dust from the hem of her skirt. She had always felt that his thoughtfulness contained an element of reproach. There wasn't a stitch on her back that hadn't been paid for by him. Her skirt and her jacket, her day dresses and her cape had been made by a dressmaker recommended by Mrs Iselin. 'She is becoming almost a fixture,' Watson had remarked, catching Mrs Iselin, two afternoons in a row, poring over patterns in the sitting-room. He hadn't said it in front of her, but the way he had loped up and down, twitching the curtains straight and bending to snatch imaginary pieces of thread from the carpet, had fooled nobody. The next day one of Mrs Iselin's children had conveniently fallen sick and she had sent word round to say that she wouldn't be available for some time. She had never called again.

'I spoke to Iselin after prayers this morning,' said Watson, coming back into the room with the clothes brush in his hand. 'And again in the corridor. He didn't mention you'd been asked for tea.'

'I expect it slipped his mind,' she said. 'You men have so much to occupy you.'

'Anne,' he cried, 'Anne.'

She was forced to open her eyes; it wasn't like him to plead.

'Anne,' he repeated, though no other words followed. He sat down at the table and then jumped up and came back to the fireplace. There was a button missing from his coat. At last he said, 'What's wrong, Anne?'

'Wrong?' she said sullenly. 'What should be wrong?'

'I feel it,' he said. 'And your remark this morning ... all day I've been thinking about it. I've been unable to concentrate on my work.'

She shrugged her shoulders in disbelief.

'It's true,' he persisted. 'Why, today Munford came and I found myself listing the books for the examinations. He knows them as well as I do. They are always the same –'

'I am alone all day,' she interrupted. 'What do you know of my life?'

'I too am alone,' he protested, and at this, outraged, she shouted at him, 'Nonsense, fiddlesticks. By your own admission you spoke to Munford and to Iselin and to Williams –'

'Williams,' he said. He couldn't think how she knew.

'And Grey never leaves your side. There are any amount of people creeping around you, bringing you gifts, asking your advice –'

'Gifts?' he said.

'Day after day I sit here and see no one. I have no servants to instruct, no household to run –'

'It was you who insisted we leave the School House,' he said, growing irritable now that she was heaping it all on to him. She reminded him that they hadn't received a penny of profit from the boarders. He had never stopped complaining at having to dip his hand into his own pocket to provide paraffin oil.

'Yes,' he admitted. 'Yes, it's true.'

She explained that the boredom she felt arose not from an inevitable withering of love but from her inability to affect him. He simply never took her into account.

He was so taken aback at her pessimistic view of marriage that he scarcely heard the rest of the sentence.

'You never ask my opinion of anything,' she said. 'Unless it's to do with inkwells or text-books or some dreary altercation you've had with Grey. And then it's no more to you than giving your gloves away to a beggar.'

'I don't understand,' he said.

'You never feel the cold,' she retorted. 'You don't need your gloves.'

He was speechless.

She went on to accuse him of becoming overwhelmed with fatigue whenever she attempted to talk of things which interested her. He had a way of biting on his lip to stop himself yawning. He needn't think she was unaware of it.

Even as she spoke he felt a muscle twitching in his cheek.

'Today I met Dr Munford coming away from the school. Consider what I felt when he complimented me on a geranium I had never set eyes on. You told him I'd grown it.'

He was bewildered. 'You're mistaken,' he said. 'There was no talk of gardens, only of flies.' He looked at her helplessly; he had envisaged it so differently. Uncertain how to proceed, he began to tell her about the increase of deaths in the district, of the dangers of contamination in the playground and how Munford had pushed the whole problem on to him.

'Of course he has,' she said sarcastically. 'Who else but you would come up with a thrifty solution?'

In spite of himself, he bit on his lip.

'Stop it,' she cried, and she jumped up from her chair and raised her fist, as though to strike him.

He stepped back, appalled. 'You're mistaken,' he said, 'I'm not yawning. It's simply a muscular spasm, a dependence of the platysma myoides, or what is known as the misorius Santorini.'

She ran into the bedroom and closed the doors. I am not bitter, she told herself. Only sad. She had overestimated his faculty for understanding; he had always underestimated her capacity for feeling.

From the beginning she had been so foolishly confident that her life would be lived, if not exactly as in those palmy days at Inchicore, then at least in some grey imitation of it. She hadn't asked for the moon, merely for an occasional supper party, an excursion into the country – a day at the seaside. And when even these paltry treats had been denied her, she had turned for company to Mrs Tulley, though of course the drill sergeant's wife was nothing more than a servant. With Mrs Tulley she had felt at ease, a state of mind unknown to Watson. The differences of class and experience – Mrs Tulley had lost her first husband in bizarre circumstances and been left to bring up a child – were of no importance. She herself had suffered a far greater deprivation for, in the ruination of her father, hadn't she lost a whole way of life? With Mrs Tulley she could savour the ruthlessness of Irish humour; without her she might have gone mad. The English had no wit – speculation was labelled gossip, interest dismissed as vulgar curiosity. They hadn't the least notion of how to enjoy themselves and were forever cleaning and polishing their furniture, wiping the soot from the windowsills, taking down the curtains and the blinds in spring as though there were devils lurking in the corners. As if anticipating the Second Coming, they waited in their scrubbed houses for the arrival of the chimney sweep, the upholsterer and the decorator; in the distance, like a storm brewing, the carts and the omnibuses rumbled across the city. Now and then, agitated by puritanical zeal and unable to come to terms with their own good fortune, they leapt out into the world and thrust second-hand clothing and left-over food on the great unwashed beyond the gates. Watson, spying some lout lying under the railway arch or sprawled in the gutter outside a public house, would give the coat off his back. Fresh from her buoyant talks with Mrs Tulley, reminiscing of roaring times in Ireland, she would taunt him with hypocrisy, of attempting to placate the desperate multitudes who swarmed up and down the Clapham Road. 'They will get you in the end,' she warned, 'for all your shenanigans', though afterwards she apologised because she could see how uncomfortable she made him.

'I have always wanted a cabinet made of satinwood,' she cried out, each time that fat-head Mandell or the Revd Mr Williams, thinking they were doing him a service, told her of Watson's latest act of lunatic charity. She saw how they looked at her, and when they had gone she would blame him for making her appear extreme, and he would protest that she had got it wrong, that they admired her, that she was more life-like than he. 'Why,' he would say, 'it is you they come to see, not me. I'm a kill-joy, a dry stick.'

At this moment she felt her happiest hours had been spent with the boarders, not with her husband. She had sat by the fire with Claybrooke, watching him toast bread. The boy's carroty hair, twisted into curls, had bounced on the frayed collar of his jacket. She had only to stretch out her hand to touch his cheek mottled by the flames. When he had caught his finger in the gate she had bound it up with her handkerchief. Often, confused, he had called her 'Mother'. Watson had taken against Claybrooke because she had lent the boy some tattered children's book she had found in the study. Claybrooke had been ill at the time with scarlet fever. When he was better Dr Munford had told her to put his possessions on the fire. Watson, on hearing what had become of his precious book, had behaved as though she was responsible for the burning of the library at Alexandria.

Though fond of the Besant brothers, especially Frank, who was idle and broke things and sometimes cheeked her, it was Claybrooke she had loved. Today, when she had called at his lodgings only to be told he was away in Norfolk, she had felt her heart would break.

I have not come very far, she thought. I have moved from one room with Olivia into two rooms with J.S. Watson. She had no furniture; if she died tomorrow her belongings would still fit into the trunk she had brought from Dublin. The daylight hours passed with her sitting vacantly at the window, motionless, untouched. Even those unspeakable movements accomplished in the dark had become little more than the wrigglings of fish under water. When he slipped away from her into sleep she lay stranded, looking up at the firelight leaping on the ceiling. Once only in his embrace, on her wedding night, had she felt she was not alone. I am a disappointed woman, she thought. He had never bought her a piano. She began to cry into the pillow.

Watson, hearing those noisy sobs, covered his face with his hands. He felt as if he had committed a crime. At the same time he couldn't help thinking it was all a storm in a tea cup. He had tormented himself for no reason. Her weeping, her disagreeableness – she had virtually accused him of stinginess – had in some way lessened the seriousness of her remark at breakfast. How mistaken he had been; it was, after all, only women's behaviour. And yet, listening to her, the tears welled up in his own eyes.

After a while she stopped crying, and he heard her rise from the bed and light the gas. The bed springs jangled as she lay down again. Half an hour passed. At last he went to the doors and, pushing them open a fraction, spoke to her through the gap. Uncertain whether she was even awake, he told her about Montpelier House and the empty rooms, dwelling on the spaciousness of the communal sitting-room and the size of the neglected garden. She could grow things, he said.

She asked calmly, 'And who lives there, besides your friend the Revd Mr Williams?'

'A Miss Cockshott,' he said. 'Headmistress of a ladies school in Euston.'

She enquired the age of Miss Cockshott.

'Old,' he said, hoping it was the truth. 'And there's Mrs Brewer from the Beulah Laundry.'

He opened the doors wide. She was sitting up in bed, her arms bare, her hands clasping her knees. She looked refreshed, coquettish almost.

'A woman from a laundry!' she said.

It was on the tip of his tongue to snap at her that Mrs Brewer, compared to Mrs Tulley, was a duchess. Instead he explained that she was the proprietor of the business and well-to-do. She was also fond of music. He didn't think this was the moment to mention Henry Grey or Mandell. 'You'd have company,' he said. 'And it would give me time to find a suitable house to rent.'

At this she held out her arms to him.

He sat on the edge of the bed and holding her close murmured that he had always meant to rent a house and to buy her a piano. It was his intention to take her to Hastings. They would go the instant the school holidays commenced.

She began to cry again. She was sorry for the cruel things she had said to him earlier – sometimes her life was so wretched she couldn't help being spiteful.

'It's my fault,' he said, 'my fault.' And stumbling over the words, he added, 'I was not taught how to love.'

'I was not taught to accept second place,' she said truthfully.

He said awkwardly, 'You know that I love you –'

'I know it,' she replied. 'But often I don't feel it. It isn't the same for a woman.'

She stared over his shoulder at a print on the bedroom wall. It was a view of Old London – a stretch of the Thames with some misty sailing ships in the distance. She thought the water was well done. How curious it was! She had waited, waited for him to tell her he loved her, and now that it was said it didn't seem to make any difference. Perhaps he had left it too late. When she had a house of her own she would have a series of such prints displayed along the wall and up the stairs.

Two weeks later, in reply to Watson's letter, the Standard Library wrote expressing interest in his proposed translation of Lucretius. After a meeting with Mr Bohn at his offices in Covent Garden, he decided he would start work on it immediately the school examinations were over. Perhaps too now was the time to apply for his Oxford M.A., *ad eundem gradum*, to which as a Trinity M.A. he was entitled.

Anne, when told that the holiday in Hastings would have to be postponed, said she understood. Naturally his literary career must come first. Besides, she would have plenty to occupy her rearranging their rooms in Montpelier House. Mandell was conveniently applying for a post at a school in Belgium, and she would simply ignore Henry Grey. Even before they moved in she gave instructions that the grass in the garden should be cut.

Winter 1858

Watson was staring out of the carriage window at London Bridge Station when he noticed a woman crying on the platform. She wore neither shoes nor stockings and was looking directly at him. In spite of the dismal contortions of her face, she seemed to be smiling. Still gazing at him, she exposed her breast and he saw she was holding an infant. Though it was February and bitterly cold, the child was almost naked. As the train began to draw away from the station he pushed down the window and hurled some coins at the woman. He tore the muffler from his neck and threw it towards the platform; it fell short and dropped onto the track. Shuddering, he pulled up the window and flung himself into his seat. He felt weak all over, as if he had suffered an intolerable shock. Tasting blood in his mouth he took out his handkerchief and spat into it. The train crawled across the bridge; below, specks of frost glinted on the mud banks of the river. Then the line sloped downwards, running between houses and factories, and slabs of wasteland on which the cattle and the pigs stood rooted, stiff as the branches of the winter trees. A pall of black smoke obliterated the sun. At last, passing a church and row of dwellings clinging to the bank of an oily canal, the train left the town and emerging from a brick tunnel travelled beside frozen fields and ponds, through Hither Green, Mottingham and Eltham. The sky turned blue again.

He had spent the earlier part of the morning at a dentist's in Oxford Street. Most of his life he had been plagued with toothache, and recently he had begun to be troubled with his stomach. Fearing his breath stank, he had sucked peppermints from morning till night. Reluctantly he had consulted Dr Munford, complaining of cramps and a foul taste in his mouth. Dr Munford, observing the advanced state of decay in his few remaining teeth had ordered him to have done with them. In his pocket, wrapped in brown paper, Watson now carried a complete set of vulcanite plates fitted with coil springs. He had been told he would be able to wear them in a matter of days when his lacerated gums had miraculously healed and he had mastered the instructions for securing the contraption in his mouth. He understood he was to hold the upper set in his right hand while placing the lower one in position, and that he must be careful not to entangle his lips in the springs. Before completing the transaction he had satisfied himself, as far as he was able, that the teeth were indeed false and had not come from some distant battlefield. He had only the haziest recollection of what had occurred in that torture chamber above a jeweller's shop. He remembered a great thumb and forefinger prising open his lips and then a taste of metal as the forceps probed his jaw, followed by an excruciating pressure, not in the region of his mouth but somewhere at the top of his skull. He had held onto the arms of his chair to prevent himself being dragged upright. Unable to scream he stamped his feet on the sawdust littered floor. He was convinced that the bony structure of his skull would be reduced to splinters and he had shut his eyes so tightly that stars sprayed through the agonising darkness. After each monstrous extraction he lay back, limbs trembling, his mouth warm with blood. The hatred he felt for the butcher who violated him, who straddled his thighs as if riding him to an abattoir, cheeks puce with exertion as he wrenched the stumps from his head, was immense. If he had been less feeble he would have seized him by the throat and tossed him out of the window. The dentist wore a white surplice splattered with scarlet flecks and tied at the neck like a choirboy. Watson had reached out blindly and smeared his own blood on to his fingertips.

He had intended, when it was finished, to go home; instead he found himself at the station booking-office buying a ticket to Crayford. It was a reckless thing to have done, as he now realised. His brother Abraham had given no address, and even if he was located without difficulty there would be little opportunity of speaking to him, not if he wanted to be home in time for Henry Dale. He should have gone to Crayford two weeks before when Abraham had first communicated with him. Anne had advised against it. She said there was no cause to return. It was bound to upset him – he was so sentimental about the family who had abandoned him. She told him to instruct Abraham to send back the money owed. He hoped she had chosen the wrong word and had meant to imply that he was a man of sentiment. Taking an historical view, he believed sentimentality walked but a step ahead of brutality.

'What a dreadful day,' Mrs Brewer had wailed, on learning that the head master had lost both a mother and an elder brother.

'There were some years between the two deaths,' Anne had retorted. 'And J.S. Watson can hardly be said to have known either of the persons concerned.'

Dear John Watson, Abraham had written, *One pound, four shillings and sixpence is in my keeping, being monies left over from quarterly payment and no longer expected. My mother caught typhoid fever on the first day of January and perished of it on the 20th day. She wrote you a letter that you have had January last. Alfred died five years ago of a fall against the furnace door. He lingered some days, peeling like an onion ...*

He had replied to Abraham, explaining that his was the only letter he had received and begging him to make use of the modest sum intended for their mother. He didn't feel he was depriving Anne of anything. The allowance he made to her sister, Olivia, far exceeded the miserly amount once set aside for his mother. He was sorry, he wrote, to hear of Alfred's sufferings, even so long after the event.

Having questioned the two servants and the housekeeper at Montpelier House, he was satisfied they knew nothing of the letter his mother was supposed to have dispatched. He drew a blank at the Post Office, the School House and at Park Road. Perhaps, as Anne suggested, there had never been a letter in the first place. Was it likely, seeing she was dying, that his mother could have written to him? Still, he was tormented by thoughts of what such a letter might have contained. When he confided his feelings to Anne, she told him to turn his back on the past. He felt that the manoeuvre was useless; as he grew older, whichever way he twisted, the past ran to meet him. He said he wished he had been there when his mother had died, and she reminded him that typhoid was catching and urged him to live in the present, as she herself did. Memories, she said, were often treacherous and inaccurate. He was impressed by her good sense. Half an hour later he overheard her telling Mrs Brewer, that, following the crash of the Bank at Dublin, Lord Ffrench had repeatedly called on her father, begging for forgiveness. But for Lord Ffrench's intervention, she said, the bailiffs would have carted away the furniture.

Looking out at the fields he was shocked to discover that the train was proceeding so slowly that a piebald pony under a crow-laden tree remained for several seconds within the frame of the carriage window. For once, if there had been other passengers in the compartment, he would have engaged them in conversation. Racked with anxiety about the time, he sank into a stupor. All he could think of was that he would be late home for Henry Dale. Not until a cemetery flickered past, gaudy with daffodils and sloping down to a narrow lane along which a pot-bellied man drove a bedraggled cow, did he pull himself together. Swinging his boots from off the footwarmer on the carriage floor, he released the window and stuck his head out into the icy wind. On the horizon the grey line of the marshes slid into the enormous sky. The Old Powder House, raised on stilts above the water, stood like a hump-backed beast come down to drink.

As he got out at Crayford it began to rain. From the station fence he could see the road winding to the river and the little iron bridge. Beyond, the town sprawled up to the church and the cottage where his mother had died. Before he left the platform he prudently asked the time of the next train back to London, and found he had less than an hour in which to look for his brother.

Within minutes of setting off his shoulders were drenched. Even if transport had been available to take him down the hill, he couldn't have afforded it; he had given his money away to the beggar woman at London Bridge.

He walked between hedgerows to the river, thinking of the supper party arranged for that evening. It was imperative that Anne shouldn't feel left out. When she thought she was ignored she was apt to pour herself another glass of port wine and become truculent. If he remonstrated with her, she called him hidebound – why, in Dublin a man wasn't considered a man until he had drunk so much that he fell insensible beneath the table. In her father's day at Inchicore House, they had strapped the militia man from Ballyraheen on to the back of his mare and whipped it up the front stairs. Such behaviour it seemed was only permissible in Irishmen. On the rare occasions the Revd Mr Williams imbibed too much and burst into maudlin song during supper, Anne stalked from the room in a huff.

She hadn't 'taken', as she put it, to Henry Dale, but then, as far as he could remember she had never 'taken' to any of his colleagues. He had translated six works for the Classical library in as many years, more than any other of Bohn's authors, as well as notes and a preface to Pope's edition of the *Iliad*, and now he and the head master of Blackheath were supposedly grappling together with the complexities of the *Cyropaedia* and *Hellenics*. It was hardly the collaboration he had expected. In November Dale's health had broken down, and apart from a lengthy correspondence of apologies and excuses, he hadn't contributed a word on the subject. With luck Anne and Mrs Brewer would retire early to the sitting room, and he and Henry Dale could discuss the matter. He was determined that the completion of the second volume, even if he had to do it all himself, should not be prolonged beyond the ending of the summer. He was now fifty-four years old and hadn't yet written an original book of his own. He had reached that middle season when the crowd must be content to remain at the foot of the mountain. Of course a man's age, he told himself, in regard to his work, was only relevant if he hadn't long to live.

Just then he saw a large black crow lying on the road ahead of him. Examining it, he concluded it had been struck down by the wheel of a cart. Its head was crushed. He shoved at the bird with the toe of his boot and its wing slid away from its body. Only the night before he had been working on Xenophon's account of the death of Abradates during the retreat of the Ten Thousand. Cyrus, seeing his lifeless friend laid out on the ground attended by a weeping woman, had dismounted from his horse and, kneeling, taken Abradates' right hand in his own, at which the hand had come away from the arm, and the arm from the shoulder. The woman, finding the body hacked to pieces by the Egyptians, had fitted it together like a puzzle.

Standing there looking down at the dismembered bird, Watson shivered. On either side of him he could hear the rain drumming on the frozen earth and it was like a death rattle in his ears. He kicked the two black lumps into the ditch beneath the blackthorn hedge and walked on. In all that funereal landscape there was not a soul about save himself; each step he took left him feeling more uneasy. Simply being in the vicinity of his birthplace oppressed him.

He had last visited Crayford shortly before his ordination when proof of his baptism had been required. Half fearing he was illegitimate, he had gone to St Paulinus' church and asked to be shown the register. There was his entry for December 30th, 1804, and the names of both father and mother. On leaving the church he had cut across the fields rather than pass the house in which his mother lived.

He had never discovered why his grandfather had taken him away. It was common enough, he knew, for parents in straitened circumstances to give up their children, but his vanity bucked at the idea that it should have happened to him. Though he had been too young to remember either occasion, his mother had twice come to Dartford to see him. On his eighth birthday she had sent him a child's book with an inscription on the fly leaf – 'To John Watson from his mother'. He had turned to the words again and again, and, closing his eyes, touched with his finger the loops and lines of her handwriting as if tracing the contours of her face. In his heart he had carried the image of a frail, milk-white girl too delicate to lift an infant in her arms. Then, at the burial of his grandfather, he had seen for the first and last time a tall, stout woman with a brick-red face, a button nose and a tattered bonnet in which a broken feather blew. She had chucked earth onto the coffin as though settling a score. When he was twelve years old she had given birth to his brother Alfred, and later to Abraham, and then to two other children. She had kept them all.

Without realising it he had crossed the bridge and reached the timber yard outside the town. He had thought of his mother as living a rustic existence and was astonished at the factories and at the noise of machinery. In spite of the rain the air was filled with the stench of bleach and nitric acid. In places the creek which ran beside the High Street had overflowed, and now the bottoms of his trouser legs were spattered with mud. He spoke to no one and was hardly noticed. Arriving at the row of cottages below the church, he glanced at them briefly and pressed on up the hill to the Vicarage.

The old woman who answered the door stared at him in alarm. She tried to shut him out, but he stuck his foot in the door and pushed past her, demanding to see the Rector. While waiting in the hall he glanced at his reflection in the looking-glass and understood her reluctance to admit him. His forehead was streaked with coal smuts and his lips caked with dried blood. He removed his hat and, placing it on the hall table, took out his stained handkerchief and attempted to clean his face. He was sickened by the sunken appearance of his cheeks and did not dare look inside his mouth.

The old woman returned and said the Rector was not well. She asked him his business.

He told her impatiently that he was looking for Abraham

Watson. His voice sounded muffled and he found it difficult to pronounce his words. Appalled, he ran his tongue over his raw and toothless gums and repeated as best he could, 'Abraham Watson. Son of Anne Watson who died of typhoid last month.'

At this the old woman replied, 'He's gone from here.'

'Gone?' he echoed. For an instant he thought she meant that death had struck a further blow.

The woman, eyeing him curiously, said Abraham Watson had sailed on an immigrant ship to America a week before. The parish had paid for his passage.

He enquired whether Anne Watson had a head stone yet in the graveyard.

'She's not buried here. She died in Bexley, in the workhouse. She were laid out by Eliza Maynard, who caught the fever from her. There's a daughter married to a stone carver living by the Iron Mill in Skibbs Lane, and another in service in Greenwich ...'

But he had stopped listening. He had taken it for granted that his mother had died in her own home, surrounded by her family. Now he saw her, stripped naked by strangers, tipped into a pauper's grave.

He went out of the door and down the path under the dripping sycamore trees. He could hear a voice shouting after him, but he hurried on. He walked at a tremendous pace through the town, over the bridge and up the road to the station. He had left his hat behind at the vicarage and the rain beat on his unprotected head.

Once on the platform he slumped exhausted against the fence. The pain now raging in his gums caused his eyes to water; it seemed as though every nerve in his body was exposed to the brutal air. He was persecuted by images, by visions of beds of death, each one more frightful than the last, until, as the train shrieked in the distance, he saw himself, for one clear and ghastly instant, bent over a woman who lay in pieces on a workhouse table.

Summer 1861

Mr Bush ran to tell his son, Fred, who was sitting at his easel in the garden sketching the Torfield, that the Watsons had arrived from London. He had seen Mrs Watson on the front porch being greeted by Mrs Merryville, not five minutes before.

83

Mr Bush had been expecting the Watsons for some days. His friend, Mr Williams, had advised him that they would be coming to Hastings on Thursday, and here it was almost noon on Saturday. 'They have hardly any luggage,' he said, 'apart from a quantity of books lying in boxes in the drive. There's no sign of Mr Watson.'

'Is Mrs Watson young?' asked Fred.

'No,' said Mr Bush. 'She is inclined to stoutness, and both hair and brows are turning grey ... but her eyes would do justice to a gypsy.'

Later, in the dining-room, Fred saw her for himself. She sat alone at the window table, dressed flamboyantly in a pink dress with green satin trimmings. As it was such a warm day the doors on to the terrace were propped open; several bees had blundered in and now hummed about the ceiling. Mrs Watson remained calm; when they spun lower she flapped her napkin carelessly in the air and went on eating.

'Her dress is not the right colour,' murmured Fred.

'Possibly it suits her temperament,' Mr Bush said, pushing back his chair. 'I shall make myself known to her.' Mr Williams had pointed the head master out to him in the street but he had never before encountered Mrs Watson.

Fred returned at once to the garden. He was forty years of age and his father was past sixty, and often he felt some mistake had been made and it was the other way round. Two greenflies had settled on his sketching pad; he squashed them with his thumb and settled down to work. By the time Mr Bush came in search of him he had completed the outlines of the spires of All Saints and St Clement's.

'Mr Watson has taken to his bed,' announced Mr Bush. 'He is worn out.' He looked critically at Fred's drawing, and continued, 'Judging by appearances he is a very studious man. The boot boy is still toiling up the stairs with the boxes.'

He wandered away and reaching the shade of a maple tree at the end of the garden sat down on the grass with his back to the trunk. It was exceptionally hot. Last week the temperature had reached 102° in the sun and 99° in the shadows, and he believed it was not far short of that now. All over the country people were dropping from heatstroke. He himself when young had lived in Southern Italy and could stand any amount of sunshine. It was just as well, he thought, considering the tropical conditions, that the head master was resting. In his debilitated state – Mrs Watson had hinted at other things beside overwork – he could go out like a candle.

He had been delighted at Mrs Watson's conversation; she was obviously a woman of character. After he had introduced himself she had asked him to sit with her. He had answered that he would wait until Mr Watson came down. To which she had replied, 'Then you will be standing there for some time, Mr Bush. We will not see the head master for a day or so.' The Revd Mr Williams had given an entirely false impression of her. He had implied that she was severe and often moody.

In the late afternoon, striding along the Parade, Mr Bush met Mrs Watson coming up the steps at the side of the bandstand. She had changed into a blue dress with yellow facings and wore a bonnet the colour of a buttercup. She seemed glad to see him and agreed to accompany him along the Promenade. As she walked she waved her hand in time to the military music blaring behind them; the blue satin reticule which hung from her wrist swung back and forth.

'How peaceful it is,' she said, stopping and leaning against the railings. 'How calm.' Indoors she had looked her age; now, in the sunlight, shading her eyes from the glare as she gazed out over the bright sea, the years fell away from her.

He apologised for staring at her too intently. He said that an artist was never on holiday.

'I don't object,' she said. 'In my younger days in Dublin I mixed almost exclusively in artistic circles. My father was a connoisseur as well as a patron of art.'

'I am glad to hear it,' he said. He was an old man, carelessly dressed, and in the heat his white hair was sticking to his forehead, but when she spoke to him he found himself drawing in his breath to minimise the portly curve of his stomach.

'Lord Ffrench and my father sat for the same painter in Upper Sackville Street. We lived at a large house at the top end. I have his portrait at home with me to this day.'

'I study faces,' confided Mr Bush, 'in much the same manner as Mr Watson studies books.'

'Ah, no,' she said quickly. 'You are looking outwards, observing life. Mr Watson looks inwards. The people he studies are invariably dead.'

Mr Bush could not have put it better himself. He asked how Mr Watson was.

'He is reading,' she replied, and added with a pleasant smile, 'Not an unusual occupation for him.'

Mr Bush admitted he had given up on books; he had to think of his eyes. But he was full of admiration for those who persisted. Only last week Mr Williams and he had discussed the head master's literary endeavours. He waited for Mrs Watson to respond to this but she looked steadily out to sea. He gathered that she wasn't altogether aware of his connection with Williams, nor had she known, until he told her, that he lived round the corner from the school in St Martin's Road.

'What a coincidence,' she cried out, clapping her hands excitedly. 'We are practically neighbours.' She said she hoped that when they returned to Stockwell she might be allowed to see some of his work. He protested that he was not a first-rate artist, or even second-rate. She would be disappointed. 'All I possess,' he told her, 'is a facility for catching a likeness.' He could tell that she instantly believed him and felt a little morose as a result.

That evening she didn't come down to supper. The next morning Mr Bush got up early and walked with Fred to Hallington Church, a distance of four miles. Fred made a poor sketch of the church, and Mr Bush a better job of scratching his initials on the back of a tombstone. Fred was afraid they would be caught in this act of desecration, and hid in the lane. On the way back they bathed in the sea off the White Rock, and when at last they returned to the boarding house the dining-room was deserted.

However, at supper, there was Mrs Watson seated at the window table with the head master. He had a book in front of him, propped up against the salt-cellar, and he wore his napkin tucked into his collar. Though extremely pale he didn't look in the least ill, and when he shook Mr Bush by the hand his grip was so vigorous that Mr Bush openly winced. All the same he had a melancholy air about him, as if he had received bad news and was only now getting over the worst of the shock.

'I trust the journey was not too tiring,' said Mr Bush, making small talk. He rubbed his crushed fingers into life against the hollow of his back. 'I hope it didn't take you too long to get here.'

'Eight years, or thereabouts,' put in Mrs Watson, with a mysterious smile.

'Our mutual friend Mr Williams has often spoken of you,' continued Mr Bush. 'When you feel stronger we shall have plenty to discuss.'

'I suppose so,' said Mr Watson.

Mr Bush said he understood that the head master played chess.

'I do,' he replied, brightening up. 'I do indeed.'

Mr Bush moved on towards his table by the hall door. On the way he was greeted enthusiastically by the Misses Cowper, who had spent the day at the Fishponds watching the tropical fish under glass, and more discreetly by Mr and Mrs Kenny.

'The heat,' cried out the younger Miss Cowper, fanning herself with a spoon. 'I thought we should melt.'

Mr Kenny, a retired solicitor from Guildford, had caught the sun. In contrast to his blazing face, his bald head, which had been protected by his straw hat, looked as if it had been white-washed. He told Mr Bush that there was to be a fireworks display in the town square that evening. He had seen a notice nailed to a tree outside the Post Office.

'There will be a dreadful crush,' said Mrs Kenny. 'And possibly pickpockets.' She began to remonstrate with the servant girl, who, maddened by the flies which buzzed above the gravy dish on the dumb waiter, was slicing the air with a carving knife. Taking the implement from her hand, Mr Bush wiped the girl's perspiring face with her apron and sent her back to the kitchen.

Seated at last, he put on his spectacles and looked at the cardboard menu which leant against a vase of cut roses in the centre of the table. There was roast beef and Yorkshire pudding.

'There is certainly nothing convalescent about his appetite,' he remarked to Fred, glancing out of the corner of his eye at the munching Mr Watson.

The Revd Mr Williams had told him, ten days before, that the head master had written no fewer than three books this year and that all of them had been unfavourably reviewed. Their brutal reception, however upsetting to him in other ways, had evidently not put him off his food.

'Socrates,' said Fred. 'Snub nose, prominent eyes under shaggy brows, large full mouth. Bearded, and later, bald.'

'Mr Watson has plenty of hair,' objected Mr Bush.

'It's early days,' said Fred, and remained silent for the rest of the meal.

As soon as the pudding was cleared away Mr Watson left the room. He was mopping his face with his handkerchief and still reading as he went out into the hall. A short time afterwards Mrs Watson followed him.

Mr Bush played a game of cribbage in the sitting-room with the elder Miss Cowper. Now and then small explosions were heard outside the French windows, and the distant sound of cheering. The garden was lit intermittently with flashes of light; coloured stars burst above the trees and trailed downwards. Through the open doors Mr Bush caught a glimpse of his son Fred standing on the flickering lawn, his head tilted to watch the fireworks.

* * *

Mr Bush had understood from the Revd Mr Williams that the head master was reserved; he hadn't expected that it would be an easy matter to get on with him. But over their very first game of chess Mr Watson confided to him that there was something about the sea air that was doing wonders for his spirits.

'Normally,' he said, 'I prefer to be on my own, but here it seems natural to be friendly.' It appeared he hadn't had a holiday in fifteen years, and since arriving in Hastings all desire to open his books had left him. Before the week was out he was talking to Mr Bush as though he had known him for a decade.

In company with Mrs Watson they walked along the shore and over the rocks to St Leonard's and back again, climbed the West Hill, explored the ruins of the castle together. Fred scrambled behind them, clutching his sketchbook and complaining of fatigue. They visited the Martello Towers, the Town Hall and the fish market – where Mr Watson bought Mrs Watson a lobster and Fred was persuaded to run home with it before it went off in the sun.

In the evenings, sometimes accompanied by Mr and Mrs Kenny, they sauntered along the Parade, followed at a courteous distance by a young man dressed in Cavalier Spanish fashion, strumming on a guitar and singing. He never asked for money and none of them could decide whether he was doing it for a living or because he was mad. Once Mr Watson left some coins on the wall by the promenade – the young man had dogged them that far – but when they returned the money was still there and the troubadour had leapt down on to the beach and was singing to himself in the starlight. Mr Watson explained that the guitar was a modern extension of the ancient Greek *cithara*, though the *cithara* had a shallower sound chest. He had always been interested, he said, in musical instruments.

It seemed he was interested in almost everything, although he insisted he was an unimaginative man and constantly on the war-path, as he put it, to stamp out prejudices within himself. His mind was so crammed with learning, with scientific concepts and philosophical ideas, with facts and anecdotes, that an hour spent with him was enough to make Mr Bush giddy. He talked of politics, of butterflies, electrical currents, agriculture, the problem of setting words to music, the law. He often discussed crime and punishment, and while he conceded the latter was probably necessary on moral grounds, he believed there wasn't a shred of evidence to prove it was a deterrent to the former. Besides, the law was an ass. Take the case, some years back, of the Reverend Samuel Smith, a Cambridge scholar who had made the lamentable discovery that his wife was having an affair with a porter called Leech. Having found her out he persuaded her to write to Leech and arrange an assignation in a secluded spot. This was done, and at the appointed time Smith jumped out and inflicted grievous injuries on the unsuspecting porter. Poor Smith was given five years penal servitude and his wife, the cause of all the trouble, a woman who had previously served behind the counter at Swan & Edgar's, was let off scot-free. Homer, Mr Watson said, had made it clear that the avenging of crime on earth was an important matter, though the fall of Troy was obviously dictated by divine justice. It must never be forgotten that the Greek gods were essentially cruel and wayward – if a man could grasp the appalling reality of antiquity he would turn from it in horror. He did not pretend to have fully grasped it himself.

He was not a good speaker – often when he talked his hand hovered over his mouth – and many of his allusions to classical literature left Mr Bush in the dark, but his curiosity was infectious. He had the startling conviction that animals had the ability to reason. Dogs, of course, were particularly canny in this respect. A dog, Mr Watson claimed, could sometimes sense the premeditation of an act of violence. Various theories existed as to why this should be so, but Mr Watson thought it had much to do with a particular odour believed to be emitted by a person with criminal intentions. As to larger animals, he told a moral and gruesome tale of an elephant whose keeper was saddled with an unfaithful wife. One day the elephant secretly tracked the woman and, finding her lying beside a water hole in the arms of her lover, lowered its tusks and ran the guilty pair through.

Fred, to whom Mr Bush repeated this information, allowed that dogs might behave in the manner described, but discounted the last story out of hand on the grounds that no one, unless stone deaf, was likely to be *secretly* followed by an elephant.

Mr Watson maintained that it was much the same with birds. Mr Bush and he spent an entire morning watching gulls dropping mussel shells on to the rocks below the headland.

'In New Holland,' he said, 'there is a species of buzzard, which, spotting the eggs of another bird, will carry a stone aloft in its talons and drop it from a height so as to smash the eggs beneath and suck out the contents. In the one case,' he concluded, indicating with his stick the industrious seagulls wheeling about the headland, 'the food is made to fall on the stone, in the other the stone is dropped on the food. In both the knowledge of cause and effect is much the same. Does this knowledge proceed from reason or instinct?' Fortunately he answered the question himself.

It was true that he had a disconcerting habit of correcting Mr Bush's choice of words, but it was a small price to pay for such stimulating chat. He noticed the shape of rocks, the gradations of colour where the sea met the sky, the form as opposed to the mass of the landscape. Mr Bush listened and nodded; not for one single instant did he feel either patronised or bored. Having begun by merely admiring the head master, he quickly grew fond of him, and in the process became protective towards him.

No sooner had this happened than it was apparent to him that Mrs Watson was neither as entertaining nor as equable as he had at first supposed. More than that, he believed she actually disliked her husband. It wasn't so much what she said, though now and then a tone of bullying insistence crept into her voice, but rather the way she looked at him. A less observant man, Mr Kenny for one, or the Revd Mr Williams for that matter, might never have noticed the mild curl of her lip, or the almost imperceptible raising of her eyebrows whenever she spoke to him. Nobody, however, certainly not Mr Watson, for whom they were intended, could possibly ignore those occasional and searing glances of calculated insolence.

'Whenever the poor man asks her opinion of anything,' he told Fred, 'she withers him with her eyes.'

'I have never heard him ask for anyone's opinion,' said Fred.

'Surely you've noticed the way she stares at him,' Mr Bush insisted.

'She regarded me in much the same way last week,' said Fred, 'when she sent me packing with the lobster. I don't take any notice.'

Mr Bush found it increasingly difficult to be in the same room with Mrs Watson, let alone give her a civil word. That frankness of speech which he had once admired, now seemed rude and overbearing. There was something offensive, indelicate almost, in the bold way she looked at people. He felt she was always demanding attention. There was a dreadful greediness of spirit inherent in the way she poured salt on to the meat on her plate, or held up her face to the sun, or childishly pleaded to be escorted home. 'I'm tired,' she would say. 'Poor little me.' As her face darkened – she hardly ever put her parasol to its proper use and merely twirled it in the air over her shoulder – Mr Bush fancied she was changing into one of those reasoning animals Mr Watson was always discussing. With her sharp muzzle and her cunning amber eyes, he began to think she resembled a fox. Fred, usually so snappy in observation, couldn't see it. He said his father was obsessed.

Mr Bush took to pressing Mr and Mrs Kenny to join them on their walks about the district, and then he would seize Mr Watson by the elbow and either surge ahead, leaving the vixen to follow with the others, or else deliberately delay him on some pretext and so manage to trail with him in the rear.

Several times he tried to draw Mr Watson out on the subject of his wife. He would say, 'Mrs Watson, I think, is of a nervous disposition,' or, 'Mrs Watson, being Irish, is possibly hasty', but each time the head master cleverly substituted one word for another, such as 'sensitive' for 'nervous' and 'impulsive' for 'hasty', and cutting him short pointed out the lichen on a rock or the presence of a bee hovering above a gorse bush. Attempting a more general tack, Mr Bush wondered aloud at the different nature of man and woman. To which the head master replied that in his view they were similar, only a woman had more to put up with.

One morning, sitting in the garden waiting for Mrs Watson to come downstairs, Mr Watson drew from his pocket a bundle of newspaper cuttings. He looked at them gloomily, and said, 'I have turned over half a library to make one book, and they have dismissed it in a few words.' He quoted: *'We cannot in all truth say anything which would imply that we could not have done very well without this book.'*

91

'Surely not,' protested Mr Bush. He had no idea to which book Mr Watson was referring.

'Here,' said Watson, throwing the bundle carelessly on to the grass. 'Browse through them. Read and digest.'

Mr Bush put on his spectacles. The cuttings all seemed to deal with the biography of Richard Porson, Greek scholar and author of the letters to Archdeacon Travis. To Mr Bush's way of thinking, leafing through them, there appeared to be a great many words. Unfortunately the ones that hit the eye were generally uncomplimentary ... *We sincerely hope that it will not stand in the way of a better work on the subject ... He is a very useful author who has the art of research. Mr Watson has not this gift ... A good hand at gossip ought to be good at the point of a joke. Mr Watson is not. The old reports of a criminal case used to say that the prisoner had been examined before torture, during torture and after torture. Mr Watson produces Porson before drink, during drink, and after drink.* There was much more, columns of it. Mr Bush seized on a last line and recited triumphantly, '*He deserves a merciful sentence as a man, and a high pedestal among scholars.*'

'They are talking of Porson, not me,' said Watson.

'I'm not a drinking man myself,' remarked Mr Bush, after an embarrassed silence.

'Porson could drink six pots of porter for breakfast,' said Watson. He sounded as if he admired the feat. 'The wife of Dr Parr, in whose house Porson stayed so that he could use the library, had never known such quantities of brandy to be drunk. Porson drank like an Irishman, and brandy and Greek acquired such an association in Mrs Parr's mind that afterwards, when any visitor was introduced to her as a Greek scholar she rushed to see if there was enough brandy in the house. She got rid of Porson by putting a close stool at the table in place of his chair.'

'Dear me,' cried Mr Bush.

'I don't have an inflated opinion of my abilities', said Watson, 'but I *know* it is a good book. But then my critics belong to the Cambridge faction – and Porson was a Cambridge man. No doubt they feel such a biography should have been left to one of their own men. They think I'm an upstart or an outsider – although I was ordained by the Bishop of Ely, and taught at Charles Parr Burney's School at Greenwich before I went up to Trinity: those were the happiest days of my life. Burney is now Archdeacon of Colchester. He took the school over from his father, who had

been one of Porson's intimate friends, and he supplied me with a
great number of letters and anecdotes from his father's papers
relating to Porson. That's what those Cambridge people don't like!
By the way, there was no whipping at Burney's establishment. Dr
Johnson used to say of the school, in the elder Burney's time,
criticising the lack of discipline, that what the boys gained at one
end they lost at the other. But we continued the tradition – and
I have continued it at Stockwell. What a contrast to the Public
Schools! Have you heard of Flogging Keate? He was only five feet
tall – "Pocket Hercules" they used to call him – and he tanned
eighty boys at Eton in a single day. The whole school cheered
him when he had finished.'

'A standing ovation, I suppose,' said Mr Bush nervously.

'They say he had no favourites and flogged the son of a duke
and the son of a grocer with equal impartiality.'

'At Stockwell, I imagine, all your pupils are the sons of grocers,'
said Mr Bush.

Watson knew it was a weakness in him that let him confide in
such an uneducated man as Bush, but he couldn't help himself. He
said: 'Mrs Parr was a woman of violent and overbearing temper –
she hanged her husband's cat in his library. No man can know,
who hasn't experienced it, the mischief such a woman can cause
between a man and his friends.'

Mr Bush fidgeted on his wicker chair. He felt enormously
dejected on Mr Watson's behalf.

Watson stared at the parched grass. He said quietly, 'Porson
wrote to Dr Parr and said how difficult it was for a man to *renovate*
his spirit once it had been broken.'

At that moment Mrs Watson was heard talking to someone on
the terrace. Watson abruptly snatched the cuttings from Mr
Bush's knee and stuffed them back into his pocket.

As Mr Bush later told Fred, it was obvious he didn't want Mrs
Watson to be reminded of the reviews. She probably never lost an
opportunity of throwing them in his face.

'He is protecting her,' said Fred, absurdly. 'They must have hurt
her as much as they hurt him'

*   *   *

At the close of the third and last week of the Watsons' visit to
Hastings, Mrs Kenny suggested that it would be nice if they all
spent an afternoon on the beach. The sun was now less fierce, and

they could take a picnic.

They were sitting on the shore on canvas chairs under two umbrellas, when Mr Kenny politely asked Mr Watson what he was working on at the present time. 'I suppose,' he said, 'that a man of your talents must always be searching for the next subject.'

Mr Watson looked at him as if measuring him for some dark corner. He was dressed, as usual, in black, but he sported a straw hat which was unravelling at the brim. 'I am engaged on a biography of Warburton,' he said. 'He had the most extraordinary ideas on the influence exerted by men on women, and regarded woman, in her natural state, as similar to one of those pictures that were once used for experiments in optics.'

'What pictures?' asked Mr Kenny.

Watson explained that a number of colours, thrown together at random on a board, could, by the use of a cylindrical mirror, instantly reflect a pattern of order and design. 'Warburton was under the misguided impression,' he said, 'that a husband could perform the function of a cylinder.'

Mr Kenny nodded wisely. Mr Bush could tell that the exchange had gone over his head; he was all at sea in more ways than one.

'One day,' said Watson. 'I hope to write an essay explaining why there has to be an Established Church. Warburton's best book was his *Alliance Between Church and State*, in which he steered a middle course between the Puritans – like Fox, the Quaker – who claimed that the law had no concern with religion, and political philosophers like Hooker and Hobbes who said that the State had a natural supremacy over the Church. Warburton's theory was that Church and State were mutually dependent, and that the Anglicans had a right to be established because there were more of them than there were Papists or Dissenters. The book got him a bishopric. Things have changed now in this age of progress and unbelief, and something new is needed to justify the union in modern terms. I am of humble origins like Fox – and Porson – but I speak for the Established Church.'

No one felt qualified to respond to this disquisition, and Watson proceeded: 'How indeed is it possible that a man of education who has read enough to understand the effects of human action on human society, should feel within himself other than Conservative tendencies? Fox of course was something of a genius, or madman. He was obsessed by light. Even the heathen, he thought, could be saved by the portion of light vouchsafed to him, if he did not resist it. His life is interesting as showing how much may be effected by the resolute perseverance of one man, notwithstanding opposition, insult, ridicule, and vexation of every kind. But he was bound to fail, for human nature remains always the same: the world was intended to be as it is, and whatever is opposed to the common sense of mankind must inevitably decay. Worldly radicals, on the other hand, are worse. Take Wilkes, with his notorious cry for "liberty". The great characteristic of the demagogue, from the earliest times to the present, has always been the same: a desire to gain advantage for himself under pretence of benefiting a multitude too short-sighterd to discern his real aims, by opposition to authority that he stigmatises as oppressive. Cobbett was better, and his egotism is as often amusing as offensive. But though many of his attacks on men and things have been attributed to love of sport rather than love of mischief, the savage earnestness of his invective, especially after he became a thorough radical, shows that the love of mischief predominated. Wilkes and Cobbett would make a good pair for a joint biography.'

There was a pause, and he pressed on hurriedly. 'Another good subject would be the Scotch rebel Sir William Wallace – whose first adventure was to kill the son of one of my ancestors: Selby, constable of Dundee. After hanging and beheading him, the English burnt his heart, liver, lungs and entrails, whence his wicked thoughts had come.'

A gust of warm air blew inland. It was sufficient to ruffle the fringes of the umbrellas, and to lift Mr Watson's hat. He clamped it on more securely, but not before Bush had noticed a white scar high up on his temple. He asked what had caused it.

'I was attacked,' replied Watson.

Mrs Watson, who until then had appeared to be dozing, rose from her chair and walked down to the water. Earlier she had paddled in the sea and her feet were still bare. She stood with her back to Mr Watson, the hem of her damp skirt encrusted with sand. The sky was washed blue all over, without cloud.

'On the other hand, whatever may be said against Cobbett,' said Watson, 'he was a true husband to a good wife.'

'Who attacked you?' asked Mr Kenny.

'I was living in Eltham at the time,' Watson told him, and then stopped. Mrs Watson had returned and was holding out a shell for Mrs Kenny to look at. It was quite a large shell and Mrs Kenny took it from her and held it to her ear.

'I have a curious shell on the mantel-shelf at home,' Mrs Watson said. 'Lord Moran, a friend of my father's, bought it at a sale of effects at Ballyraheen. It belonged to an old militia man who had defended the slopes of Vinegar Hill. Lord Moran gave it to me on my sixteenth birthday. I was his favourite god-child.' As she spoke she looked steadily at Watson. Taking the shell from Mrs Kenny she sat down again and wriggled her toes in the warm sand.

'The attack,' repeated Mr Kenny. 'Who attacked you?'

It seemed for a moment as though Watson hadn't heard, but then he said, 'Marines', and began his history again. 'I was living in Eltham, having graduated a year before from Trinity College. I had been teaching for two terms at a school in Woolwich. It was a summer's night and I was returning home after coaching a university candidate. Coming down Well-hall Lane out of the Dover Road at about half past ten, I was overtaken by a man who was lame. There was a moon and I clearly saw that the man was walking in a lopsided manner. I was considerably in advance of the crippled man when two soldiers came towards me. As they separated on the path to allow me to pass, one of them said, "Goodnight." It was at this point that I was struck on the head.'

'How dreadful,' murmured Mrs Kenny.

'I was hit with something heavy. I have no idea what it was. I was knocked down in the dust and became unconscious for a matter of seconds, perhaps a minute.'

'Did you bleed much?' enquired Mrs Kenny, leaning forward on her chair, her cheeks red with second-hand excitement.

'When I came to myself, the two men were going through my pockets. I remember having the ridiculous notion that they were tickling me. I didn't feel any pain. I tried to cry out but the one who held me down put sand into my mouth. I was convinced I should choke to death. Having emptied my pockets they ran off towards Woolwich. I knew they were marines because they wore scarlet jackets, though at the time of choking I thought they were toy soldiers marching out of some dream. I think they wore white trousers ... at any rate they were of a lighter colour than their jackets. I got up and walked towards Eltham. I was staggering.'

'Sand in the mouth,' shrieked Mrs Kenny.

'Thinking they might have left something behind, I went back and groped on the ground in an attempt to salvage something ... some coins or my keys. They had taken my keys. As I crawled there in the dirt the lame man came up and assisted me back to

Eltham. I was bleeding like a pig. The clock struck eleven just as we entered the town.'

Mrs Watson again rose from her chair. Picking up her towel she draped it over her yellow bonnet and strolled to the water's edge.

'I went to the house of Mr and Mrs Crawley,' said Watson. 'Later they took me to the hospital. I had been robbed of a considerable sum.'

'Were the men ever caught?' demanded Mr Kenny.

'They were,' Watson said. 'They drew attention to themselves by spending my money in the Black Boy at Greenwich. One of the men was transported for life.'

'Wherever there is greed,' put in Mr Kenny, 'there will unfortunately be violence.'

'They had been drinking,' said Watson. 'The lame man remembered them singing in the distance.'

Fred, who had been sitting some yards from the rest of the party, suddenly fell from his chair and rolled in the sand. Mr Bush's first thought was that he was having a fit. Mrs Watson was walking back towards the group beneath the umbrellas, the towel still draped over her bonnet. Fred was now squealing in a peculiar way. Mr Bush, momentarily rigid on his chair, decided he was being stung by invisible and silent bees. He was just struggling to his feet when Fred, pointing his finger at Mrs Watson, sat up and bellowed with laughter. One side of his face was veiled in sand.

'Tell that fat simpleton to keep quiet,' said Mrs Watson. She flung the towel from her head and strode away towards the rocks.

Nobody uttered a word. The squealing and the laughing continued for several long seconds, during which age Mr Watson dug a hole by his chair with the tip of his walking stick. Mr Bush was sorry it wasn't deep enough to bury the wretched Fred.

Afterwards he was not sure of the sequence of events that preceded the accident. Certainly Mr Watson had been looking in the direction of the rocks a moment before his wife screamed. Her forehead was badly gashed. The blood ran down her face and dripped onto her blue bodice, and she made little moans, one after the other, all the way along the beach and up the steps to the Parade. A crowd of onlookers gathered and Mr Watson waved them away with his stick. As she was helped down the road under the avenue of limes, Mrs Watson dashed her head from side to side and splashed blood on to the dappled ground. The whites of her eyes flashed in the green tunnel of the trees. Fred, carrying the folded umbrellas, remained mercifully silent, though he was smiling. When Mr Bush got him back to the boarding house he sent him straight upstairs to douse his head in a basin of cold water.

Mr Bush did not go down for supper that night; he was too ashamed. Mrs Merryville sent up a plate of cold meat, and when he had eaten he climbed into bed beside Fred. The undersheet was sprinkled with grains of sand, but he fell asleep immediately.

In the middle of the night he was woken by voices and the slamming of doors. He put on his flowered dressing-gown and went out on to the landing. The lights were turned up and the head master was walking along the corridor in his nightshirt. Mr Bush noticed the reddish hairs on his stout calves and the threadbare condition of his slippers.

'My wife is delirious,' said Mr Watson, 'I have fetched the doctor.' He went to the head of the stairs and slumped down on the top step. Mr Bush stood behind him and stared miserably at the carpet. The front door had been left open and the hall was full of rustlings as the wind fluttered the trees in the drive. He could hear the sea sweeping the shingle on the beach.

'An hour ago she started to talk to me in a deranged manner,' said Mr Watson. 'In an almost biblical manner.'

'Biblical?' said Mr Bush.

'Thou must go into the garden. Thou must not stay indoors on such a fine day. Dost thou think thou canst escape me?'

'Ah,' murmured Mr Bush.

'I have always been too self-reliant,' Mr Watson said. 'It is my main fault.'

'You shouldn't blame yourself,' protested Mr Bush. 'There are always two sides to every problem.'

Watson groaned and beat the banister rail with his fist.

This is too dreadful, thought Mr Bush, and he wedged himself beside Mr Watson and patted him awkwardly on the shoulder.

'She has a swelling above her eye,' Mr Watson said. 'It pains her.' Mr Bush could bear it no longer. Mrs Watson's act was quite incomprehensible to him. He blurted out, 'She did it to herself. My son Fred tells me so, and he is not a boy for lies. He saw her drag her face against the rock, and then she butted her head like a goat.'

'I know,' said Mr Watson. 'I saw her too. But intentional or otherwise, the result is the same. She has hurt herself and is paying for it.'

There were tears in Mr Bush's eyes, though they were not for Mrs Watson. He cried out that it was a tragedy.

'Apparently so,' Mr Watson said. 'At least to the spectators. God knows what it was for her.' He stood up and returned to his pacing of the corridor.

Mr Bush settled himself on the cane chair in the alcove and wiped his wet cheek with the tassel of his dressing-gown. The thought came to him that never again, after tonight, would Mr Watson confide in him. They would possibly remain friends, but further advancement was impossible – a man could only reveal so much of himself.

Presently Mrs Merryville came out of the bedroom carrying a basin filled with pink water and scraps of blood-stained lint. She was followed by the doctor.

'The wound is superficial,' he declared, 'but she has heatstroke.'

When the doctor had gone, Mr Bush thanked providence it was not more serious. Mr Watson shook him by the hand. He said, 'You're a good fellow. You take things to heart.'

'I blame myself,' stammered Mr Bush. 'Or rather I blame Fred.'

'Fred had nothing to do with it,' said Mr Watson. 'I believe you already know that.' He looked searchingly at Mr Bush and added, 'Tired of the raging sea I'm getting sane, and my old scars are quite skin-whole again.'

Mr Bush went into the bedroom and woke Fred. 'Mrs Watson has sunstroke,' he told him, 'and the head master is a little mad. He's just informed me he's recovering, and that his old cuts are healing. I imagine he's thinking of those marines.'

'He's talking about love,' said Fred.

Winter 1866

Mrs Tulley and Mrs Watson were sitting at the breakfast table when the head master burst into the room. Both women pretended to be startled, though both had heard his thunderous descent of the stairs. The moment he entered, Mrs Watson, who a moment before had been discussing some scandal involving the music teacher over the road, launched into a description of the dress she intended to wear that evening at the school.

'It's blue,' she said, looking directly at Mrs Tulley. 'Blue has always been Mr Watson's favourite colour.'

He interrupted her sharply, demanding to know whether she had given the servant girl permission to go into the library.

'No,' said Mrs Watson, 'I haven't budged.' She seemed to be smiling, though it was possibly from nervousness. 'Mrs Tulley and I have sat here talking of the prize-giving.'

'Ink has been spilt on my letter to the Bishop of Winchester.'

Mrs Tulley made a mewing sound, expressing sympathy. Several times she had attempted to rise from her chair and each time Mrs Watson had prevented her.

'That in itself,' Watson shouted, 'is hardly a disaster. But ink has dripped down on to the spine of one of my books. It is a library book.' He was so angry he pounded the table, and a pearl-handled butter knife bounced off the cloth and fell to the carpet.

Mrs Tulley wanted to follow it and sink through the floor. She hadn't seen him to speak to in years, but obviously his temper hadn't improved. He was actually grinding his teeth with rage.

'What of it,' said Mrs Watson. 'You are always knocking over things.' She continued to prattle on about her dress, as if hoping to stupefy him.

He stood there looking at his wife, his fists clenched and a muscle twitching in his cheek. He had been so sure that he was in the right, questioning her in that hectoring way, and now she had cut the ground from under his feet. Mrs Tulley felt almost sorry for him. In spite of his lowered brows and the rat-trap set of his mouth, his eyes were bewildered.

He turned and was half way through the door when Mrs Watson called his name. He waited, his back to her and his head bent. He was looking down at his ink-stained hands.

'John,' Mrs Watson repeated. 'John. Please.'

He stepped into the hall and put on his hat. He was punishing her for something. The front door slammed shut and they heard him marching down the path.

Mrs Tulley said perhaps she had best be on her way. Her son Henry had recently married and there was a child expected – she liked to keep an eye on her daughter-in-law. Mrs Watson protested that she hadn't yet seen over the house, but Mrs Tulley could tell her heart wasn't in it. There were beads of perspiration on her upper lip.

'Shall I just peek at the garden?' suggested Mrs Tulley. 'I remember you were always a dab hand with the flowers.'

'It's a poor enough plot,' said Mrs Watson listlessly, and she went out into the hall and stood there, waiting for Mrs Tulley to leave.

When Mrs Tulley had gone she ran upstairs and tried the handle of the library door. It was locked. He is taking no chances, she thought, and crossing the landing she went into the dressing-room. She began to pull out the drawers of the mahogany chest by the window. She couldn't see any dust, though she lifted up Watson's shirts and blew on them. There was nothing in the top right hand drawer save a few scraps of material and those old pistols his grandfather had left him. If the drawers were less than spotless, she told herself, it was because the chest was second-hand. It had come from a saleroom in Clapham, along with the bedside table, the chairs and the wardrobe. Watson had rented the house last October, and before they had moved in he had promised her all new things. Later he had changed his mind. He had worried in case she would be annoyed at the lack of a proper garden, but she hadn't minded the dark little back yard. She was done with gardens. They had left South Lambeth Road because the absentee landlord had sold off the grounds of Montpelier House to the speculators. She had put so much of herself into that flourishing acre of colour and beauty – everyone said so – that when she heard that it was to be torn up and built over she had taken to her bed. She would never hold a pruning knife again. Mrs Brewer had said that with her connections in Ireland it was a wonder she didn't bring pressure to bear on the landlord – he was a member of Parliament for an Irish borough. Her phrasing had sounded malicious. They had fallen out over it.

She went through into the bedroom and was about to lie down when she heard the servant girl clearing away the breakfast dishes. Going out on to the landing, she shouted down the stairs that she had a headache. 'I don't want to be disturbed,' she called. She was exhausted. After their altercation last night she had tossed and turned until dawn.

Watson had been sitting at his desk, as usual, and she had accidentally knocked over the fire irons. He had swung round, demanding to know whether there wasn't something she could occupy herself with. When she had replied that there wasn't, he suggested she should clean the house. 'At nine o'clock at night?' she had retorted. He complained that the servant girl was hopeless. 'You should supervise her,' he said. 'It is your duty.' 'I supervised the last one,' she protested. 'And the one before that. They didn't stay long enough for us to reap the benefit.'

Quick as a flash he had blamed her for their leaving. She had started to weep, not loudly, but audibly sniffing and gulping – he found it difficult to concentrate when she cried. She had thought he was working on his book about the reasoning power of animals, or his history of the Popes, but later it had turned out that he was only writing his never-ending letter to the Bishop.

'There are mouse droppings in the wardrobe,' he had shouted. 'And the chest of drawers is full of dust.' She had jumped up, outraged, and told him that in Inchicore House platoons of mice had run between the floorboards and nobody had cared a fig. Why, in Upper Sackville Street, this whole room would have fitted into the corridor outside the butler's pantry. To which he'd replied that if the library was so distasteful to her, why didn't she go downstairs to the drawing-room and give him some peace.

She said that she would never give him that. Never. Once she had loved him, then she had detested him, and for a time she had been afraid of him. She spat out the words, though none of them were true. 'If you had advanced further,' she cried, 'we could have afforded a housekeeper instead of workhouse girls.'

Adopting a sarcastic tone, he said that he pitied her for having fallen into the hands of someone who could make very little money and who had no aptitude for success. She had cut him short and informed him that she wasn't going to build up his self-esteem or act as a buffer against the world. 'You are responsible for me,' she ground out. 'I will not be left in a corner to rot.'

Trembling with fury he retaliated by saying unforgivable things about her father. His greed had been his downfall, he said. As a mere rent-collector he must have been despised the length and breadth of the county. An intelligent man, he said, would have thought to make provision for his family ... She had run at him then and, snapping her fingers in his face, cried out, 'At least I knew my father.' And so it had gone on.

It was she who needed to be given peace, not he. By some atrocious quirk of fate he had become her whole life. Whatever emotion she had substituted for love, it now consumed her. She could not bear to let him out of her sight.

Two years before he had packed her off to Dublin to visit Olivia. A week spent with her sister had brought back the empty past before she had known him. They did not go out, because there was nowhere to go. Mrs Quin was dead. Quin also, and Aunt Lawson, and Edwin; and for all the life that was in her, Olivia might as well have been dead too. Anne had told her that in London she was asked to functions several times a month. Being a head master's wife, she said, was not always a bed of roses. It could be tiring. But then, of course, her husband cherished her. 'You surprise me,' Olivia had said. 'You don't look like a woman who is cherished.' Insufferable as ever, she had even dragged up County Cork. Then, when it was perhaps too late, Anne had returned home determined to be a loving companion to her husband.

When he worked at his desk she took to sitting at his elbow, listening to the sound of his pen scratching across those endless sheets of paper. If he was reading she watched his fingers turning the pages, and waited, for it seemed to her that among all those millions of words printed in all those hundreds of books on his shelves he must eventually come across one simple sentence which would enable him to understand her.

At church on Sundays, kneeling at his side during prayers, she leaned so heavily against him that sometimes he lost his balance. She accompanied him on his constitutional walk of a morning and evening, hanging on to his arm and trotting to keep up with him as he strode morosely round and round the Crescent. She knew that he didn't want her with him. If she had stayed behind he would have slipped off to call on the odious Mr Bush further down the road, or Mr Anderson at Herne Hill, or the Revd Mr Wallace at St Andrew's church. Since Williams had retired and gone to live with his sister at Hastings, he had chummed up with Wallace. For a man with such a passion for solitude it was extraordinary how many people he visited.

Often during the night she clamped her leg over his, and wound her arm so tightly about his neck that in his sleep he fought her off, half throttled in the small hours.

Somewhere in the room beneath her she heard the girl knocking the sweeping brush against the skirting-board. Sleep was impossible, and yet unless she rested she wouldn't look her best for the prize-giving. She put her fingers in her ears, but still the knocking persisted, and now there was a rattle of milk churns.

At last she rose from the bed and went through the double doors into the dressing-room. She walked very slowly, as if hoping someone would catch up with her. The window overlooked the road beyond the back yard; she could see the horse and cart from the dairy, milk churns flashing silver in the sunlight, disappearing round the corner. She hesitated a moment, gazing regretfully at the empty street, and then opened the wardrobe door.

* * *

After taking morning prayers Watson told Grey he was going out. He would be gone an hour. Grey didn't conceal his annoyance. He had found two women, both the worse for drink, loitering outside the gates before eight o'clock that morning. They had wanted money, of course, and were bound to come back. He was tired of being accosted at the school, and on his own front door step. He continued to lodge at Montpelier House, and often when he returned home he was forced to run the gauntlet of unemployed persons, miserably dirty and cut about the face, who clustered outside in the belief that the head master still lived there. Watson gave the Secretary two shillings in loose change and asked him to share it between the women should they appear again.

He hurried back to St Martin's Road. On the corner he met Henry Rogers, manager of the Beulah Laundry, who wished him good morning and whom he ignored. Passing his own house without looking up, he walked further along the row to No. 32.

Mr Bush's son, Fred, answered the door and said his father was out. Watson explained that he had a sitting for his portrait that afternoon, but owing to the preparations for the prize-giving he would have to cancel it. Fred said his father was expected at any moment and why didn't he stay and deliver the message himself. The Revd Mr Anderson was already waiting.

'No,' replied Watson. 'I can't stop.' But hardly had Fred closed the door before he changed his mind and knocked again. He was told to go through to the studio, where he found Mr Anderson seated in a leather armchair daubed with yellow paint and reading a newspaper.

Watson's portrait was set up on the easel by the window. It was a full-length pose with the subject wearing a degree gown and clutching a book.

'It promises to be rather good,' said Mr Anderson, 'though the flesh tones are somewhat livid.'

'He works in glazes,' Watson told him.

Anderson thought it must be tiring, being painted. 'I don't think

I could take the standing still,' he said. 'I should probably become giddy.'

Watson said he didn't mind it. He had plenty to think about, and at any rate it got him out of the house. He had meant to say 'school', not 'house', and bothered by this slip of the tongue he turned too quickly and brushed his shoulder against the painting. The canvas was still wet; he rubbed at his coat sleeve, and now he had crimson paint on his hands as well as ink.

'Wipe it off on the chair,' suggested Anderson, when no suitable cloth could be found.

Watson said that today was to have been his fourth sitting. Last week Mr Bush had gone to Brighton for a few days and this week he himself was forced into a postponement.

'Bush is always going somewhere,' Anderson said. 'The man's a marvel of energy for his age.'

'But then he's not married,' said Watson.

'No,' agreed Anderson, and after a pause asked how Mrs Watson was keeping.

'Exceptionally well,' replied Watson. 'She will be at the ceremony tonight.' He said he would be grateful if Mr Anderson could tell Bush that he wouldn't be able to come this afternoon. 'I've already given the message to Fred,' he explained, 'but one never knows with him.'

If it had been an ordinary day, to be followed by an evening at his desk – he had set himself to write four pages a night, both sides – he would have called in at home on his way to the school and made his peace with Anne. Tonight, however, work was out of the question.

Last night she had accused him of meanness again, this time over the matter of a housekeeper. Alarmed, he had tried to change the subject, but she had driven the issue through to its obvious conclusion and pushed beyond endurance he had said things best forgotten. As usual she had put the words into his mouth. Afterwards he was filled with remorse, followed by pity, and then, naturally, he'd been unable to write one page, let alone four. He had made a botched job of his letter to the Bishop of Winchester. She'd said she was sick of the sight of him labouring away at his desk. She didn't realise that the labour lay not in the writing but in the effort required to placate her and maintain her in a reasonable frame of mind.

And yet it was hard on her; he did see that. Every year she

anticipated the publication and reception of his latest book. It was always his next book that was bound to be greeted with acclaim and sell in thousands. Though it was kindly meant, he could have done without her telling him so. For when the mixture turned out as before, lukewarm reviews and no more than a hundred copies sold, she suffered twice over, for herself and for him, and he had to bear the brunt of this double, crushing disappointment.

Arriving at the school he found that there was some confusion over the number of chairs needed in the Gymnasium. There were at least three rows too many. He couldn't understand Grey's insistence that the extra chairs were necessary. For over twenty years they had been involved in the prize-giving arrangements, and during the last ten the number of parents expected had hardly varied. There was something odd about Grey's behaviour. As a rule he was more than anxious to share his duties, and yet today he went missing at intervals, and once, when Watson walked into his office, he jumped almost a foot in the air as if he had been caught in some guilty act. Perhaps it had something to do with his having recently gone into print. He had published two books, *Trowel, Chisel and Brush* and *Resting without Resting*. Watson had been presented with copies of both, fulsomely inscribed – they had always disliked each other – only two weeks before. He still hadn't bothered to cut the pages.

He had meant to go home for his dinner, but there wasn't the opportunity. One of the presentation books turned out to have its centre pages missing, and another copy had to be fetched and the rest examined in case they were similarly flawed; and then later on Matthews, the head boy, son of a local grocer and exceptionally brainy, was found to have developed a spectacular rash on his face and trunk. Fortunately he was a spotty boy in his own right. Watson said the rash wouldn't be noticed under the lights and advised him to say nothing about it to anyone.

Before he went home to change his clothes he tidied his desk. The President and the Board would be drinking a glass of wine with him before the start of the ceremony. He was putting the contents of the drawers into some sort of rough order when he came across an envelope. It was addressed in his mother's hand. He no longer had in his possession the book she had given to him in childhood – Anne had given it to a boy with scarlet fever – but he would have known her handwriting anywhere. Deliberately he tore the envelope into pieces. He had found it in Anne's trunk when they had moved from Montpelier House to St Martin's Road. He had never told her of his discovery – what purpose would it serve – and perhaps it was as well that she had destroyed the contents. There was possibly a sort of love buried under her reasons for getting rid of the letter. He was putting the pieces into the wastepaper basket when Grey came in and asked him if he had prepared his speech for tonight.

'What speech,' he said, all at sea. It was not up to him to make a speech.

'One never knows,' muttered the Secretary, and he went out again.

Watson thought the man was ill. The President usually spoke for twenty minutes, then the chairman of the Proprietary Committee, then the chairman of the Examining Board; and lastly the wife of the chairman of the Proprietary Committee was brought to her feet. Hers was a mercifully short oration. She was required merely to say thank you for the bouquet of mixed flowers handed up by the blushing, and in this case infectious, head boy. Never, at any time, had the head master been called upon to speak.

He left the school at five o'clock. He had an hour in which to change his clothes. St Martin's Road was just round the corner; in the summer months when the dressing-room window was open, he could hear the hand bell ringing for morning school. He was not worried about Anne's reception of him; she so enjoyed going out and feeling herself the centre of a crowd that once over the doorstep she would forget their quarrel and behave towards him with almost embarrassing solicitude.

As he entered the hall he saw her at the top of the stairs, looking down at him. He knew at once she was unwell. If he hadn't run up and caught her, she would have fallen and rolled to the bottom. She was actually swaying as he took the stairs two at a time.

He helped her to her bed and fetched a cloth from the dressing-room. He was dreadfully moved by her condition. 'Anne, Anne,' he murmured, and pressed the cloth to her forehead. She was in her petticoats and there was a mauve stain on the front of her bodice. She was sixty years old and she looked at him as though she believed she was a girl. Evidently she had begun to get ready for the evening – he could smell scent in the room and there was a dusting of powder on her flushed face.

'I love you,' she said. 'Remember that.'

'No,' he cried, 'No.'

'I love you,' she repeated.

Sickened, he longed to tell her that love was not the problem. Love dropped out of the sky, unsought, enearned. He had loved his mother. It was liking someone that was the difficulty.

'I must go,' he told her. 'I have to go.' He pulled his hands from hers.

'Of course you have,' she said. 'Of course, my dear.'

He ran down the stairs and called the servant up from the basement. He asked her to make her mistress some chicken soup and to take it in to her when he had gone. He avoided looking at the girl.

It was now twenty to six. As he dressed he could hear Anne talking to herself. At such times she usually spoke bossily to Olivia, ordering her out into those faded gardens of Inchicore House.

It doesn't matter, he thought. Tragedy, though hard to contend with, was an affirmation of life. At that instant, brushing the shoulders of his best black coat, he could think of despair in such terms. There was still time for him to achieve something; time still for him to do his best work.

Anne was asleep when he went in to say goodbye. Her arms were raised up on either side of her head and her mouth was open. He turned her on to her side in case she vomited.

As soon as he climbed on to the rostrum in the Gymnasium he understood the business of the extra chairs. The first three rows were entirely filled with former pupils of the school. He recognised the Woodley brothers, Frank and Walter Besant, the Holroyd boy, George Hunter, Fraser, young Taunton, Daley's son. Taunton, at fourteen, had climbed onto the roof and hurled stones at the drill sergeant. He had offered no excuse for his behaviour beyond claiming that the hot weather had affected him. Anne had said she was sure that it was Taunton who had caused the fire at the school. The Committee had wanted him flogged but had given way in the end. He seemed tame enough now, with his pince-nez, his watch chain and his little fluffy moustaches.

There were some faces that Watson looked at perplexed, so changed had they become, and others whose eyes, staring up at him out of those altered, manly countenances, betrayed them instantly for the boys they once had been. He could not imagine what they were doing here in such numbers.

The President, who was a hat manufacturer and only slightly

more efficient than the late Mr Dalton, made the opening speech. The orations were delivered, the prizes given. The President was a cheroot addict, and though no one else would have thought it proper to light up in the presence of ladies he puffed his way through three hours. The air above the rostrum rolled blue with smoke. Mrs Rawlings, the wife of the chairman of the Committee, fanned herself with her chamois gloves. Old Dr Munford, finding himself in a bar parlour, had taken out his handkerchief and was clasping it to his nose.

Watson thought of Anne. By now she would be out of bed and sitting in the dressing-room, in the dark, watching out of the back window for a sight of him. For a time she would be filled with remorse; if he delayed much longer she would feel self-pity. Anger would undoubtedly follow. He was glad that he had locked the library door. There had been a boy at St Elizabeth's College, he remembered, who had come under suspicion of tampering with an exam paper. Though there was no positive proof of guilt, Davies, the Principal, had expelled him on the spot. Le Courtois and himself had put up a petition and gathered statements from senior boys, to no avail.

He was thinking about his life at St Elizabeth's, various pictures passing before his eyes – the sea breaking against the rocks, Le Courtois throwing up his arms and pretending to go under for the third and last time, a particular corner of the beach one rainy afternoon – when he became aware that the President was again on his feet, smiling and gesturing, not at Mrs Rawlings, whose moment of glory should have arrived, but at him. And then Matthews, the head boy, came up the steps of the rostrum without his bouquet of flowers, carrying instead an object shaped like a tray, loosely wrapped in tissue paper. From the hall came a tremendous scraping of chairs on the wooden floor. The old boys were rising to their feet and starting to clap. Even the smaller boys, sitting cross-legged at the front, were beating their fists against the base of the rostrum and cheering.

The President, his bald head wreathed in smoke, held up his hand for silence. He said that it was his pleasant duty to make a further presentation, one which in his opinion was highly merited. For twenty-two years the Reverend John Selby Watson had occupied the post of head master at the school, and there were many here tonight, and still others out there in the world, who could bear witness to his scholarship, his patience and his devotion

109

to the sacred task of education. He went on in this vein for some time, and when he had finished such a roar of approval came from the old boys, that, swayed by their enthusiasm the body of the audience rose too and for over a minute applauded the head master. During this tumult, Matthews, his face scarlet with excitement and undiagnosed fever, handed over the wrapped object. The tissue paper dropped away and a silver salver was uncovered, highly polished, and engraved. Watson, clutching the shining dish to himself like a breastplate, found he was near to tears. He had not suspected that he could feel such gratitude, nor take such delight in being appreciated.

At last he too held up his hand – Mrs Rawlings noticed that he had both ink and blood on his fingers – and when the clapping had died away he began to make a speech. He said that it was obvious that the tide of change was sweeping in to erode the shores of education. There were some who believed this change was for the better and others who believed the opposite. Ultimately the position of Latin and Greek was imposed by History. We could no more say goodbye to Latin and replace it with Russian or Sanskrit than we could wipe out the History of Europe for the last two thousand years. He would not join in the controversy, he said, nor bring up the tired old argument that a boy's mind was best trained by the instrument of Latin. For himself, to know Greek and to read the Tragedies was to begin to understand his own nature. The purpose of Tragedy was not to free one from pity or terror, nor to purge one by allowing the discharge of such feelings, but to bring one face to face with the awful truths of human existence. 'Let us then,' he said, 'pursue these truths with our whole powers, and strive for eloquence, without which all nature would be mute, and all our acts deprived alike of present honour and commemoration among posterity; and let us aspire to the highest excellence, for, by this means, we shall attain the summit, or at least see many below us.' He faltered, not sure whether he was hitting the right note, and looked down at the salver in his arms. He was dazzled by its brightness. 'Greek,' he said, 'is a musical and prolific language, that gives a soul to the objects of sense, and a body to the abstractions of philosophy. As to the learning of Latin,' he concluded, 'the point of it is simple. It is so that we can read Horace.'

Afterwards he was convinced that Anne, crouching at the open window, must have heard the ovation they gave him.

Henry Grey was shown a copy of the letter which had been sent on the 30th September, 1870, and affirmed that he had written it:

Dear Sir

In conformity with the annexed resolution, which was unanimously adopted at a meeting of the Committee last evening, I hereby give notice that they will not require your services after the expiration of the present term.

I am, yours faithfully,

Henry Grey. Secretary, Stockwell Grammar School.

(Copy of resolution) That the Secretary be instructed to inform each of the present masters that owing to the continuous falling off in the number of pupils, and the consequent insufficiency of the income to meet the current expenditure, the Committee feel themselves most reluctantly compelled to give notice to each of them that their services will not be required after the expiration of the present term.

Henry Grey said that Mr Watson had replied to the Committee on October 17th, 1870. The letter was read out as follows:

Dear Sirs

Your resolution has taken me greatly by surprise, as I had thought that, considering the long time I have conducted the school, and the way in which I have constantly endeavoured to maintain its character and excellence, the Committee would have allowed me the courtesy of some communication with them, after which I might have, if necessary, tendered my resignation.

I am shocked that the notice of dismissal was accompanied by no expression of concern, or any single word which might soften its intent.

So far from any any accusation of neglect, or failure of duty, having been brought against me, the Committee in July last congratulated the proprietors on the untiring exertions of the highly talented head master.

I am at a loss to understand what it is I have done during the last few months to cause the Committee to withhold all confidence from me, and request that I should be allowed to tender my resignation.

I am, yours faithfully, J.S. Watson.

111

PART 3

He showed the letter of dismissal to anyone who would spare the time to read it – Wallace, Murdoch from King's College, the Revd Mr Anderson at Herne Hill, colleagues at the Royal Society of Literature, even Mr Bush's son, Fred. Each one professed to be as baffled by it as he was. He couldn't forgive the Board for not taking him into their confidence. He knew as well as they that the school, once anchored in a quiet village and now adrift in a metropolis, was something of an anachronism. He knew better than they that the old order was changing and that a classical education was no longer essential to advancement in the world; but to cast him out, half way through the school year and in such an abrupt manner, was beyond belief. Did they think they were terminating the services of a lamp-lighter or a crossing-sweeper, that they could get rid of him in so few words?

He still had to work the term out at the school, and this was the worst part of his humiliation. He patrolled the familiar corridors believing that he was part of a conspiracy, a practical joke almost, which might yet be explained to him.

In the night he woke from bad dreams, hoping the letter was a fragment of them, and when he stumbled through into his study and saw it lying there on his desk he covered his face with his hands and groaned aloud. In the past, if sleep eluded him he had been used to reading; during the three months remaining to him at the school he was unable to touch the books on his shelves, not even the ones he had written himself and which once had given him such pleasure to hold, for now it seemed they represented some thing and some time which was irretrievably dead and lost to him. In his blackest hours he thought of burning them.

There had been talk in the beginning of organising a meeting at the school and getting influential parents to agitate on behalf of himself and the other masters. But when it came to it, the younger masters backed off. He didn't blame them. If they were to get further employment they needed recommendations from the Committee.

He corresponded with numerous people in high places, but he had always been too self-sufficient and had never troubled to ingratiate himself with anyone. He received few replies, and those, beyond expressing a distant sympathy for his plight, offered no solution to his difficulties.

Two days before the end of term, in the middle of morning service when the choir was singing Adeste Fideles, he walked out of the school, leaving his books and his belongings behind. It was not like him to act impulsively, but then he was no longer himself. Someone had dropped a paper lantern in the snow in the yard; he crushed it into a ball and threw it over the railings. He felt he was hurling his own life away.

Later, Grey packed his books and papers into two boxes and sent them round with the drill sergeant. Looking at the boxes, Watson was surprised how small they were, considering they contained the debris of twenty-six years.

He was not yet desperate for money, but it was obvious that he couldn't continue to lay out sixty pounds a year for a large house in which only he and Anne lived. They would have to find somewhere more modest – somewhere, above all, as far away from the school as possible. He wrote to Mrs Hill, the owner of 28, St Martin's Road, and told her he would quit the premises the following June, and might, if she wished it, do so even sooner.

In the meantime economies should be made, though it was puzzling to know in what direction. He could not in all charity cut the allowance he made to Olivia Armstrong in Dublin; since the death of her brother she was wholly reliant on him. Nor could he cancel his subscriptions to various societies and to the London Library. His survival depended more than ever on his being able to borrow books and to meet people in the literary world. He told Anne that he would sell the silver plate which the school had presented to him four years ago, but he didn't mean it. She suggested that they get rid of the younger of the two servant girls. The boarders had left some time before and it was surely an extravagance to keep both servants. He dithered, feeling that it was unfair to dismiss one of them so hastily – and besides, he preferred Ellen Pyne to her sister Margaret. Then the accident occurred, and Margaret Pyne went of her own accord.

Anne had been unwell that day. She had called out to him that Snap was standing on the top landing, whining and scratching at the attic doors. Mr Wallace had given him the dog some weeks before, having found it starving in a brick field. Anne said she was certain someone was trying to break in through the trapdoor in the loft. The dog's behaviour was proof of it. He knew she wasn't telling the truth. Only a minute before he had gone through into the room behind the library and looked out of the window; he had seen the animal down in the yard. Anne had continued to make a nuisance of herself, roaming the house and blundering into things, and complaining of a slithering noise on the roof. He had called Margaret to help her to her room – she wouldn't allow either Ellen Pyne or himself to see to her – and some sort of scuffle had taken place at the head of the stairs. The girl had fallen awkwardly and sprained her ankle. He had fetched Dr Rugg from Stockwell Villas to attend to her. The next day, when Anne was better, she had insisted on waiting on the girl herself. She gave her a brooch as a present and two weeks extra wages when she left. So much for economy.

Once he had removed himself physically from the school, his misery, though not his bitterness, lessened. He began to take an interest in his books again. During the day he locked himself in his library. When Anne objected, he said she must pretend he was keeping school hours. He allowed her in after five o'clock on a week day and all day on Sunday. He told himself that he locked the door in order to be left in peace, but in his heart he knew it was a precaution against his own lunacy. He was afraid he would walk to the Crescent and loiter outside the ornamental gates of the school like a beggar. In her worst moods Anne stood on the landing and beat on the panel of the door.

One morning in January young Fraser called at St Martin's Road. He was now a solicitor in his father's firm in Dean Street, Soho. He was also a member of that shameful Proprietory Board which had ousted Watson from his post, though he had spoken out against the manoeuvre. He was anxious to be of assistance; he thought Watson had been harshly treated. He found his former head master in a better state than he had expected. Watson spoke enthusiastically of his *History of the Papacy*, and said he was translating a collection of the songs of Béranger. Towards the end of the year, when his history was finished – it covered the whole period from St Peter to the Reformation – he had another commission from Bohn. He was also contemplating an essay on the relationship between Church and State.

Fraser enquired whether he had given up all hopes of returning to the school.

'It is out of my hands,' replied Watson.

'It could be,' said Fraser, 'that we can apply different tactics.' He hesitated to ask, but he wondered if Mr Watson had enough funds set by to make a proposition to the Board. In the financial position in which the school found itself, the Board might be persuaded to let it out of their control. He said he would be willing to put up money himself.

Watson was elated at the idea, and immediately suggested they should send the Board a copy of the letter he was writing to the Bishop of Winchester. He had composed it some years before but had never sent it because he was not yet satisfied with its construction. Only recently he had added to it a passage from Lucian, in which Jupiter lamented to the Cynic Menippus, the time when, far from being thought of as old-fashioned and decrepit, he was looked up to by all, and sacrifices had been so general that one could not see for the smoke.

'Jupiter,' he explained, making a small circle with the thumb and forefinger of one hand and closing it with the palm of his other, 'showed Menippus how prayers came up to him through holes with covers to them. In this way foolish petitions could be shut off and he need only listen to the reasonable ones.' The letter was in Latin, and he believed that the Board, as well as the Bishop, couldn't fail to grasp the aptness of its classical references.

Fraser, beyond admiring its style, could think of no useful purpose that the letter would serve in this instance – the Board was mainly made up of shopkeepers and brewers – and instead drafted a letter to the Proprietors which read as follows:

Having fully reviewed the state of finances at the school, it is proposed that the Board should relieve themselves of all existing and future liabilities by allowing the school to pass into other hands. I am prepared to negotiate for the lease of the premises, for the sum at which it was valued in the late Report of the Committee to the Proprietors, and to relieve the Proprietors of all liabilities from next Christmas.

When Watson had signed it, Fraser cautioned him not to raise his hopes too high, warning him that further disappointment might be in store.

'I am not a fool,' Watson assured him. 'I was never one for optimism and am even less so now. Once a man's spirit has been broken it is not easy to renovate it.'

The negotiations came to nothing. The Committee thought that the amount offered wasn't large enough. They didn't absolutely repudiate the idea in principle, but considered that the terms were not good enough to accept.

Watson believed it was he they were against. However much he offered they would in the end turn it down. Fraser was inclined to agree. Still, now that the idea of taking over the school had entered his head, Watson would not give it up without a struggle.

In May he met by appointment in the offices of Bisson, the Scholastical Agent near Oxford Street, a gentleman of means from Liverpool called John Brindley. They had corresponded through the Agent, with a view to Mr Brindley's taking over the lease of the school and putting Watson in as head master.

Mr Brindley smelled of spirits. He had fallen into schools by accident, having inherited two in the north of England at the death of an uncle. He was not against making a further investment.

'Have you any fixed ideas on education in general?' asked Watson.

Mr Brindley confessed he hadn't, beyond the ordinary ones concerning the importance of the new sciences.

'And have you any knowledge of the classics?'

'Not a great deal,' admitted Mr Brindley cheerfully.

Mr Bisson intervened and questioned Mr Brindley on the returns he was making on his other investment, and the amount of control he exercised in his establishments.

'He means interference,' said Watson, and he rose from his chair and walked about the room. He did not see how he could do business with such a man; his voice was so nasal it was hard to understand a word he uttered.

Mr Brindley wanted to know the reasons for Watson's leaving the school in Stockwell. Watson said irritably that he had already explained the circumstances in his letters.

'I had some difficulty in reading them through to the end,' replied Brindley. 'The handwriting was very cramped, and there was all that underlining of words.'

'I am the victim of Philistines,' Watson said. 'Men who put their pockets before traditions or scholarship.' It was obvious to the Agent that he thought the man from Liverpool was of the same breed. He was pressing his fist to his temple agitatedly. 'Think of it,' he cried. 'They thought nothing of dismissing seven masters only six months before the University examinations. What sort of men would do that, do you think?'

At that moment he was distracted by the presence of a large fly which had flown out from behind the window blind and was buzzing above his head. Seizing his hat from the table he proceeded to swipe the air with it. 'I would have been willing,' he continued breathlessly, 'to have taken a drop in salary, had I been asked. I would have been willing −' here he began to pursue the fly about the room, slicing his hat ferociously from side to side − 'to have worked for a period of time, if absolutely necessary, for no reimbursement whatsoever.' Exasperated, he flung his hat at the ceiling.

Arriving home, he wrote to Mr Bisson complaining that Mr Brindley was not a desirable person to be on a scholastical list. Was there anyone else more suitable to his requirements? Mr Bisson never replied.

* * *

In August the weather became very hot. Anne suffered a great deal from headaches, brought on, she claimed, by the thunderstorms. They were still living at St Martin's Road. He had meant to look for somewhere else but he had been too busy working on the second volume of his book. It was now finished, and had been for a week, but he was loath to let it go. He was convinced Longmans must take it. They had published his life of Warburton and of Porson, and though the Porson had sunk like a stone, the Warburton had been respectfully reviewed in all the leading journals. According to the *Athenaeum* he had drawn the character of his hero with a 'firm, if not a very tender, hand'. They had debated whether Warburton deserved the 'zeal, labour and ability of such an author as Mr Watson'. The book had even proved to be something of a commercial success, and he had no reason to suppose that his *History of the Papacy* would not do even better.

At last he took the manuscript, loosely wrapped in brown paper, to Turner's the trunkmaker on the Clapham Road.

The shop was next door to the Post Office, and over the years he had got into the habit of giving Turner a few coppers to dispatch his parcels for him. The Post Office was usually crowded, and he detested waiting. Having instructed Turner as to the exact amount of string and sealing wax needed to make a secure job of his package, he decided to call on Mr Bush. It would be in the nature of a celebration – it was not every day he sent off a book to the publishers.

As he turned into Lansdowne Road a funeral cortège approached from the direction of the Crescent, and he halted and removed his hat. When the procession had gone by, he saw Anne on the opposite pavement. He was not surprised: she could sense a funeral a mile off. No sooner did a hearse appear in the street than she ran from the house as if tugged on strings. She was not wearing her bonnet. Hands piously clasped on her protruding stomach, she bobbed along in the wake of death. The dog ran ahead of her.

Watson called out to her, and she stopped, her face losing its rapt expression and becoming sullen. She turned and made her way back to the house, keeping a few yards in front of him. He did not dare escape up the road to Mr Bush and was forced to follow her indoors.

'I have sent off my manuscript,' he told her. 'Now, I'll have time to look for somewhere to live.'

She said nothing. Possibly he should never have mentioned his book – he did not want to set off that painful process of hope and dread.

'You will have to come with me,' he said. 'It will be your choice as well as mine.'

'You won't want me to,' she replied. 'Not when it comes to it.'

He went up to his study. Any discussion with Anne as to where they might go, or what sort of accommodation they should look for, usually ended in a quarrel. She insisted that she liked Stockwell; once she had foolishly said it was where her friends were, and though he hadn't twitched an eyelid, let alone corrected such a preposterous statement, she had burst into tears and flung a glass at him.

Sometimes she still begged him to comfort her, and when he tried to do so she screamed out that she didn't want his pity. Sometimes she told him to leave her alone, and when he did just that she rounded on him and accused him of treating her worse than the dog. Often she asked him what it was he wanted, as though his expectations were somehow beyond human understanding, when, God knows, all that he had ever hoped for was a modest income and a quiet life. She thought she was acting out of love; that was the cruellest part of it. In spite of all her insults, her tricks, her friendship with the scandal-mongering Mrs Tulley, she believed she doted on him. If he didn't unlock the library on the stroke of five o'clock she took a hammer to the door. It wasn't her irrational behaviour which was upsetting – indeed, she had hardly behaved any differently in all the time he had known her – it was the increased frequency of her fits of 'illness' which disturbed him. He did nothing about it, and was afraid that his passiveness was deliberate and malicious.

Now that his manuscript was gone from his desk he didn't know how to occupy himself. He tried to concentrate on Béranger, but his mind wandered. There was some controversy over whether the coquettish Lisette of the later songs was in fact the Mademoiselle Judith, whom, it was said, Béranger had loved as a pure and tender friend. Watson thought they were one and the same. He didn't think there was a woman alive capable of pure and tender friendship, though she might give an imitation of it.

They had tea, as always, at six o'clock. Afterwards he said he would take Snap for a walk. Anne decided she would come too, and later he told her that he had changed his mind and was feeling somewhat tired. He went to bed before her. She was downstairs for a while, and just as he was falling asleep he heard her moving about in the library, opening the drawers of his desk. In the middle of the night she urinated in the bed.

At breakfast he told Ellen Pyne that the dog had upset the slop pail. He instructed her to take the mattress down into the yard and let it dry out in the sun. He had to help her; she couldn't shift it past the bend in the basement stairs. He thought of Mrs Parr humiliating poor, dead Porson, and felt enormous sympathy for him, though he had none for Anne.

He never uttered a word of rebuke to her; it wasn't necessary. She was pitifully embarrassed and wrote him a note which she slipped under the door, begging him for forgiveness and telling him that she was moving one of the beds from the attic into the dressing-room behind the library. She added a pathetic postscript, to the effect that when it was less hot she wouldn't need to drink such quantities of barley water.

The dressing-room contained some of his books and papers, and she herself cleared them out, after five o'clock, and stacked them neatly under his desk. She called her new retreat the 'glory hole', a name once used by her father for a room in the house in Upper Sackville Street. He had kept his guns in it and his saddle.

As Watson told Mr Bush later that evening, as they drank

champagne under a chinese lantern in the painter's little back garden – Bush had insisted on celebrating the sending off of the manuscript – she had never recovered from losing her position in life. It had warped her. 'I understand it,' he said. 'Not to have one's expectations realised is a dreadful thing.'

'Not everyone takes it quite so badly,' objected Mr Bush.

'I have done her a great wrong,' Watson said. 'In the beginning I didn't do so badly – better than Porson, for instance, who forgot to go home on his wedding-night. But I haven't done so well since. Mrs Watson is a difficult woman – but who knows, a different husband might have made her easier to live with.'

'Or worse,' said Mr Bush, though he didn't think it likely. His being an artist, and therefore outside rigid society, put him in a privileged position. Watson could confide in him and speak his mind – he knew the poor man would have found it impossible to talk of his wife in such terms to Anderson or Wallace.

'She has taken herself off into the dressing-room to sleep,' Watson said. He didn't say why, though in the past they had discussed both his marriage and Anne's 'illness'. There were some things best left unspoken. Besides, Bush disliked Anne, and sometimes Watson felt guilty at giving him so much domestic information. He had never allowed him to say a harsh word about her. He himself might criticise Anne till the cows came home, but he wouldn't stand for it in others.

'You'll be able to read more,' Bush said. He hesitated, and then asked, 'Do you still miss the school?'

'Not as much as I would have supposed,' said Watson. 'But then, though I have always been interested in people, I have never needed them. Last month the pupils got up a collection for me. They wanted me to attend the presentation, but I wouldn't. Fraser brought a purse round. The whole thing smacked of charity.'

'Never,' cried Mr Bush. 'If the Committee had instigated it, you might be right. But it was the boys.'

'Exactly how young Fraser saw it,' Watson told him.

There was a scent of nightstock in the garden. In the house next door someone was playing the piano. He had a sudden, melancholy vision of a young man standing in a drawing-room, gazing with infatuated eyes at a girl in a pink dress by a window. He said: 'She stole money from the purse Fraser brought. A guinea almost, a bit at a time.'

'Of course,' said Bush.

'Ellen Pyne goes out for her. I don't say anything to the girl because I don't wish to shame Anne behind her back. But the situation is terrible.'

'Terrible indeed,' agreed Mr Bush.

'I should have bought her a piano.'

'It hardly seems a priority now,' murmured Mr Bush.

On the doorstep, when he was leaving, Watson said he had been wrong to describe the taking of the money as stealing. He was ashamed to have implied that his wife was a thief. 'I did not hide it,' he said. 'Nor forbid her the use of it. In marriage there can be no such thing as private money.'

He was miserably aware that his meanness of spirit was not due to the crushing disappointment he had suffered over the loss of his school, nor to his lack of literary success, but rather to an accumulation of little wrongs done to him – a spoiled page, an intercepted letter, a burnt book. My marriage has destroyed me, he thought. I am buried under trivialities.

*   *   *

He waited three weeks for an acknowledgment of his manuscript from the publishers, and when nothing came, he went to Longman's offices and was treated offhandedly by the Secretary, who seemed not to have heard of him and curtly told him that he would doubtless receive a communication when, and if, his parcel arrived. Almost demented at the thought that his manuscript might be lost, Watson demanded a search be made, and when it was found in a cupboard, unopened, beneath at least twenty other such packages, he left without asking for a receipt.

He took the whole incident very hard. In a flash it was apparent to him what lay ahead, and he began seriously to worry about money; he had visions of the workhouse. His savings were dwindling, and still he had not looked for a cheaper place to rent. Catching sight of himself in the mirror in the drawing-room, he saw an old man. He was old, in years, but until now had not felt it. He believed he was sliding towards a pauper's grave.

For a whole week he avoided Mr Bush and the Revd Mr Armstrong. He was afraid he would break down in front of them. Once he found himself almost at the gates of the school, and he turned and ran headlong in the opposite direction, the dog leaping up at his side and barking. He cursed aloud, and out of the corner of his eye saw Henry Rogers, manager of the Beulah Laundry, tipping his hat to him as he passed.

At last he went to St Andrews Church, and painfully, because it distressed him to show his feelings to an equal, begged Mr Wallace to help him get employment.

'There's a Mr Ingram,' said Wallace, 'who keeps a list of relief clergymen who may be called on. I will have a word with him.'

Anne said his low spirits were due to the hot weather – he hadn't told her of his reception at Longman's. She too stayed indoors. She thought the air in the streets was infected, and she sat at the window with a handkerchief to her nose, fanning herself with a tattered remnant of blue silk. During the day she locked the door of the glory hole. She had forbidden Ellen Pyne to go in there. She told Watson that the girl had enough to do looking after the house, and that she preferred to clean the room herself. He was not sure he believed her; he was afraid there was a more devious explanation for her sudden attack of thoughtfulness. She had removed the oyster shell, of which she was so fond, from the mantel-shelf in the library and had taken it into the back room. 'You have *your* possessions crowding *you*,' she said, looking at his books and his bust of Homer. If I wake in the small hours I find it comforting to have it near me.'

She still undressed in the front bedroom and dropped her dress and her petticoats on the floor by the window. He thought she was compelled to do this, rather as an animal was driven to stake out its territory. He had stopped putting her clothes away years ago, and now he flung his own on top of hers. It was only in those delicious, solitary moments before he drifted into sleep that he gained any advantage from the new arrangement. She was back in the morning, waddling about the room in her torn nightgown, her bare feet slapping against the oil cloth; and if she retired before him, or if he worked late, he heard her beyond the double doors, sighing in her single bed, and occasionally sobbing. He stuffed his fingers into his ears but he couldn't blot her out.

To his dismay, in this period of gloom he kept thinking about the intimacy they had shared when they were first married. He remembered that far-off time when he had known hate and love and not the reason for it, save that he burned and felt it so. Catching sight of her when he woke – her swollen eyes, her faded hair – he wondered at his sentimentality. Of course it worked both ways. In the shaving glass of a morning his face was so altered in appearance that he hardly recognised himself, though inside he remained the same, forty-years-old with success ahead of him.

Some evenings Anne crouched quiet as a mouse in her chair by his desk. Other times she raved of Inchicore House, and Henry Boxer, and of a boy in a boat on a lake. Either way, Watson sat there and faced the disintegration of his life.

Then, quite suddenly, his depression lifted. Perhaps it had had something to do with the weather after all. Whatever the reason, he felt sufficiently recovered to finish his Latin letter to the Bishop of Winchester, and to answer several advertisements for accommodation in North London. He began work on Valerius Flaccus for Bohn. Hope, that best comfort of an imperfect condition, once more bore him up.

* * *

By the first week in October he had finished the manuscript. He thought that he had done a good job. He was so pleased with himself that on the Saturday he decided to take a morning away from his desk and go to Herne Hill. He had heard of a house there with rooms vacant. It wasn't the area he wanted but it wouldn't do any harm to make enquiries. He asked Anne to come with him.

'Why pretend my opinion is of any importance,' she said. 'Leave me alone.'

His good humour drained away. He slammed the door after him and struck savagely at the privet hedge; he no longer felt like looking at houses.

Then he remembered Mr Hall, a tea-dealer of Brixton, who had called on him earlier in the year to ask for a recommendation for his son. At the time, coming so soon after his dismissal, Watson had hardly known to which boy he was referring. Now he would go and see Hall and offer his help. He still had influence in the district.

When he got to the address both the boy and his father were out. He thought that the woman who opened the door looked at him oddly. It took all his strength to be civil to her.

He was walking back along the Clapham Road when he saw a ragged procession of working men coming towards him, carrying placards. They were ill-clothed and unprotected from the rain, and as they drew nearer an omnibus overtook them, throwing up such a deluge of spray that the men, further saturated, flung down their banners in the gutter and, dispersing on the wet pavement, shook themselves like dogs. Surely, thought Watson, the day will come when the persecuted – he was not alone – would demand a place in the sun. And if it wasn't allowed them, why, then they would take it – roaring up from man's unconscious would come an urge towards violence, a determination to destroy. If the road had not been so busy he would have crossed it and given the men all the money he had on him.

The weather, he realised, was an important factor in war. How different it might have been for Cyrus had the clouds opened on the way to Babylon. Would the Persian king, roused by the battle hymn of Mars, have raised his glittering sword in the air and charged the Royal bodyguard if it had been raining? He suddenly noticed Henry Rogers, manager of the Beulah laundry, standing stockstill on the pavement staring at him. Abruptly he lowered his arm and walked on. The Ten Thousand, he thought, had been lucky in other respects. They hadn't needed to find accommodation; for them, it was a simple matter of pitching tents.

* * *

On the Sunday morning, having persuaded Anne to come to Herne Hill with him, Watson left the house earlier than usual. It was raining again and Anne complained that her boots were letting in the damp. It seemed to him that she deliberately stepped in every puddle.

When they reached the house she refused to go inside. She said she didn't care for the look of it. The curtains were grubby, she argued, and there were several cats sitting in the window. In all the time they had lived at St Martin's Road he had never known her to take down the curtains to be washed, not unless prompted. But he said nothing. He knew she was frightened of change, of leaving her home.

They attended morning service at St Emmanuel's. It wasn't their usual church but already it was eleven o'clock. Afterwards they walked home past St Andrew's. The Revd Mr Wallace caught up with them in the road and asked Watson if he could have a private word. He took his friend by the arm and led him a few paces further on. Anne was left sheltering under her umbrella, leaning against a wall and eyeing them suspiciously.

'Word has got through to me, as it will,' said Mr Wallace, 'that perhaps you were not quite yourself in Kent.'

'Not myself?' said Watson.

'Not altogether yourself.'

'In Kent?' Watson said.

'At St Martin's Church. In September.'

'Oh, there,' said Watson. 'What do you mean, not myself?'

'I understand,' said Mr Wallace, 'that you were unable to preach the sermon.'

'Not unable,' protested Watson. 'Unasked. He insisted on doing it himself.'

'The Revd Mr Baugh apparently thought you were somewhat unemphatic when reading the Lessons.'

'I should hope so,' said Watson. 'I detest emphatic scripture readings. The congregation fixes on the reader rather than the words.'

Mr Wallace apologised for having brought up the subject. 'You do see that I had to,' he said. 'After all, it was through my recommendation that you were used.'

'I may have been thinking of something else,' admitted Watson. 'I had Hercules on my mind.'

Anne was convinced that Wallace had been talking about her. 'I don't know why you pretend,' she said. 'You know he has never liked me.'

'He has never had any reason to like you,' protested Watson. 'You have invariably given him the cold shoulder.'

'Then he did say something,' she cried. 'What is it? I demand you tell me!'

'You're not in a position to demand,' he said.

They walked on in silence, until, taking pity on her, he told her that Wallace had merely discussed his visit to Chelsfield the month before, when he had been employed as relief clergyman.

'You wouldn't allow me to come,' she said bitterly.

'You yourself,' he reminded her, 'said two train fares would be a needless extravagance.'

At dinner time he refused to open the wine cupboard; it was Ellen Pyne's afternoon off and he didn't want Anne sitting too long at the table and delaying the girl. He liked Ellen. When she had first come to the house he had caught her in the library, reading; it was a harmless enough book on agriculture. He had talked to her and formed the opinion that she was a bright girl. When told that Xenophon could be read, in translation, for his guidance on the subject of household economy, she had asked to see the appropriate passages – this was in marked contrast to Anne, who, given the same information some years before, had struck him on the ear with a bound edition of the *Memorabilia*. After that he had shown Ellen Pyne the correct way to turn pages, and allowed her to borrow whatever book she wanted. She treated her mistress with patience and kindness, and he was certain she had never divulged to anyone that Anne had pitched Margaret Pyne down the stairs.

Later, when they had withdrawn to the library, he relented over the wine, and giving Ellen the keys told her to bring it up with the dessert.

Immediately Ellen left the house Anne said she wanted more to drink.

'No,' he told her. 'You've had enough.'

'I want more,' she repeated.

He stacked the port-wine decanter and the pudding plates on to a tray and took it downstairs. She followed him into the dining-room and watched him locking the wine away in the cupboard. He took the tray to the basement, and when he came back she was standing there with a knife in her hand, attempting to prise open the cupboard door. He said nothing to her and went upstairs.

Presently she came into the study and said, 'I can't continue.'

'Continue what?' he asked.

'My life,' she said.

He thought this was a preparation for one of her scenes, but mercifully she left him and, crossing the landing, went into the dressing-room. He heard her opening the wardrobe door; some minutes later she hurried downstairs.

He had been sitting at his desk for over an hour when he imagined he heard a knock at the front door. The dog, though it pricked up its ears, remained comatose on the hearthrug. He went to the window and peered into the street, but he couldn't see anyone. He sat down again and tried to concentrate on the book he was reading. Then he wondered whether the noise had been caused by Anne – sometimes she fell over things. He was worried she might have hurt herself, and he ran downstairs into the dining-room. She was slumped at the table; though the wine cupboard was still locked she had a glass and an empty bottle in front of her. The room reeked of spirits. He was so angry he flung the glass on the carpet. When he had gained control of his voice he ordered her to her room.

'Go to your room,' she mimicked, still sitting there, and louder: 'Go to the glory hole, you naughty girl.'

He tried to pull her from the chair but she clung on to the edge of the table.

'You're incapable,' he cried. 'You are always incapable.'

'Yes,' she agreed. 'Yes, I am.'

He could not understand how he had got himself into such a position of useless superiority. She had never been astute enough to marshal her arguments correctly and had always muddied the issue with imagined slights and false evidence. Often, simply to test her, he had admitted that he was guilty of making her unhappy, but she had always missed the point and followed a red herring. He knew he was a clever man, a thinking man, and yet neither his cleverness nor his ability to reason affected his situation with Anne. If he had been in conflict with Williams or Grey or the priggish Anderson, he would have put his case, judged himself in the right and forgotten the whole business within the hour. With Anne he could never resolve anything. In spite of reason, against all logic, he felt he was in the wrong. It was not something an ordinary man could live with and remain sane. The fact that he had held on to his sanity confirmed his belief that he was extraordinary.

It was growing dark; he moved away from her to light the gas, and as he reached up he thought he saw a face at the window. Startled, he went and stood beside the curtains, staring out at the gloomy little garden.

'What is it?' asked Anne.

At that moment the door bell rang, followed by a rattling at the letter box.

'Don't answer it,' she cried. 'If you do you will be overpowered.' She was cowering on her chair; he couldn't tell whether her fear was real or assumed.

'Go upstairs,' he hissed. He did not want Anderson or Wallace to see her in this condition. The bell rang again; reluctantly he went into the hall and opened the door. It was Mrs Tulley.

He called through to Anne. She ran from the dining-room and, seizing Mrs Tulley by the arm, told her she was frightened.

'Frightened of what?' asked the Irishwoman.

'It would be so easy for a man to climb the back wall and break into the house,' Anne said. 'The dog is worse than useless. It hardly ever barks.'

She took Mrs Tulley into the drawing-room. The fire was almost out and she did not bother to light the lamp.

Mrs Tulley wasn't asked to sit down. Watson hovered in the doorway, unable to leave the two women alone together; in her present state Anne might say anything. Once she looked over her shoulder and gave him a small, cruel smile. He was obliged to stand there and listen to the inane chatter of the drill sergeant's wife. It was typical of his existence, he thought, that while men of intellect had been discouraged from visiting the house, he was forced to make conversation with an illiterate and bigoted woman from the bogs of Connemara.

When at last Mrs Tulley had gone, he rushed into the drawing-room and, taking out his keys, unlocked the cupboard door and flung it open.

'There,' he said, 'there!' And pointing a trembling finger at the decanter he told Anne to take what she wanted. 'Drink yourself to death,' he shouted; and afraid he might do her an injury if he stayed in the same room, he swept past her and up the stairs.

He was shaking with rage at Mrs Tulley's insolent reference to Messrs. Johnson and Son – the idea of a woman like that putting in a good word for him! He had never forgotten Anne telling him that Mrs Tulley had been a crony of Mrs Gallagher's all those years ago in Dublin. She had often come to the house in Great Britain Street, being in a demented state after the death of her first husband. Anne and she had never met then, but Anne thought it a grand coincidence. He thought it insufferable that Mrs Tulley had been there right from the beginnings of their life together.

No sooner had he sat down at his desk than Anne had the audacity to come after him. She was cradling the decanter in her arms as though it was an infant; the wine was dribbling on to the floor. She swayed on her feet, and as she did so a further quantity slopped over the crook of her arm.

'Anne,' he protested. 'Where is the stopper? You are spilling it.'

'It will do the carpet good,' she said. She began to wander about the room, peering short-sightedly at the books on his shelves. 'When the time comes for us to leave our lovely home,' she said, 'you will need several trunks in which to cart the wretched things away.'

'It is not sensible to remove books in trunks or boxes,' he replied. 'The accumulated weight would be too much. It is far better to tie them into bundles of twelve or so.'

'But of course,' she said. 'I might have realised there was a sensible way to do it.' Without warning, though he should have known it was coming, she reached up and, tugging at a volume of essays, sent it tumbling to the floor.

'Don't', he cried.

'I am helping you,' she said, 'towards your first dozen.'

'Please,' he said. 'Leave me alone.'

'Please,' she repeated mockingly. 'How polite we are to each other.'

He tried to take her by the elbow and lead her to the glory hole – he couldn't allow her to run amok in his library – but she broke away from him and stumbled to the window. He heard the wine splattering on the floor. 'I'll leave you alone in my own good time,' she told him.

He returned to his desk and pretended to be absorbed in his book. He had his back to her. Now and then he made senseless jottings in the margin. He had read two pages and taken in neither of them, when she asked, 'How long will this go on?'

'What do you mean?' he said, stammering, because he couldn't cope with her.

'The Popes,' she said. 'The Blessed Popes.'

'I have sent it to Longman's,' he said stiffly. 'You know that.'

'Then why haven't they replied? I have looked for the post every day, as you have.'

'I haven't been counting the days,' he said.

'Probably,' she said, 'they haven't anyone clever enough to read it.'

He tried to close his ears to her but she was relentless. The drink had affected her speech; she was slurring her words. 'I don't know why you bother,' she said, 'considering no one has ever taken the slightest notice of your work.'

'Please stop,' he muttered under his breath. 'For the love of God, please stop.'

'But then when one thinks how abruptly you were got rid of, you were scarcely more successful as a schoolmaster.'

'Shut your mouth,' he said. He sat hunched over his desk and heard her go out of the door. He hoped she was tiring; sometimes she gave up and, sprawling fully dressed on her narrow bed, slept and snored the night away. He didn't think she had gone in search of more to drink; the decanter was still a quarter full. He listened at the open door and heard her rummaging about in the dressing-room.

He wondered if he dared leave the house to call on Mr Bush. At least there he was approved of; the old man never allowed him to feel he was in the wrong. But then how was he to get out of the house without being detected? As soon as she heard his footsteps Anne would run down the stairs in pursuit; she could lose her balance and fall. There is no way out for me, he thought. He would stay with her not only tonight but for the rest of his life. It was his burden to protect her from herself.

Anne was looking for the letters he had written to her before they were married. She couldn't remember where she had put them, only that she had wrapped them in something. There was a sentence in one of the letters which had never been explained. It had to do with someone's having been unfaithful to somebody's image. She had hidden the letters because she was afraid a housebreaker might steal them.

Even as she tugged at the top drawer of the chest she distinctly heard a clatter in the back yard. She gazed into the darkness, trembling. A man was out there, poised on the top of the wall, ready to leap down. There were two women talking to each other under the street lamp on the corner, and she signalled to them, trying to draw their attention to the figure on the wall, but they didn't see her. The man's shoulders bulged under the black sky. She shrank back from the window and fell onto her knees, staring transfixed at the floor. No one has ever seen me, she thought. I have always been one of those players situated at the back of the stage. When violence struck she would be crushed, not because she was the central objective but because she was in the way. Soon would come a splintering of wood as the yard door was forced inwards. J.S. Watson, forever reading, everlastingly scribbling, would fail to hear the stealthy footsteps in the hall.

Summoning all her strength, she reached up and felt for the pistols in the drawer above her head. She crawled on to the landing and scuttled past the head of the stairs.

'For the love of God,' cried Watson, swinging round from the window and seeing her on all fours like an animal. He dragged her upright and made her sit in the chair by the fire. Her teeth were chattering.

'There's someone out there,' she told him.

'It's cats,' he said. 'Cats prowling.'

'They are after my letters,' she moaned.

He didn't know what she meant. He had been rubbing with his

handkerchief at the wine stains on the carpet, and now he began to wipe the surrounds.

'I have become invisible,' she said, and she held her hand out in front of her and, spreading her fingers, peered at him as if through a grill. All at once she wailed, 'I have lost them. They were important to me.' He took no notice and asked her what she was doing with his grandfather's pistol.

'I need protection,' she said. 'I am alone in there.' She waved the barrel in the direction of the glory hole.

'You would be better off taking the dog in with you,' he said, and, as though it had understood, the dog got up from its place beside the hearth and slunk from the room. He called its name and clicked his fingers, but it backed away from him along the passage. He grew irritated and slammed the door.

'Snap has never liked me,' she said. 'You saw to that. You've never allowed anyone to like me.'

'No,' he agreed, 'I am a wicked man, and will no doubt burn for it.'

She watched him for a while and it maddened him. The sight of her slack mouth, her plum-coloured cheeks, filled him with revulsion.

At last she said, 'I shall go away. You don't want me here. I shall leave in the morning.'

'Good,' he said. 'I shall be able to get on with my work.'

He heard her attempting to rise from her chair and the grunt which escaped her as she fell back again. He knew now that she would keep on at him until it was time for bed.

'And which of your many friends,' he asked, 'will have the honour of taking you in?'

'Mrs Tulley will have me,' she answered. She sounded subdued.

He hoped she wasn't intending to weep. More than anything he distrusted her tears, suspecting that they sprang to her theatrical eyes at will and had nothing to do with her dry heart, which lay like a stone in her breast.

'On second thoughts,' she said, 'I shall go tonight.'

'Do as you please,' he muttered.

'Mrs Tulley,' she said, 'leads a normal life. She goes out. In the daytime, and in the evening.'

'I'm glad to hear it,' he said. 'I'm all in favour of a normal life.' He put away his handkerchief and picked up the book she had earlier pulled from the shelf.

131

'My mother made my father happy,' Anne said. 'I remember a particular smile.'

'You won't remember mine,' he replied, 'particular or otherwise. You've not caused me to smile in twenty years.'

* * *

He was on the landing, on hands and knees, when Ellen Pyne came back. He called out to her that she must wait. He was dipping a rag into a basin of water and wiping the skirting board clean. But she didn't hear, and knocked again, louder than before.

After a few moments he went downstairs and let her in. She wanted to know what was wrong with the gas-mantle in the hall.

'What do you mean?' he said.

'It's given up, Sir. It went out when I was on the step.'

He didn't reply. She went into the dining-room and he followed her. Here too the gas was unlit, though there was a glimmer of light from the lamp in the street outside. She could see that the tea things hadn't been touched, and exclaimed, 'You haven't taken tea, Sir.'

'I didn't think of tea,' he answered.

She bent down and picked up a glass from the carpet. 'Will you be wanting supper, Sir?' she asked.

'What?' he said, and then, 'Yes, of course. Some bread and cheese.'

He was fingering his ear and she thought that his cheek was swollen, though perhaps it was a trick of the lamp-light.

He left her and began to climb the dark stairs. 'The mistress has gone away,' he said, 'for a day or two. I am cleaning some port wine that has been spilled on the landing. In the morning you had best go over the paint work again. There's also some spilt on the threshold of the library door. I'm telling you in case you should wonder what it is.'

She half followed him up the stairs. 'Won't you leave it, Sir,' she said. 'I'll see to it in the morning.'

'I know what I'm doing,' he replied.

She went down into the hall again. She was shivering; the house seemed colder than usual.

The master, she thought, was obviously upset. Probably the mistress had thrown wine over him. Such things had happened before.

She laid the tray and prepared supper. Poor man! What a life he led! She respected him, though she had never felt easy in his presence, unlike the mistress, who was a different kettle of fish and whose nasty little ways made her all too human. When the mistress enquired how her mother did, or what Margaret was doing, it was simple to answer her. If the master asked a question, even something as ordinary as 'How are you this morning, Ellen Pyne?', it always sounded as if he was seeking deeper information, nothing to do with her health, more with her character. It made her uncomfortable; she didn't like to feel stupid. But then nobody could read the books he did without being a cut above everyone else. The things locked up in books made people ask clever questions. And yet, when the mistress had one of her turns and he had to pick her up off the floor, he carried her to her room with such a hang-dog expression on his face that it was plain that none of his books were of much use to him. Not at that moment. Sometimes, when the mistress had been particularly cruel and he had shouted back at her, he wandered up and down the stairs like a lost soul. She longed to tell him that he was in the right of it, that among the people she knew the mistress would long since have got a black eye for her pains, if not worse. Her mother had once given her father a piece of her lip and he had kicked her down the stairs, even though she was expecting a child. The master and mistress were poorly matched. For all her boasting it was obvious that the mistress came from a lower class than he and found it hard to keep up with him.

While the master ate his supper, Ellen saw to the fire in his bedroom, and drew the curtains.

He had left his Sunday boots by the door and she took them through into the dressing-room and put them away in the bottom of the wardrobe.

The master stayed up very late. Though she pulled the coverlet about her ears she could still hear him in the rooms below, pulling out the drawers of his desk and talking to himself.

* * *

At breakfast he asked Ellen what she would do when he gave up the house.

'I shall go home, Sir,' she said. 'For a time.'

'To New Cross?'

'Yes, Sir,' she said. She explained that her mother was in poor health and that she would look after her if it could be managed.

'Are you fond of her?' he asked.

'Yes,' she said.

She had evidently been crying; her eyelids were red and she had recently bathed her face. He hoped she wasn't in some sort of trouble – she was generally so cheerful. 'The greatest misfortune which can happen among relations,' he told her, 'is a different way of upbringing and an habitual blindness to certain defects.'

'Yes, Sir,' she said.

He would have continued the conversation but she was looking anxiously at the door. He could tell that she was afraid that Anne might come back and scold her for not getting on with her work. Even now there were tears in her eyes. Perhaps mention of her mother had upset her. It was difficult to know with women whether they were actually distressed or merely indulging in female emotions. He dismissed her, and she turned away with such a woe-begone expression on her plump face that he felt uncomfortable. He thought something had been expected of him.

After breakfast he went upstairs to the library. The dog was crouching on the landing with its head on its paws. Watson reflected that he hadn't yet told Mrs Hill when he would be quitting the house, and sitting down at his desk he began to write her a letter. He gave up before it was completed. His hand was so unsteady – he hadn't slept well – that what he had written was illegible. He stuffed the letter into a drawer, intending to finish it later in the day. Tidying the surface of his desk he noticed a smear of ink on the title page of Valerius Flaccus. The appearance of a manuscript, to the ignorant eye of a publisher, was almost as important as its content, though in this case he was far too useful to Bohn's Library for them to be put off by a single sheet of spoiled paper. All the same, he would have to write out the page again. He would have done it there and then – he could have held his wrist with one hand to guide his pen – but he was restless. The window was open and yet there didn't seem to be any air in the room.

He went downstairs and whistled for the dog to follow him. It took no notice, though he heard it growling in its sleep. Before he left the house he called out to Ellen Pyne that the key to the store cupboard was on the hall table and that she could take the candles she wanted.

He thought he would go into town and call on William Longman at Paternoster Row, and he walked in the direction of the railway station. Half way there he decided that he was wasting his time. There wasn't a more despised creature than an author, particularly one without any advantages of birth or fortune to set him off. Longman was bound to be too busy to see him, and he was in no mood to be treated like a tradesman; it wouldn't help him to lose his temper with the secretary. Besides, it was more urgent that he should go to Turner's on the High Street.

Once there, he made some calculations in his head and, after discussing the matter with the trunk-maker, left the shop without having come to a decision.

It was a blustery day and refuse sailed up from the gutters; ribbons of paper fluttered at his knees. He had to hold onto his hat as he turned the corners. Usually his head was so full of words, of sentences he was trying to wrestle into shape, that he was hardly aware of his surroundings, but now his mind was curiously blank and he was overwhelmed by the noise in the streets. There was such a roaring and rattling all about him that he felt giddy. He stumbled into a side road, and still the sounds followed him, increasing in volume as though a monstrous wave reared up behind him; soon it would break over his head and smash him to the cobble-stones. He walked faster and knew he was listening to his own blood pounding in his ears. In spite of the cold wind the sweat dripped into his eyes.

At last he stopped in the doorway of a dark little shop and fumbled in his pocket for his handkerchief. A pigeon flew out from the ledge above his head; he started so violently that he almost lost his balance and tumbled from the step. His heart beat like a drum. He took off his hat and was about to wipe his forehead when he saw the stains on his handkerchief. An old woman passed, carrying firewood, and for an instant the doorway was filled with the stench of her clothes. I am no better than she, he thought, and he dropped the handkerchief to the ground and rushed out into the street. More than anything he wanted to lie down and sleep.

All the same, when he came to St Martin's Road he walked straight on past the house and rang the door bell of No.32.

Mr Bush was out; his son Fred was in the studio painting a stormy sky above a windmill. Watson immediately began to complain of the disgraceful state of the roads. 'The dirt,' he cried, 'the potholes. Above all the noise.'

'I don't know when my father will be back,' said Fred. 'Possibly not for hours.'

'Twice this morning,' Watson said, 'I was almost run down. Once by a Vauxhall omnibus, and again by a dray horse.' He had no idea why he had made such a remark – it was untrue. Confused, he lowered himself into Mr Bush's armchair by the easel and wiped his forehead with a paint rag. 'I wanted to call last night,' he said. 'I should have come but was prevented.'

'You wouldn't have seen my father,' said Fred. 'He was at a musical evening.' He looked over his shoulder at Watson who was lying back in the chair with his eyes closed. There was a shred of old newspaper caught in the laces of his boots. It was plain that he might sit there all day.

Several minutes elapsed, during which time Watson struggled to remember the name of a student he had once known in Dublin. He could see his face quite clearly; even the room he had lived in was familiar to him. There had been a green ottoman under the window with a book propping up one leg because the floor sloped.

'Is this a large house?' he asked suddenly.

Fred said he supposed it was. He hadn't measured it.

'And does someone live in the attic?'

'Two people,' said Fred. 'Both women.'

'And what about Mr Williams in Hastings?' demanded Watson.

'What about him?' asked Fred.

'Has he an attic?'

'He lives in a cottage,' replied Fred. He wished his visitor would go away or else keep silent. He had no interest in attics himself.

All at once Watson started to talk about a silver dish which someone had presented to him. On receiving it he had made a speech which had gone down exceptionally well. By all accounts the clapping had been heard in St Martin's Road. 'I borrowed most of my words from other authors,' he admitted, 'but I do not think anyone noticed. I would like your father to have the dish.'

'It isn't his birthday,' said Fred. 'However, he will be in this afternoon. I should come back then.'

'There is also a chair,' said Watson. 'A very special chair. I should like him to have that also, although I would not like him to sit on it.'

He got up and glanced at the painting on the easel. He frowned and walked to the door. Fred had never known him to make any comment on either his father's work or his own. It was a point in his favour. When he had come to collect his portrait he had complimented Mr Bush on the frame. Grateful that Watson was leaving, Fred wished him good morning.

'If you ask me, it's goodbye,' said Watson. He was smiling good humouredly. 'Be sure to tell your father about the salver and the chair.' He knew perfectly well that Fred would forget that he had even called.

He went home and spoke to Ellen Pyne in the dining-room. She was laying the table for dinner and he could tell she was still upset; her hands shook as she took up the cutlery from the sideboard. He didn't want to pry, but he felt it was his duty to assist her in whatever way he could. 'There is something troubling you,' he said. 'I know it.'

She protested that there was nothing the matter; she couldn't meet his eye.

'You mustn't worry about your mother,' he persisted.

She admitted she couldn't help feeling anxious. Her mother had grown frail. She had borne eight children.

'I expect she finds it was worth it,' he said. 'They must be a comfort to her now that she is old.'

'Not all of them have turned out as she would have wished, Sir.' the girl said. 'Though she has loved them all.'

Suddenly he grew impatient. 'It is often harmful to be loved,' he said severely. 'And always harmful to love.'

She seemed to be paying particular attention to his wrists. Scowling, he pulled down the sleeves of his coat.

He took no more than a mouthful of soup. Then, his mind made up, he threw down his spoon and rushing from the room seized his hat and coat. He heard Ellen coming up the basement stairs, and he slammed the front door after him, not wanting to face her, though it was surely none of her business if he hadn't time to finish his dinner.

He returned to Turner's shop, and having told the trunkmaker what he had decided walked for several hours about the district. It was strange knowing that he could go home and work undisturbed at his desk, and even stranger that he hadn't any inclination to do so. He was irritated at the way people looked at him as he passed. He was wearing a suit of clothes that he had bought thirty years before. The coat jacket was too tight across his shoulders, and the trousers were frayed at the bottoms.

In the evening he wrote letters. The decanter of wine that Anne had brought up from the dining-room was still on the library table. He drank two glasses and slept a little, his head resting on his papers.

He woke up thinking of death, and scribbled sentences across a page torn from a notebook:

Of the dead in general the voice of mankind exhorts us to say of them only what is just. Have we not a conviction that in every right-constituted person there is far more good than ill? Are we not anxious, after their deaths, to look on their virtues only and to pass over those imperfections which were in their characters? Are we not desirous to remember only the sweet scent of the rose, and to forget the thorns among which it grew?

Somewhere on the top shelf he knew there was a book on the cultivation of herbs. He couldn't reach it without standing on Anne's chair. He was about to drag the chair away from the window when he grew suddenly faint and was afraid he might fall down.

* * *

On the Tuesday, sometime in the morning, he bought a hammer and a length of rope. He unwrapped the parcel in the hall and left its contents on the small table beside the coat-stand.

Later, Ellen Pyne asked him if she should put the hammer and the rope away in the cupboard.

'No,' he said. 'Leave them where they are.'

'There is another hammer in the house, Sir. Had you forgotten?'

'Of course not,' he said. 'But that is in the Mistress's room and she has locked the door.'

At dinner time he told Ellen that he would be going away for the night. She gave a small moan; her hands shook as she put the dishes on the table.

'You can ask somebody in,' he said. 'To keep you company.'

'It's not being alone that frightens me,' she blurted out, and he looked up, startled. She turned and busied herself at the sideboard.

'Are you crying?' he asked.

'I can't help it, Sir,' she muttered, and tried not to sniff.

After a moment, he said, 'It's true. Being alone is not the worst thing that can happen,' and added, 'You're a good girl, Ellen.'

She left the room, her face quite calm, as though everything was all right.

He felt very unwell that evening. Earlier, he had gone to Brixton station, determined to go on a journey, but at the last minute he drew back.

At eleven o'clock he heard someone moving about downstairs. He went on to the landing and called out, 'Anne, is it you?'

'No, Sir, it's Ellen.'

He looked down at her, frowning. 'Whoever you are,' he said, 'I don't feel well.' She asked him if she should bring him some hot milk.

'I don't want milk,' he said, 'I want peace. Is the street full of people?'

'People, Sir?' she said.

'Go and look,' he shouted. 'Send them away. I am not a peep show.'

She opened the front door and peered out at the dark road. There wasn't a sound to be heard save the rustling of the holly bush by the gate. 'There's nobody there,' she told him, and closed the door.

'In the morning,' he said, 'if you should find something wrong with me, go and fetch Dr Rugg.'

'Shall I fetch him now, Sir?' she said.

'It's not urgent now,' he replied. 'But I may require medicines in the morning.'

That night he dreamt he was running behind a young girl whose hair streamed in the wind like a horse's tail. He tried to catch up with her but she was too swift for him. In the distance the arms of a windmill combed the sky. As he ran, he shouted for the girl to wait for him – he had been told there was something she could tell him. A quantity of golden apples spilled from the basket she was carrying and bowled down the lane towards him. He leaped over them, and a strand of hair blew from her head and lashed his face; it cut his cheek. It was hardly a nightmare but he woke trembling, his shirt sticking to his back. There was something he had forgotten, either a portion of his dream or something that had happened earlier, some dark event which hovered at the edges of his mind. Finally he got up and, lighting a candle, went through into the library to find a suitable book to read. The window was open and yet there was an unpleasant smell in the room. He realised that it was the smell of his own clothes; he had worn the same shirt for three days. He was perplexed by a sheet of paper, covered in his handwriting, which he saw lying on his desk.

Examining the last line he could make nothing of it: *Are we not desirous to remember only the sweet scent of the rose, and to forget the thorns among which it grew?* He thought the style deplorable.

At daybreak he found himself sitting in the chair by the banked up fire, staring at the window. The most frightful image jigged before his eyes. Suspended between the desk and window he saw a naked figure, portly, pale as milk, obscenely sighing. He jumped to his feet and the figure vanished, and now there was only the blind with the new day behind it, puffing outwards as the wind blew.

* * *

Ellen got up, as usual, at six o'clock. She let the dog out into the yard and it padded straight to the border of sooty earth by the back wall and began to dig a hole. It was raining; she didn't want Snap coming in with muddy paws, and she tried to shoo him away on to the flagstones. The dog bared its teeth at her and growled, and she ran indoors half afraid of it, though it had always been as soft as butter.

At eight o'clock she knocked on the Master's bedroom door and told him his breakfast was ready.

He said he would be down directly. His voice sounded quite normal.

But he didn't appear for another three-quarters of an hour, and when finally he rang the bell for her to come up and she entered the dining-room, she couldn't help staring at him. He didn't look ill at all; there was even a dab of colour in his cheeks.

She said, 'I'm glad to see you well, Sir', and all at once he gave her a ferocious smile, his lip curled back over his teeth. It was a terrible smile. She was shaking so much that she splashed hot water on to the cloth. She left the room as quickly as possible and whimpered as she ran down the basement stairs. She wanted her mother.

Shortly after ten o'clock she heard him go out. She went up to the dining-room and stacked the dishes and put more slack on the fire.

The master came in an hour later when she was dusting the drawing-room. She had expected him, but at the sound of his step on the path her heart leapt in her breast. She wasn't afraid of him; she was afraid for him. He came into the drawing-room and said

140

calmly, 'If I should be ill before dinner, send for the doctor.' He was holding a small paper bag, twisted into a cone at the top.

'Please, Sir,' she said. 'Won't you tell me what is wrong?'

'I know what I'm doing,' he said. 'Don't be alarmed.'

He went upstairs, and she stood on the threshold of the drawing-room and waited. Afterwards she couldn't remember what had gone on in her head, only the sound of the ormolu clock ticking the minutes away on the mantel-shelf.

She had been standing there for perhaps an hour when she heard him groaning in the room above. She climbed the stairs and went into the bedroom. He was lying there, propped on pillows, looking at her. There was a medicine glass and a green bottle on the chair by the bed, and a phial on the floor.

'Oh Sir,' she cried, and she ran to him and clasped his hand, the tears spilling down her cheeks.

He stared past her and feebly indicated with his head that she should go to the wash-stand. She did as he wished and saw some letters lying there, among them an envelope with her name on it. She picked it up and read what he had written beneath her name, and dropped the envelope as though it had burned her fingers.

'Tell them nothing of my domestic life,' he said. 'For my sake. Be truthful as regards the events of the past few days but remember I have always been a private man.'

She stood at the end of the bed, wringing her hands and sniffing. She hadn't the education to comfort him. He had closed his eyes, and his face was the colour of the sheet about his throat. She thought he had fainted, but suddenly he said, 'I have put the pistol back in the drawer in the dressing-room.'

'Pistol, Sir!' she blubbered.

'When I took off the shirt,' he murmured. 'I thought I should bleed to death.'

She waited a short while longer and then crept to the door, watching over her shoulder in case he stirred. She was certain he was asleep; otherwise she wouldn't have left him on his own.

He was unconscious when the doctor arrived. Dr Rugg did what he could for him, and then read the letters shown to him by Ellen Pyne. He sent her downstairs. Taking the key from the washstand he opened the door of the room behind the library.

After a few minutes he went down into the hall and told Ellen Pyne that he was going out. She must stay where she was. She was crying, and he was so distracted that he lent her his handkerchief, though he had a heavy cold on him.

In the early afternoon, when Watson had sufficiently recovered, Dr Rugg hurried home to tell his wife that he wouldn't be available for the rest of the day. She should send his patients on to Dr Rose in Clarkson Avenue.

On coming back to St Martin's Road he found Dr Pope, the surgeon, waiting for his opinion on whether Watson was fit to be moved. Reluctantly he agreed that he was.

Watson asked if it was absolutely necessary for him to leave the house. 'I don't like being away from my books,' he said, 'or my dog.' The dog was barking outside on the landing, and he called out to it and tried to coax it into the room. He seemed amused when it backed off, whining, its ears laid flat to its head.

In spite of being somewhat unsteady on his feet he didn't need any assistance while dressing. He fussed over which boots he should put on; there was a special pair which suited him. He was quite lucid. Pointing at the chest of drawers, he drew Dr Rugg's attention to a large oyster shell.

'Ah, yes, most interesting,' remarked the doctor, humouring him.

'It's a curious thing,' Watson said, 'but I cannot be sure where I picked it up. Some say Ireland, others the South Seas.' And he smiled, as though he had made a joke.

He took particular pains over his appearance. He had two silver-backed hair brushes, and he used them vigorously. Dr Rugg wanted to know whether there wasn't someone he should get in touch with on his behalf.

'To what end?' asked Watson.

'To let them know what has happened,' explained Dr Rugg. 'And you must have advice.'

'I don't feel it will be of much use,' Watson said.

'What about Mr Fraser?' persisted Rugg. 'He was a pupil of yours and is a clever young man.'

Watson shrugged his shoulders and continued to brush his hair. Dr Rugg himself wrote a note to Fraser and took it downstairs to Ellen Pyne. He told her to run all the way to the solicitor's house. When she opened the door he saw half a dozen people gathered in the street, mainly young boys and old women. He changed his mind about the note – he was afraid Pyne might drop it and that it would fall into the wrong hands. He took it from her and tore it up.

He mentioned to Dr Pope that there were people in the road; he tried to keep his voice low in case Watson should hear.

'What's that?' demanded Watson. 'What's wrong now?'

'There are some boys in the road,' Dr Rugg said, and added hastily, 'They are not from the school. They are mostly ragamuffins.'

Watson became agitated. He rushed to the window and made as if to pull aside the blind. Dr Rugg took him by the arm and spoke soothingly to him. 'The boys will be sent away before we leave the house,' he assured him.

A cab arrived some minutes later. Dr Rugg took leave of Watson in the hall. He said the servant was very distressed and that he would stay and attend to her. It was an excuse. He shrank from seeing Watson exposed to the salacious gaze of that excited crowd.

He thought that Ellen Pyne was a courageous girl. Though she was in a state of shock she refused to go home to her family, saying she preferred to be in the neighbourhood in case there was anything she could do for her master. 'He'll be worried about his books and papers,' she said. 'Someone ought to keep an eye on them.'

Dr Rugg enquired whether there was anyone nearby who could take her in.

'There's a girl in service further up the road,' she said. 'Her mistress has already sent word to the door that I can stay there for some nights.'

'You understand,' Dr Rugg warned, 'that it would be better for all concerned if you said as little as possible, at this time, of what you know?'

'I know nothing, Sir,' the girl said.

Dr Rugg went home to have his tea. There were still people in the road, standing on the opposite pavement staring at the house. It was raining heavily, but they stood there, gawping up at the windows.

In the evening he walked to Fraser's house and was told that he was out and wouldn't be back until ten o'clock. Next he went to Brixton and was allowed to see Watson, who was brought out to him with a shawl draped over his shoulders; he was eating a sandwich and frowning. Dr Rugg asked him if he had anything particular on his mind.

'I asked for lean beef,' Watson said. 'This is too tough.'

'I mean anything to do with the situation in which you find yourself,' said Rugg.

'How would you feel?' countered Watson. He looked down at his sandwich in disgust.

Dr Rugg told him he would return the following day. He was on his way to Fraser's; when he learned what had happened Fraser would be sure to come and see him. Watson said he didn't think Fraser would bother.

Dr Rugg called at Fraser's house again, some time before eleven. Fraser was dreadfully concerned. He had been round to St Martin's Road and seen the house bolted and barred. He said it was unendurable to think of a man like Watson kept from his books. What he must be suffering!

'He seems comfortable enough,' said Dr Rugg. 'I saw him two hours ago. The meat sandwich sent in by Ellen Pyne seemed to be his main preoccupation. I had some hopes that he might have suffered an epileptic seizure. Epileptic mania would, I think, be sufficient evidence of a state of temporary insanity.'

Fraser began to talk about the character of Mr Watson, his kindness, his ability as a teacher, his commitment to his pupils. He had never allowed flogging. 'Once,' he said, 'when I was a new boy, a junior master wrongly accused me of some trivial offence. He hit me on the cheek and put me out of the room. I was thirteen and big for my age, but I cried.' He faltered, and looked perplexedly round the room, at the cheerful fire in the grate, the gasolier burning above the polished table, as though he couldn't understand what he was doing in such pleasant surroundings now that the world was turned upside down. He blurted out: 'I cannot believe it. It doesn't seem possible. It's unthinkable that he should be considered insane. I have know him since I was a child. He is saner than most men.'

'I fear he is,' remarked Dr Rugg solemnly. 'And I'm afraid epilepsy must be ruled out. I found no evidence of it.'

'We must all help him,' said Fraser. 'Many, many people have reason to be thankful to him. He has always been the most generous of men. I have seen him give the shirt off his back to a beggar in the street.'

'Hardly the class of person who will be of much use to him now,' objected Dr Rugg, but the young man wasn't listening. He had left the table and now stood in front of the drawn curtains, his back to the doctor.

'You don't know him as I do,' he said. 'He is an unusual man.' His voice shook. 'He has a peculiar sweetness of character.'

'So I have heard,' murmured Dr Rugg, and he looked thoughtfully at the floor, remembering a woman under a filthy blanket, jack-knifed in the corner like an old battered doll.

*　*　*

The next day Fraser visited Watson. He didn't expect it would be an easy matter to get him to speak of the events of the previous day and had thought out his approach carefully. He was taken aback, when, after complaining that he wasn't allowed to shave, Watson began immediately to talk of his wife. 'I cannot pretend I have been a good husband,' he said. 'I have always been a man out of the ordinary for silence and reserve, and yet she was worried about some letters I had written to her in happier times. She said they were important to her. Do you think an unfeeling woman would concern herself with old love letters?'

'I suppose not,' said Fraser.

'Only an hour before she was helping me gather my books together, in readiness for our move from the house. She wanted me to tie them into bundles – I admit it hadn't crossed my mind. Books are much easier to transport in bundles of a dozen or so. She is a sensible woman, don't you agree? No doubt she felt she was in a desperate situation. To have no home, no place to go – can you imagine how she felt? It is a dreadful thing for a man to lose his position, the roof over his head – but for a woman, just think of it, and for it to happen twice in a lifetime! It was the same for her when she was a young girl in Dublin – cast on to the world by an improvident father. Why else would she have married me? I should have lived my life alone. She could not resist saying hurtful things – there was more of aloes than of honey in her character. She would be the first to tell you that she wasn't brought up to take second place. She always wanted more –' Suddenly his mouth twitched; he looked bewildered. He was sitting opposite Fraser at a small table in a windowless anteroom.

'Her words,' prompted Fraser. 'Her attitude. I would spare you if I could, but you must see that I have to know everything. I need to know the facts. The details.'

'I don't think I can remember them,' replied Watson.

It was not true, but he didn't see why he should enlighten Fraser. What good would it do either of them? Details were a matter of subjective preference and merely reflected personal prejudices.

'Do you remember feeling confused?' asked Fraser.

'In dealings with my wife,' said Watson, 'confusion was a daily occurrence. Sunday was no different in that respect. I had been working on a story about Hercules, I think, or perhaps that was the day before. As you know I've recently finished a translation of the expedition of the Golden Fleece and the two things may have merged in my mind. As far as I recall, the only moment of confusion, as you put it, was when I imagined that I was wearing the shirt of Nessus.'

'And on the Sunday afternoon, Mrs Watson was sitting with you while you worked?'

'The idea of love being harmful to the beloved is an interesting one,' said Watson. 'In my own experience, injury has been gradual rather than immediate.'

On the rickety table stood a jug and a metal cup. All at once Watson dipped his finger into the jug and flicked out a dead fly. It landed on Fraser's papers and wobbled there in a drop of water. 'My wife always sat with me,' he said. 'Sunday or any other day you care to name.' He smiled, but almost at the same moment his face became serious again. Fraser had the oddest feeling that his client was play-acting, though it was difficult to tell whether it was madness or sanity that he imitated.

Suddenly Watson demanded, 'What has happened to my dog? Where have they put him?'

Fraser told him that Ellen Pyne was looking after it. It was on a chain in the backyard. He said, 'I beg you to think of your position, head master. A motive will be sought, an intention –'

'*Cui bono?*' murmured Watson. Jumping to his feet he brushed a speck of dust from his trouser leg.

'You must defend yourself,' said Fraser miserably. 'If not –' he shrugged his shoulders and looked down at the fly.

Seated again, Watson leaned across the table and asked who was taking care of his books and papers.

Fraser thought it was a grotesque question. Dr Rugg was right – Watson was surely mad.

'I will see to them,' he said. 'They will be quite safe for the time being, though I expect the owner of the house will want the contents cleared as soon as possible.'

'Is it that urgent?' demanded Watson. He seemed put out.

'I'm afraid it is,' replied Fraser. 'You must realise that it may be some time before she will be able to rent the property again.'

Watson said he didn't see why. Notwithstanding certain irritations he had always found it a very pleasant house to live in.

Fraser stood up, and rapping on the door waited to be let out.

'I don't think I will have anything more to tell you,' Watson said. 'It is, after all, a personal matter.' Whether Watson was genuinely mad or not it was obvious to Fraser that the only possible line of defence was one of insanity. Witnesses must be found to say that the marriage had always been harmonious and medical men produced to speak of a sudden outburst brought on by melancholia. Later that day he spoke to Ellen Pyne; and he found her as uncommunicative as her master. 'I know nothing, sir,' she said, 'beyond what Mr Watson has probably told you.'

The day before, when Ellen had fetched Dr Rugg, she had given way to hysteria, but it had only been for a minute. She wouldn't let her master down again, not after that one momentary lapse when she had gabbled of bonnets in the wardrobe and someone being shot and the dog digging a grave in the yard.

Excerpts from some writings found in a carpet bag in Horsemonger Lane Gaol, said to have been written by Mr Watson while waiting trial for his life and entitled: 'Dead. A Contemplation.'

I

She is dead. She lies motionless. That which once animated her, animates her no longer. Thou canst not disturb her. Thou canst not touch her cheek and awaken her, and call upon her face, as thou wast wont, a smile answering to thine own. No; no feature, no limb will she stir more

Nor will she utter a sound. The voice which for so many years addressed thee so familarly is dumb. Thou dost address her; thou callest her by name; thou lavishest on her the terms of endearment with which thou wast accustomed to please her ear; but the only reply is silence.

II

She is dead, but not gone. She will live in the memory of many, and especially in thine; she will live in thine to the end of they life, an oft-recurring object of contemplation to thee

Thou canst not free thyself, as it were, from her presence. Sleeping or waking, she is with thee wherever thou goest. She cannot be excluded.

III

Thou goest into another room. Thou rememberest the place where she used to sit, and the seat which she most frequently occupied. Was it this chair that was her favourite? No, it was this, with the peculiar wavy marks in the wood. The door opens. You look round. But no, it is a living member of the household that comes in. You seem half-disappointed. You had almost allowed yourself to think that the dead was coming to resume her place in her chair

The seat which she loved you will regard as sacred to her. You will perhaps put it in a place by itself; so that no one can violate it.

IV

Thou venturest to inspect her little boxes and cases, the recepticles in which she treasured up gifts from friends. The things themselves may be of small value, but they had powerful charms in her eyes

Here is something which thou recognisest with surprise. A scrap of paper, a little note which thou hadst utterly forgotten.

V

Thou sittest and reflectest upon her character, and upon the time which she passed with thee. Thou knowest that she was not quite perfect, and thou art at times disposed to let thy thoughts dwell upon her faults and imperfections. Was she not occasionally wayward, somewhat perverse, and difficult to persuade to comply with that which thou desirest? But what were these failings, which were but those of an hour, in comparison with the whole course of her married life? Was she not devoted to thy interests, and desirous to promote they comforts, though sometimes it was difficult to perceive those feelings in her. Thou wilt not meditate on these little imperfections of a woman's nature

Are we not disposed, in regard to those who are deemed the good in mankind, to look, after their deaths, on their virtues only, and to dismiss from our thoughts whatever faults there were in their characters? Are we not desirous to remember only the sweet scent of the rose, and to forget the thorns among which it grew?

VI

The time for the funeral approaches. Those who once quarrelled now cease from discord. Thou bearest her in memory and will always bear. Thou art now at peace with her. She will offend thee no more in this life. Thou wilt not suffer they memory to dwell on her failings

She is dead, but thou dost not think of her as gone.

149

The strange murder at Stockwell must for the moment engross attention, and throw a distressing gloom over all thoughtful minds. It is one of those tragedies, happily rare, which reveal the possibilities of human evil, of moral and mental disease, or of both, under circumstances of everyday life, and which seem, therefore, to come close home to us like spectres dogging our steps.

When some wretched, unintelligent, half-brutalised ruffian butchers his wife in a fit of drunkenness or rage, we feel divided by a great gulf from the very possiblities of such an outrage. He is an animal and has lived like an animal, and we seem simply to behold a more terrible and furious kind of wild beast among us. We view all such horrors as fearful spectacles, but we fail – perhaps more than we ought – to feel that community of nature and similarity of circumstances which could bring such crimes and miseries home to our own imaginations and could at once deepen and sober our horror by some dim sympathetic dread.

Are these the possibilities which lie hidden in ordinary flesh and blood, in simple circumstances, and in ordinary middle-class life? Is our everyday human nature such a mere crust over a seething abyss? We fear such a lesson needs to be taken to heart. We have smoothed down our lives by civilisation to such a decent and regular exterior that we are apt to feel rather injured by the plain words and broad denunciations which ancient authorities, and even modern poets, are occasionally heard to mutter against us. Our novelists and would-be moralists play with the vices of the heart and body as mere materials for an amusing tale, fit to be read even by boys and girls. Our philosophers contemplate with serenity the emancipation of men, women and children from the old restraints and the stern regulations of tradition. It is only unscrupulous kings who set continents in flames, and we are thought to need nothing but a little education and political economy to keep the people steady and prosperous.

Amid these flattering fancies we are startled by a deed which, at first glance, recalls nothing so much as the primaeval murder; and it occurs not amid those dens of violence or in those haunts of malicious crime which are nearer hell than earth, but in a decent neighbourhood, at a clergyman's hearth, on a Sunday afternoon after a morning's visit to church, associated with grey hairs and honoured age ...

PART 4

Having pleaded 'Not Guilty' at the November Sessions, Watson was not asked to plead again. On being asked whether he wished to challenge any of the jury, he simply shook his head.

The Hon. George Denman, Q.C. with Messrs Poland and Beasley, conducted the Prosecution, instructed by Mr Pollard, Assistant Solicitor to the Treasury. Mr Sergeant Parry, with the Hon. F. Thesiger, conducted the Defence, instructed by Mr Fraser, solicitor, of Dean Street. Mr Justice Byles presided.

The Hon. G. Denman, in opening the case to the jury, said: 'Gentlemen of the Jury, the prisoner at the bar, Mr John Selby Watson, is a clergyman of the Established Church, and, I believe, a man of about 67 years of age. He stands charged upon this indictment with the wilful murder of his wife, Anne Watson, who was 63 or 64 years of age at the time of her death. He himself, being a clergyman of the Established Church, and having been a school master, and being a man of learning and education and culture, stands charged with this offence.

'Gentlemen, I need say nothing more to ensure your best attention to this case. I fear upon the facts it will be terribly clear that by the hand of the prisoner, and by his wilful act, the deceased came to her death; and so far as I am instructed, and so far as I can form any guess, the only defence that is at all likely to be set up is one frequently adopted in cases of murder; namely, that at the time the offence was committed the prisoner was not responsible for his actions. I am heartened to know that the prisoner is in the hands of one of the most powerful and eloquent counsels who ever conducted a case in a court of justice, and that the case is to be tried before a humane, learned, and experienced Judge.

'The prisoner – Mr John Selby Watson – was appointed in 1844 as head master of Stockwell Grammar School. In September, 1870, he received notice that his services would be no longer required. At that time, and I believe for some five or six years previously, he had resided with his wife at 28, St Martin's Road, Stockwell, and so far as external appearances went, they lived in a friendly and affectionate manner, the sort which subsists between a man and his wife, and especially so in the case of an aged couple. From the middle of 1870, at the beginning of the hot summer months, they slept in different apartments, and strange to say the servant was not asked to take any part in the cleaning of Mrs Watson's room. This curious arrangement might possibly be due to the straitened means which had resulted from the prisoner losing his situation. However, as I told you, they lived on affectionate terms, though I should state there were no children born to the marriage. Nothing, as I will prove to you, indicated anything contrary to ordinary relations between the parties down to the 8th October, 1871, to which I am now about to call your attention.

'The servant had been in the habit of taking a holiday every other Sunday, and the 8th of October was a Sunday. The prisoner and his wife went to church as usual, had their dinner as usual, and wine was taken to them in the library. The servant went away at four o'clock and did not return until nine, when certain things occurred which are of great importance in this case. The only person whom I am able to bring in communication with the prisoner and his wife, between the departure of the servant and her return, is an old lady named Tulley. Mrs Tulley will tell you that she went to the house at five o'clock and was kept a long time waiting at the door, and that she heard some confusion before she was let in.

'When the servant returned at nine o'clock, she saw nothing at all unusual, except that she was informed that Mrs Watson had gone out and would not be back until next day. As she was going upstairs to bed the prisoner called her attention to a mark on the stairs outside the library door, and told her port wine had been spilt on the landing. In so doing, he was stating something he deliberately knew to be false.

'On Monday the 9th the prisoner went to Turner's on the Clapham Road and asked them to furnish him with a trunk or packing case. The box is here if it is necessary for you to see it. It is a box which is undoubtedly capable of holding any person of Mrs Watson's size, if the object for which it was ordered was to place a corpse in that box. The same afternoon the servant asked if her

152

mistress would be back that day and the prisoner said she would not; whereupon she remarked it would be awkward, because there were candles or something of the kind which she wanted.

'On Tuesday, the 10th October, the prisoner told the servant he would be away that night and advised her to get somebody in to keep her company. In the event, he did not go out; at about eleven o'clock he called out to her that if there was anything wrong with him in the morning, he should go for Dr Rugg. You will hear from the evidence that later that night he took some prussic acid with the probable intention of destroying his life.

'On Wednesday, the 11th October, the prisoner went out both before and after breakfast. On his return he again told the servant that if he should fall ill she should go for the doctor. An hour or so later she heard him groaning, and subsequently fetched Dr Rugg. Dr Rugg found the prisoner unconscious, and after doing what he could for him he was shown some letters by the servant. Having read the note addressed 'To the surgeon', he went into the room behind the library and found the body of the deceased in a corner, in a sort of sitting position   in fact the sort of position which would have made it easy to dispose of the body by placing it in just such a box as I have described being ordered at the trunkmakers. Dr Rugg will tell you of the curious remark the prisoner made while dressing. He pointed to the chest of drawers and said, "Isn't that a curious oyster shell?" He said it coolly and in such a way as you would hardly expect from a man, unless he were of a very great nerve indeed, who had committed a very horrible crime. It made a great impression on Dr Rugg, and in that way he will to some extent be a witness on behalf of the prisoner, his impression being that his coolness indicated the existence of insanity.

'There was another document found, and as far as I can make out, it gives a clue to an expression, otherwise unintelligible, with regard to the exception of his happiness and felicity. It is in Latin and is as follows – *Felix in omnibus fere rebus praeterquam quod ad sexum attinet femineum. Saepe olim amanti amare semper nocuit.* The former part means – "Happy in all things except that pertaining to the female sex". The latter part may be said to be ambiguous. The sentence is one capable of three or four interpretations. I should say a scholarlike translation would be, "To a person who has loved often in former times, loving has never been anything but a trial and an injury."

'In these cases it is often common for the counsel for the

prosecution, having stated the facts of the case, to stop and tell the jury that it is for the prisoner or his counsel to make out the case for insanity, to do no more than prove the facts of the case, and to throw the burden for defence entirely on the counsel for the prisoner. But, having had ample notice, from what has previously occurred, that the defence to be set up is one of insanity, it is necessary for me, I think, in the first instance, to call witnesses with regard to that issue which is the practical one the jury will have to try. The prisoner was taken into custody and remained in the Surrey County gaol until the 14th November. I will call the medical gentleman who attended him in the gaol and who saw him every day, and he will tell you, that, doing the best he could, by conversation and otherwise to form an honest judgment with regard to the prisoner's state of mind, he came to the clearest conclusion that there was nothing in his conversation, his reasoning powers, his manner or his physical appearance to lead him to any conclusion but that the prisoner was a man of sound mind, capable of exercising his judgment, and of doing rational things.

'Gentlemen, I must remind you of the necessity of exercising extreme caution in dealing with pleas of insanity in the cases of persons charged with murder.'

George Greenham. I am in the Metropolitan Police Force – I understand the making of plans – I have prepared and produce a plan showing the position of the rooms at 28, St Martin's Road, Stockwell. On the ground floor, as you enter, the drawing-room is on the left, and the dining-room on the right, with a small schoolroom at the back – on the first floor there is a front bedroom and a dressing-room behind, also a library in front, and a smaller bedroom behind it.

Eleanor Mary Pyne. I am now living at New Cross – I am twenty years of age – I was in the service of the prisoner and his wife not quite three years. While I was there a sister of mine was in service as well – she left last Christmas twelvemonth – from that time I was the only servant there – no one lived in the same house but me and my Master and Mistress. My Master and Mistress used to occupy the same bedroom; that was the front bedroom on the first floor – they ceased to occupy the same bedroom at the commencement of the hot weather last year. My Mistress then slept in the room behind the library. She dressed in the room Mr Watson slept in, the front bedroom. At the back of that bedroom is a dressing-room. I used to attend to all the rooms on the floor, excepting the one that Mrs Watson slept in – she attended to that herself – I only went into it once or twice during the two or three months she slept there – I don't remember how recently before Sunday, 8th October, I had been in it. On Sunday morning, 8th October, my Master and Mistress went out together rather earlier than the usual church time – they came back rather later than usual – I should think it was about 1.45 o'clock – that was their dinner hour at that time. I had prepared dinner in the dining-room on the ground floor; that is the room on the right, as you come into the house. Mrs Watson took off her bonnet and things, and they sat down to dinner – I attended to them – they had no wine for dinner, they had some after dinner – I am not certain what wine it was – after dinner they went upstairs into the library. I do not remember seeing them again – it was between 2 and 3 o'clock when I left them in the library – up to that time I had not noticed anything in their manner or demeanour to attract my attention   they usually lived on very friendly terms. They were generally very quiet. I went out that afternoon, about 4 o'clock – I let myself out – before I went out I had prepared the tea in the dining-room – 5.45 was their usual time for taking tea. When I returned, at 9 o'clock, I knocked at the door, and Mr Watson let me in, and he said my Mistress had gone out of town and would not be home till tomorrow. I don't remember his saying anything more then – I went into the dining-room and he came in with me – I noticed that the tea things had not been touched; I looked at them, and he said "We have not taken tea" – he said nothing more – I passed some remark, a word or two – I forget now what it was – I asked him if he would take some supper, and he said yes, he would take a little bread and cheese – it was usual for him to take supper – he then went upstairs into the library. I went down to the kitchen and took off my things, and took some bread and cheese up into the dining-room – I then went upstairs to settle the bedrooms as usual – I went into Mr Watson's bedroom. I don't remember going into the library that night – I did not notice anything about the bedroom different to what I had left it – that was the front bedroom – I did not see Mr Watson then, he was taking his bread and cheese in the dining-room – I had told him it was ready, and he went downstairs and had his supper in the dining-room. I saw him

155

again at 10 o'clock that night. He came out of the library as I was going up to bed, he opened the door and said, "This stain on the floor is port wine your Mistress has spilt. In case you might wonder what it was I have told you." I could not see any stain then, it was under the carpet as you are walking into the library, at the side of the door, under the door – he also pointed to the next room door, the small bedroom at the back of the library, and said, "Do not go to that door, your Mistress has locked it" – I said "No," and went up to bed – that was all I saw that night. On the following morning, Monday, I got my Master's breakfast in the dining-room – I am not certain if it was that day or on the Tuesday that he said my Mistress would not be home for a day or two – I don't know how he came to say that – I did not ask him any question – I wanted some candles and I said to him, if she would not be home till dark I should want some candles out, and it was upon that he said that she would not be home for two or three days – he did not say where she had gone. My Master went out on the Monday, and he had his meals as usual – he went out on the Tuesday – I almost forget now the times at which he went out – he said on the Tuesday that he was going out, and would not be home all night – it was after dinner that he said that – he had been out before dinner – and he went out after he had said that – he went out about three times after that – I went out in the afternoon to try to find somebody to sleep there; but I was not able to get anyone. I told him at night that I was unable to get anybody, and he said that I should have to remain by myself – I went downstairs, and waited to see if he would go out, but he did not go; I remained up till about 11 o'clock, when he called me over the stairs. He was standing on the staircase, the first flight from the hall – he said, "If you should find anything wrong with me in the morning, send for Dr Rugg" – I said "Are you ill, Sir?" – he said, "I may require medicine in the morning"; nothing further took place. I went downstairs, and he went upstairs, to bed, as I supposed; I did not see him after he went from the stairs; it must have been after 11 o'clock when he went to bed. On the Wednesday morning I came down about 6.45 – near 8 o'clock I went to the door of his room; I knocked at the door, and Mr Watson answered me; he was dressing himself, I could hear – it was not quite 8.30 when he came downstairs – he went out, before breakfast, for about ten minutes; he breakfasted as soon as he came in – after breakfast he went out again, between 10 and 11 o'clock – he came back about 11 o'clock;

I think he went up to the library; I don't remember his passing any remark at that time – between 11 and 12 o'clock he called me, I saw him in the hall; he said, "If I should be ill before dinner, go for the doctor" – I said "Yes" – he said nothing more; he went upstairs. Some time after, I heard a groaning – I should not think it was an hour after, about half an hour, or more, I should think – I was in the drawing-room and the groaning came from overhead, in the front bedroom – I went up to my Master's bedroom, he was lying in bed, undressed – I spoke to him, but he was unconscious, he did not know me – I went for the doctor at once – I left him in the house by himself. Before I went for the doctor, I noticed three papers in the chair, and a small phial on the drawers, and there was a glass on the chair by the side of the bed – I took up one of the papers, this is it; I took it up, thinking it might be some message for the doctor, and read it – it is in my Master's writing (*Read*: "For the servant, Ellen Pyne, exclusive of her wages. Let no suspicion fall on the servant, whom I believe to be a good girl.") That was sealed; a £5 note was enclosed in it – I don't think the "No.3" was on it when I opened it; I don't remember seeing it, it might have been there. I went out and fetched Dr Rugg – I had known him before, he had been to the house before to attend my sister, who was ill – he went into my Master's bedroom, and he afterwards went out and fetched the police. I went into the room afterwards, and spoke to my master; I spoke to him once or twice before he answered me; then I asked him if he was cold – he said "Yes" and I put something more on the bed. When the police came I went into the library with them – I showed them some marks there; there were some splashes about the window, which I supposed to be wine that had been splashed about, I mean on the library window – I think I first noticed those marks on the Tuesday, I had cleaned the window – the marks were by the side of the skirting; I did not touch them; I don't remember any being on the glass – I did not see any other marks in that room – I did not notice the furniture; I did not notice the chair – I had not done anything to the carpet before that, I had only done the fireplace – I did not see the body of my mistress that day, I did afterwards. One quarter's wages was nearly due to me at this time; it would be due that day month that my mistress died, that would be 8th November. I did not know that my master had any pistols; the pistol in the possession of the police I had never seen in my master's possession, I did not know where it was kept. This paper, headed "For the surgeon", is in my master's writing. This letter in Latin was left on the library table, I saw it found – I remember seeing that paper on Tuesday, on the table; I saw it on the Wednesday as well – it is my master's writing. The police afterwards showed me some clothes, and a shirt – they were my master's; they looked like the clothes he used to wear.

Cross-examined by Mr Serjeant Parry: I never saw any pistols in my master's possession, I never saw them till they were found by the police – I was the first that went to the drawer and saw them there – I think somebody told me they had been found in the drawer, and I went and saw them; I am not certain, but I think I was the first person that found them – I called the attention of one of the policemen to the fact that I had seen some pistols in that drawer – it was in Mr Watson's dressing-room, the drawer of a chest of drawers – it was shut; it was unlocked, I could open it easily and look – there was nothing to prevent anyone opening the drawer and looking into it. I had been in the habit of attending to my master's dressing-room, putting it to rights in the morning; that was a part of my duty – I had access to it constantly; if I had been curious I might at any time have seen these pistols, but I never opened the drawer till that day. This Latin paper was left on the library table, the corner of it was put under a book, I think, or something was across it – it was placed so that you could read the writing; it was open – I noticed it, and looked at it, but I could not read it – that was on the Tuesday morning. It was in the hot weather that they first ceased to sleep together – about July – the reason of their ceasing to sleep together was the hot weather, and then my mistress attended to her own bedroom; she said I had enough to do, and she would help me – sometimes she would behave to me with great kindness, sometimes she was hasty. My master always behaved to me with great kindness; I considered him to be a kind-hearted gentleman – I never noticed any quarrelling, or any angry feeling between them, while I was attending upon them – they always appeared to me to live happily and comfortably together. Mrs Watson always seemed to have her own way, that is all I know. My master was a very reserved man; I may have noticed it more by their being so quiet, by their not having much company; there was no company at all – after their meals they used to sit together in the library; that was their common practice – when I went up there Mr Watson was always either reading or writing. When I saw the pistols in the drawer I did not move them – I went down to Sergeant Giddings, and told him.

Dr George Philip Rugg. I am a doctor of medicine, living and practising at Stockwell Villas, Clapham Road – I know Mr Watson – I have known him for years as the head master of the Grammar School, at Stockwell – I have not attended him professionally, but on one occasion I attended the sister of the last witness, who was a servant with her, and who left at Christmas. I have an impression that the last time I saw Mr Watson was the day before the transaction in question – I did not speak to him – I was on the opposite side of the way – whether it was that day or two days before, I don't know, but I saw him that week. On Wednesday, 11th October, I was called to Mr Watson's house, about 11.30 – I was fetched by the servant Pyne – when I got there I found the prisoner in bed; he was unconscious, breathing heavily, with difficulty – his eyes were turned up, there was a cold clammy perspiration on him, and he had a weak, soft, compressible pulse, an intermittent pulse – I thought he was labouring under an attack of epilepsy at first – he was probably a quarter of an hour or twenty minutes in that unconscious state. Pyne put three letters into my hand – one was addressed "For the surgeon" – it was sealed with an adhesive envelope, this is it. (*Read*: "I have killed my wife in a fit of rage to which she provoked me; often, often has she provoked me before, but I never lost restraint over myself with her till the present occasion, when I allowed fury to carry me away. Her body will be found in the room adjoining the library, the key of which I leave with the paper. I trust she will be buried with the attention due to a lady of good birth. She was an Irish-woman. Her name was Anne"). The key was enclosed in that paper – there was something scratched out, and I asked Mr Watson what it was; but he did not enter into it at all, in fact I had my doubts at the time whether he was married or not, from that being scratched out, and I asked him the question afterwards, and he said he was married, certainly; but he did not tell me what it was that he had scratched out. I have the envelope, it is addressed "For the surgeon" – this was also one of the papers handed to me, it is marked "Statement for such as may care to read it" on the envelope.(*Read*: "I know not whose business it will be to look to my property, my books and furniture. My only brother was living, when I heard of him, five or six years ago, in America, at 82 Grand Street, Williamsburg, and a niece with him. He is my heir, if still alive. I know not if I have any other surviving relatives. One quarter's wages will soon be due to my servant, and I should wish the sum to be more than doubled for her, on account of the trouble which she will have at the present time, and the patience with which she has borne other troubles. In my purse will be found £1.10s. I leave a number of letters, many of them very old, with which I hope those who handle them will deal tenderly. The books are a very useful collection for a literary man. The two thick quarto MS books, marked P and Q, might be sent to the British Museum, or might possibly find some purchaser among literary men, for whom they contain many valuable notes and hints. Among the other MS is a complete translation of "Valerius Flaccus" in verse, which I think deserves to be published. Messrs Longman and Co. also have in their hands for inspection 2 vols. of manuscript, containing a complete history of the Popes from the foundation of the Papal power to the Reformation. There is also ready for the press a tale entitled "Hercules". I leave, too, in the bookcase, several books of extracts and observations marked with the letters of the alphabet, the oldest being that I believe marked M, and the most recent that marked P. There is an annotated copy of the "Life of Porson", with a book of addenda and a copy of the "Life of Warburton", with a few annotations and a book of addenda. There will be found, in loose sheets, in the press at the side of the fireplace in the library, a complete translation of Béranger's songs, with the exception of "Mes Derniers Chansons". Some of these have been printed. The house is to be vacated at the half-quarter. For the rent to Michaelmas I have sent a cheque today. There will be some small bills, but when all claims are satisfied there will be a considerable sum left, besides what will arise from the sale of books and furniture. I have made my way in the world, so far as it has been made, by my own efforts. My great fault has been too much self-dependence, and too little regard for others. Whatever I have done I have endeavoured to do to the best of my ability, and have been fortunate, I may say, generally, but with one great exception. In the paper-cases lying about and elsewhere will be found some MSS which have been used, and others intended for literary purposes.") I found out Mrs Watson's room from the servant – I opened the door with the key and went in – it was the bedroom at the back of the library. I found Mrs Watson dead, huddled up in one corner of the room – she was covered over with a blanket – I examined her, to see what was the cause of death, and found several wounds on the scalp, and a fracture of the bone – there was blood on the floor, and her gown was covered with blood, saturated with blood – there was a good deal on the floor – I can't say how much, it was congealed, and the clothes all saturated. The body was stiff – she must have been dead a day or two at least, on account of the congealed blood and the stiffness of the body – death was no doubt caused by the fracture of the skull by some blunt kind of instrument. A horse-pistol was shown to me the next day at the station. The wounds I saw were most likely to have been produced by such an instrument as that. The body was dressed in the ordinary female dress, she had a gown on. I afterwards returned to Mr Watson's room, where I found a glass of this description and a bottle, which were on a chair beside his bed – this phial was on the chest of drawers, it was half full – it holds two drachms; there was a slight drain in the glass, scarcely a drain, apparently the same kind of liquid that there was in the bottle – I did not examine it then – I could only tell by sense of smell at that time, and I had a very severe cold, therefore I went to the chemist's to discover whether he had purchased poison, and he smelt it for me – that was Mr Lewis, another chemist – I found it to be prussic acid – I was away about five minutes when I went to Mr Lewis – I then came back again, and went into Mr Watson's room, he was recovering his consciousness, but he was talking in an incoherent way – I spoke to him – I told him that I knew he had taken poison, and I also knew it was prussic acid, and that he had been to the chemist's that morning to purchase some. He did not make any remark at that time, that I remember – I asked him where he had purchased the prussic acid and he said he did not wish to get the chemist into trouble, and he told me where he had purchased it. I sent for a policeman, and I told him what I had done – I told him there was a policeman in the next room, that he would be given into charge, that he must be aware what it was for. He did not make any reply to that, he simply put up his arms and made an exclamation of that sort, "Ah", but he did not make any remark. I left him then in charge of the police. I thought he was not in a fit state to be removed at that time, he had scarcely got over the dose of poison – I returned afterwards. The police surgeon was there; he wished to see me, to know if he was in a fit state to be removed – we examined the flooring and the spots of blood, the chair in the library, and the woodwork about the window – the window frames were spattered with blood. The prisoner told me he had taken prussic acid the night before, but he had not taken a sufficient dose, or he supposed so. Dr Pope and I agreed that he could be moved, and he then got up to dress himself; that was about 4 o'clock – the police were present while he was dressing – there was no very particular conversation – he called for a particular pair of boots, which he said fitted him, that he felt easier with them, and he directed my attention to an oyster-shell that was on the chest of drawers in his dressing-room, or on the washhand-stand; he said "A curious thing" – he said very little, he was a man that never said very much – he said "A curious thing that, I picked it up" – I examined it, and said it was a curious thing; it was rather a remarkable shell, it was covered with cercules, a sort of calcareous matter made by a worm, a sort of coral. Nothing more passed, except the observations he was making while he was dressing, with regard to brushing his hair and that – he seemed to be very particular about himself before he went away; he wished to be shaved – his manner seemed frivolous to me, considering the position in which he was placed. I don't remember any further conversation that took place at the time; by-the-bye, I did mention to him that he should have a solicitor, and he mentioned Mr Fraser's name, as being an old pupil of his – he said he did not think it was any use, the deed was done – he consented to my calling on Mr Fraser, which I did afterwards, and he is the gentleman who is now conducting the defence. He asked the police to deal gently with him, and to get the matter over as quickly as they could – he did not quite seem to understand that he was to be removed to the police-station; he asked why he could not remain where he was. I don't recollect anything more. I next saw him at the police-station, in the evening, after that, and I told him I had called on Mr Fraser, but he was out, the servant said he would be home about 10 o'clock, and he would be there in the evening. He said he did not suppose Mr Fraser would come.

Cross-examined. I have known Mr Watson for many years as head master of the Grammar School at Stockwell – he bore the character of being a gentleman of great learning and classical attainments, and of being a kind and humane man – I always understood that he was very punctual in the performance of his duties as head master of the school – I had never attended him, or had much personal intercourse with him; he has not had much illness, I believe – I had often met him in the street, and three or four months previously I met him at a luncheon, at King's College distribution of prizes – he did not know me at first, he was very absent – he was a very reserved man, and very self-absorbed. When I was called in to see him in this unconscious state, I have no doubt that he had taken poison for the purpose of committing suicide. I asked him whether there was any insanity in his family; that was afterwards, at the police station, in the evening – he said no, he could not say much, for his father and brother were the only two members – he said "My brother was quite sane, but I can't say so much for my father." At the time he called my attention to the oyster shell he knew that he was charged with murder, and that the police were in his house. At that time he seemed perfectly oblivious to the crime he had committed; he did not allude to it; he conducted himself as if nothing of the sort had occurred – he wanted to shave himself; he said, to the police officer, why could not he shave – the officer did not allow him to do it – the policemen were in the room at the time. I don't know that I can recollect the exact language he used about the oyster shell, he simply drew my attention to it as a great curiosity, and I examined it – he did not tell me how he had got it; I rather avoided speaking to him at that time. I asked him afterwards, at the police station, in the evening, if he had anything on his mind particularly, and if his means were bad or limited – he said he had sufficient, but that his means were getting exhausted – he said that losing the grammar school had affected him very much, that he had become very much depressed and despondent; that he had been promised another appointment, but it had fallen to the ground. Those remarks seemed perfectly genuine, as really exhibiting the state of his mind, owing to the loss of the school – his age is sixty-seven, I understand. Most of the wounds on the scalp of the deceased were severe wounds; they indicated very great violence. The other marks on her person were recent – they might be the result of blows; they were abrasions, or scratches, not the same character as those on the skull. In the course of my experience the disease of insanity has come under my study, with other diseases – insanity is as much a disease as any other known to me as a professional man – it is always treated as a disease, to be cured if possible, and if not to be cured, the patient to be prevented from doing harm if he is liable to do so – there is a well-defined form of insanity called melancholia – I should say it was recognised by every medical man – a sudden shock or calamity falling upon a man would most certainly have a tendency to produce despondency and depression, which might ultimately

163

result in melancholia – a person suffering under that disease is liable to sudden outbursts and paroxysms of madness – in such a condition he has not the reasoning power which would enable him to distinguish right from wrong, or to understand the nature and quality of the act that he commits, at the time that he commits it; that is my judgment. It is consistent with my experience that after the fit of madness is over they may resume almost their normal state – it is similar to a case of epilepsy; a person may be perfectly well after an attack of epilepsy – I thought Mr Watson was suffering from epilepsy at the time I saw him – homicidal mania and suicidal mania are recognisable diseases, they very frequently go together; an insane desire to destroy either one's self or somebody else. I have not the slightest doubt that this gentleman attempted to commit suicide by poisoning himself. I have seen the prisoner since; I saw him in Horsemonger Lane Gaol – he then complained to me of having suffered from despondency since he had lost his school and could not obtain employment elsewhere – I don't recollect his saying that at his great age it was almost hopeless to expect that he could ever get any other appointment; he complained that he had been in a despondent state – he said "I wish I had consulted you before".

Inquest report by Dr Rugg on the body of Anne Watson

Body well nourished. A large, contused and lacerated wound of irregular triangular shape was found upon the posterior superior angle of the right parietal bone. In the front and to the right of the wound there was a lacerated wound to inches in length extending to the bone. Immediately in front was a wound of similar shape, also extending to the bone. To the right of the last described was an irregular triangular, contused and lacerated wound, two inches in length and breadth, causing a fracture to the bone. In front of this wound were two other lacerated wounds, each one about one and a half inches in length. On the forehead, about two inches above the brow, was an irregular lacerated wound of two inches in length. The mouth was closed and drawn to the left side, the lips compressed, and the under lip contused on the right side. There was nothing remarkable about the appearance of the face, except a small contused wound under the chin, as if bruised through falling. On the right arm there were two small wounds on its fleshy part. There were also wounds on the elbow joint of the right arm and several contusions on the hand. There were bruises on the left arm over elbow and back of fleshy part, and on the back of the hand a severe contused wound of two inches in length, and smaller marks on the knuckles. On the back of the neck there was a wound two inches in length, but only superficial and similar to the one on the chin. There was a slight bruise on the left knee cap and abrasions on each shin. Upon removal of the brain an extensive extravasation of blood was found between its convolutions and at its base. There was an extensive fracture at the base of the skull, from the anterior inferior angle of the parietal bone to the extent of two inches, through the wing of the apheroid to the temporal bone. The heart was small and covered with fat, but the valves were healthy. The liver was less than usual size, and was hard in structure (cirrhotic). The stomach contained about half a pound of partially undigested food. The intestines were healthy but loaded with fat. The kidneys were small and flabby and much congested, especially the left one. There was chronic disease of the liver, which may have been caused by the deceased taking stimulants from time to time.

George Davis (Police Inspector). On Wednesday, 11th October, I went into the room where Mrs Watson was lying dead – that was the first room I entered – Dr Pope went in with me, Dr Rugg came shortly afterwards. I saw the dead body in the corner – there were smears of blood about the room which appeared to have been caused by her clothing, which was saturated with it. On the landing between that room and the library, I saw a stain which appeared to be blood, that was outside the library door, about three or four inches from it – I had to remove the carpet. I found blood in different parts of the library, on the sides of the window, the window frame, the woodwork, also on the wire-blinds, several small spots, and also on the back part of a large armchair – I then went into the dressing-room – I there found a pair of trousers, which I produce, and a waistcoat was handed to me by Dr Pope in that room – there were stains on them which appeared to me to be blood – I am now speaking of the trousers – I showed them to Dr Pope – there were stains down the front of the waistcoat, which appeared to be blood – I showed those also to Dr Pope – I also found a pair of drawers in the dressing-room, they have marks of the same sort on the knees and inside the thigh. I also found there this sponge, it had a reddish stain on it and also some long white hairs – it appeared to have been washed out. I then went into the room in which the prisoner was in bed; he was at that time able to understand – that was about 3.40 – I told him that I should put him into custody for killing and slaying his wife on the previous Sunday – he made no reply then – he asked me where I should take him to – I said to the Brixton police-station – I then asked him for the shirt and coat that he was wearing on the previous Sunday – he said "What for, what do you want them for?" – he afterwards said the coat was hanging up in the next room – I found it, and produce it – there were a great quantity of marks on it which appeared to be blood, down the front and the sleeves, they appeared to have been wiped with something. I remained with him while he dressed, and then conveyed him in a cab to the police-station. I was present in the dressing-room while he was combing out his hair there – he dressed in his bedroom partly, and he went into the dressing-room to comb his hair. I took him to the police-station, where I charged him with the wilful murder of his wife – I asked him his wife's christian name as I was unacquainted with it – he said Anne – the charge was entered in the usual way – he made no reply, with the exception, when the sergeant was speaking to him, when I told him the name Anne, he only put down Ann, and I called the sergeant's attention to the fact, and said Anne, and the sergeant said "Annie", and the prisoner said "Anne". He wanted to know whether he could have anything brought him – I said yes, anything he required, if he put it down on paper, I would send for it. He gave me a list, I produce it – he wrote it himself (*Read:* "Mattress, two or three blankets, counterpane, pillow, clean cravat, clean collar, boot hooks, hairbrush, some slices of cold beef, b.k.f." – When I came to b.k.f. I could not understand it, and he said it was bread, knife and fork – I told him he could have anything with the exception of the knife and fork, and he had nearly all these things supplied to him. When I said he could not have the knife he said "What is the good of the bread and meat; what am I going to eat it with". I told him his servant could make some sandwiches, and he said that would do very well. Next day, the 12th, I was sent for to the house – I was shown a drawer in the dressing-room by Sergeant Giddings – I opened it, and saw in it five pistols, the one produced, and four others. I examined this one and saw what appeared to be a stain on the wood work at the side of the trigger – that was one of the largest pistols – there were two others not quite so large as this, and two smaller ones – it was a stain of a reddish colour, similar to blood – it has been scraped off for the purpose of the analysis – I noticed a stain of a similar colour on the butt end, a portion of it is remaining now – the woodwork of the handle was split in three places, lengthways, and across in two places – Giddings had seen it before me – the other pistols were rusty and dusty, and apparently had not been handled for some years I should think, and there was dirt in the drawer. I afterwards brought away the piece of Latin that has been produced – that was on the Sunday following – I saw it the day I first entered there, but did not remove it. I also found a pair of boots and some rope, the rope was in the library – it is new rope, nearly twelve yards, wrapped in brown paper, also a new hammer. There was no appearance of the hammer having been used, it was perfectly new, wrapped in brown paper, and the size marked on it, also an old hammer that had been in use for some time – there were no marks on that.

George Hazell (Police Sergeant). On Wednesday, 11th October, I was called to the prisoner's house by Dr Rugg – I went upstairs and saw the body of Mrs Watson in the room on the first floor – I afterwards went into the prisoner's bedroom – it was about 12.45 when I got to the house I saw the prisoner in bed, and told him he must consider himself in custody for the murder of his wife – he said "I suppose so, don't be violent" – I told him no violence would be used – he then turned on the other side, and said "I am ill" – Dr Rugg was there at the time – I left Dr Rugg to attend to him – I afterwards made a search at the house. On the following Sunday, the 15th, I examined a chest of drawers in the dressing-room, and in the bottom drawer I found this shirt; both the wristbands appear to have been cut off – there were marks on the sleeves that appeared to be blood – there was a quantity of shirts and clean linen in the drawers – this shirt was under some other clean linen – the drawer was not locked – there was a lock to it.

John Huey (Police Sergeant). On Wednesday, 11th October, I went with Hazell to 28, St Martin's Road – I found Dr Rugg at the door; he beckoned me into the house, and I went in, and went upstairs into the room where the body of a woman was – Dr Rugg went in first, Hazell next, and I last – I did not observe how the body was covered – it was dressed, no cap or bonnet on – the hair was very much disarranged. After leaving the room I went into the library with Dr Rugg, and there saw the servant Pyne – I then went into the prisoner's bedroom with Dr Rugg and Hazell – he was in bed – Hazell told him he might consider himself in custody for the murder of his wife – I understood the prisoner to say "Don't be loud about it" – it was either "Don't be violent", or "Don't be loud", I could not be certain, but I understood him to say "Don't be loud about it". He asked me if I had any objection to his shaving before he went to the police-station – I said "Yes, I have a very strong one" – when Dr Rugg came in he told him that I had objected to his shaving and Dr Rugg said that was quite right. His dog was on the landing, barking, at the time, and he called him by name, "Snap", and kept snapping his fingers for the dog to come into the room, but the dog did not come in.

Thomas Giddings (Police Sergeant). On Thursday morning, 12th October, I was at the prisoner's house – in consequence of what the servant said I went to a drawer in the prisoner's dressing-room, and there found three pistols – I did not touch them – I sent for Inspector Davis, and showed them to him.

Edmund Pope. I am surgeon to the W division of the police – on Wednesday, 11th October, I went to 28, St Martin's Road, Stockwell – I found Inspector Davis there – I went up to the prisoner's bedroom – I found him there in bed. Dr Rugg had been there before me – I asked the prisoner how he felt now – he said better than he hoped or expected to be – I sent for Dr Rugg, and then went into the room in which the dead body was – I found it in the crouching, huddled up position which has been described. I have this morning had pointed out to me a deal box, which is in Court – I think, with a little compression, the body could have been stowed away in that box – Dr Rugg and I went together into the room, and examined the glass that was there – I mean the glass that had been drunk from – I waited there until I formed an opinion that he was fit to be moved, and I then authorised Inspector Davis to remove him – Davis said he should apprehend him on a charge of murder, and after doing so I asked him if he would tell me where the coat was which he had worn on that day, as he wished to have it. Mr Watson objected at first to say where the coat was – he said he did not wish an exhibition made of it – he said "What do you want it for?" – I can't say the exact words – that was the purport of what he said – I left the room almost immediately after that – I afterwards saw him at the station – I heard what passed about his wife's name, and so on, which has been spoken of by the witness – the charge was read over to him –

he made no reply. During the whole of that time I saw nothing which led me to come to the conclusion that he was a person of unsound mind – I saw him in the cell that same evening – I then had a conversation with him – I asked him if he required anything, if he had been attended to – he said he had had a cup of tea, that he wanted something to eat – on that occasion I did not notice anything at all about him which indicated that he was of unsound mind. I afterwards made a post mortem examination with Dr Rugg.

Cross-examined. Those were the only times I saw him – when he said "If you wish to make an exhibition of the coat I decline to tell you," I understood him to mean an exhibition before the public – I don't think he meant Madame Tussaud's, or anything of that kind – perhaps it was an odd phrase to use, though at the time it did not strike me as particularly odd.

John Muter. I am a director of the South London School of Chemistry and Pharmacy in the Kennington Road. I have analysed the contents of the bottles found in the prisoner's bedroom. They both contained a colourless liquid which I am satisfied was a solution of hydrocyanic acid, but it was not up to the standard of Scheele's strength, which should contain five per cent of acid. No trace of the acid could be discovered, though that could be accounted for by the volatile nature of the liquid. I have also analysed the stains on the prisoner's clothes. I found some skin as well as blood on a pistol – I have also examined a sponge with grey hairs sticking to it – they were long hairs. (Results of analysis read out as follows.)

Report on the stains on certain articles contained in six parcels received from Inspector Davis in the presence of Dr Rugg on the 20th October.

No.1 parcel contained a black coat, waistcoat and trousers. The coat exhibited 132 distinct stains on the outside, and 16 on the inside, the principal stains being on the left arm. The waistcoat had stains on the outside, chiefly near the buttons and buttonholes, ranging from two inches in diameter downwards. The trousers exhibited 95 stains, chiefly on the front of the left leg. There was one small stain at the bottom of the right hand pocket. A number of these stains were examined chemically and microscopically, and were found to have been caused by blood.

No.2 parcel contained a shirt and a pair of drawers. The

wristbands of the shirt had been cut off, and the sleeves had the appearance of having been dipped in water. The drawers exhibited four stains, darker in colour than those on the shirt.

No.3 parcel contained a pair of Wellington boots, the soles of which presented the appearance of having been trodden in blood, especially near the toes.

No.4 parcel contained a sponge considerably stained, and having a quantity of hairs adhering to it. Several of them proved to be human hairs, and the remainder were short fragments of wool of various colours, similar to those which would be left on a sponge after rubbing a carpet or other coarse woollen fabric. The sponge was proved to be saturated with blood.

No.5 parcel contained an old, brass-barrelled, flint-lock horse pistol, which was found to have a clot consisting of human blood near the left hand trigger guard. Several small fragments of skin were embedded in the brass ornamentation on the left hand side of the barrel.

No.6 was an envelope containing a portion of morocco leather which was almost entirely covered with human blood.

Charles Turner. I am a trunk and brush manufacturer in the Clapham Road. On Monday the 9th of October at half past twelve o'clock, the prisoner came into my shop and asked to look at some trunks – I showed him several but he did not seem to think them strong enough – what he wanted, he said, was more of a packing case. I suggested we should make him one. He replied he wanted one 2ft 9in long and 2ft 3in wide, and 1ft 9in deep. He did not really decide then and there whether he would have one made or not. I believe he thought he might get one somewhere else. I told him if he let me know by two o'clock it should be ready the next day about the same time. He came back at two o'clock as I had asked, and said he had made up his mind to have one made – I told him it would be a very large case, and asked him for what purpose it was intended. He said he wanted to pack some papers in it. The case was made and on the following day the prisoner called at the shop about two o'clock and said, "Don't send that case round to my house, but I will pay for it." He did so; he gave me a £10 note and I gave him the change. I remarked that I supposed I was not to send it round until I heard from him. The prisoner said something which I didn't understand or fully hear as he was leaving the shop – I noticed a difference in his manner on the Tuesday – he seemed very depressed. The cost of the box came to £1. 5s. and yet he scarcely looked at his change.

MR WATSON'S LATINITY

To the Editor of The Times

Sir, It appears to me that the Latin phrase found among Mr Watson's papers has been so construed by Mr Denman as to do him an injustice. 'Saepe olim amanti nocuit semper amare.' Mr Denman construes it allowing that it must be bad Latin if it means what he thinks, 'To one who has so often loved it has always been harmful to love,' giving, to say the least, an unamiable turn to the poor man's reflections upon his life, and one by no means supported by the evidence. I would ask better scholars than myself whether it is not perfectly good Latin for 'To one who has acquired the habit of loving it has often been an injury not to cease to love.'
Yours, G.Y., Lincoln's Inn

Sir, Mr Watson's Latin seems to me very indifferent. But the most obvious construction ought to be the following: 'Saepe nocuit olim amanti semper amare' – 'It was often injurious or fatal to a man who once loved to go on forever loving', i.e. to pretend to love on, to insist on a love which no longer exists. This, of course, refers to Mr Watson's case, all whose calamities, by his own account, arose from his continuing to live with a wife whom he once loved, but life with whom had now become insupportable
It must be observed that in the two versions mentioned by 'G.Y.', no account is taken of the 'olim', which is the key-stone of the sentence
I have the honour to be, sir, your obedient servant
G., Lincoln's Inn

Sir, It is amusing to see how much mystery can be made out of nothing. If a fifth form schoolboy at Eton (which I was once myself) were asked to translate 'Saepe olim amanti nocuit semper amare', he would go it thus, and he would be right: 'Saepe' (often) 'olim' (heretofore) 'semper amare', here used as a substantive, (constant love) 'nocuit' (has been injurious) 'amanti' (to the lover). This, no doubt, is bald enough: but dress it up a little, and use Shakespeare's formula slightly changed:

Ah, me for all that ever I could learn,
Could ever read in tale or history,
True love hath often been the lover's bane.

171

In this garb, I doubt not, both Mr Denman and 'G.Y.' will recognise their own extraordinary shortcomings and a solution of all their difficulties, which they will pardon me for thinking are rather to be attributed to their acquaintance with bad Latin than good.

I am, sir, your obedient servant,

Winchilsea.

P.S.: What would Mr Watson himself say of two such versions as these?

> To one who has often loved it has always been harmful to love. Denman.

and

> To one who has acquired the habit of loving, it has often been an injury not to cease to love. G.Y.

Why, if he were an Eton Master, he would put them both 'in the bill.'

Sir, Whatever poor Mr Watson may have to answer for, he has not yet been convicted of writing bad Latin. Your ingenious correspondents from Lincoln's Inn seem, however, to impute this to him. The word 'olim', as every scholar knows, means 'in the far-off line', which may be either past or future, but the phrase 'olim amanti' involves a contradiction in terms. The moment you attach an adverb to 'amanti' you restore to it its verbal or participial force – 'one who loves in the present' – and deprive it of its abstract meaning, 'amatori', or lover.

Lord Winchilsea's construction is undoubtedly the right one. The Latin sentence, which I need not here repeat, simply means: 'Often ere now has the lover suffered from the constancy of his love.' This is good sense, applies to Mr Watson's case, and no one can fairly cavil at Mr Watson's rendering of it.

These 'nugae' may seem out of place when a man is on trial for his life, but the Law-Latinists must not be allowed to have the last word.

Yours, M.H.C..

Sir, It is hardly fair of your correspondents to assume that the line 'saepe olim amanti nocuit semper amare' must be bad Latin because they cannot interpret it satisfactorily. The Latin is good Latin, and the meaning of the words can be but one, however the application may differ. 'Saepe olim' go together, and like πολλάκις ἤδη, πάλαι in Greek, serve to state the result of experience in the form of a proverb. The apparent redundancy of 'saepe olim' is defended by such expressions as 'saepe ante', Sallust, Jugurtha 107,4, – 'saepe ante paucis strenuis advorsum multitudinem bene pugnantium'. The meaning may be explained by the Greek:

πολλάκις ἔβλαψεν ἤδη τὸν φιλοῦντ' ἀεὶ φιλεῖν

'Often in the experience of men constant love has proved the lover's bane.'

I am, your humble servant, Hertford Scholar.
Magdalen College, Oxford.

Sir, Your learned commentators assume too readily that the words in question were meant by the reverend gentleman Mr Watson to apply to himself. May I venture to suggest that they may have been intended rather as an epigraph to the tale 'Hercules' which he had just completed?

Your readers will remember that the mad Hercules – the Hercules furens of Euripides' play – was successful in all his labours but less fortunate in his dealings with the fair sex. After being required to satisfy the 50 daughters of Thespius in one night, he was forced into employment for sexual purposes by Queen Omphale of Lydia. He was brought down finally by his wife Deianira, who gave him the fatal shirt of Nessus to wear in the fond hope that it would be the means of restoring his love.

We may wonder too about the legibility of Mr Watson's handwriting in this time of stress. Did he perhaps write not 'amare' (to love) but 'amari' (to be loved) – not 'amanti' (lover) but 'amenti' (madman)? If so, the adage would fit both equally – 'Fortunate in all things except as pertains to the female sex. Often has it harmed a lover (or a madman?) to be pursued by love.'

Yours etc, CH, Camden Town

This correspondence is now closed – Ed.

Ann Tulley. I am now housekeeper to Messrs Johnson and Son, of Cursitor Street, Holborn. My husband and I lived at the Grammar School, Stockwell, with the prisoner and his wife, he as drilling master, and I as housekeeper – my husband says we lived there five years. I have been in the habit, from time to time, of paying visits to Mr and Mrs Watson – I went there on Sunday, 8th October – I rang the doorbell – no one answered it, but I heard a traffic about inside; I thought it was Mrs Watson, and that the servant was busy – I heard a sound of tramping about, and after a bit Mrs Watson's voice – I could not tell what she said just then – I rang the bell a second time, and then heard Mrs Watson say "There is somebody at the door," she said that three times continuously – no one came, and I rang a third time. Mr Watson then opened the door, and said, "Oh, it is only Mrs Tulley" – he let me in, and went into the dining-room and told Mrs Watson, in a slow tone, "Mrs Tulley." Mrs Watson came out to me, and said "How do you do, Mrs Tulley?" I said "Quite well, thank you, Ma'am," and she asked me into the drawing-room, and when I got inside, Mr Watson stood in the hall, at the drawing-room door, for a moment or so – after a bit he came into the drawing-room. Mrs Watson said "The servant is out, Mrs Tulley" – Mr Watson said "Only every other Sunday," and Mrs Watson repeated "Only every other Sunday" – she said "I am so frightened, Mrs Tulley." "Are you, Ma'am," I said – she said "I am afraid of somebody getting over the back." "What, over the garden wall?" I said – she said "Yes." Mr Watson was at the door at that time – he came into the room, and sat on the same side of the drawing-room as I was, opposite Mrs Watson, and he asked me how my husband was, and how we were getting on. I said we were quite well, and my husband was doing very well – he said "Have Johnson & Son got as many hands on as they generally have?" They are my employers; it is a large firm, they have different branches. I said, "Yes, Sir, they are at work day and night, by times; they give a large salary to clever writers." I told him that they had a part portion taken at the Exhibition, and a great many page boys and young women in the business, selling catalogues – he was very pleased about Johnson & Son's doing well. I forgot to mention that at first he was very cross; I thought, when I first came to the door, that he would not ask me in. After the conversation he seemed pleased. I thought he was very fidgety, sitting. I heard nothing more of the slightest importance said by him while I was in the room – I got up to go, and made my obedience to Mr and Mrs Watson, and thanked them for past favours to me and my husband, and he got up and returned it in the most kind and polite manner, and said they would be always glad to hear of our welfare; that is, my husband and I, I believe. I went out into the hall, and Mrs Watson went out – I said "Pray don't come to the door, Sir," as I did not want to give him trouble; so he stood close to the dining-room and drawing-room, and as I turned on the step to close the door I made my obedience to him, and he returned it with a very cross face – he made a bow as I was on the step. As near as I can tell you, I stopped in the house half an hour, or upon it; I got there about 5 o'clock, and left about 5.30, as near as I can recollect.

Cross-examined. I had been at the grammar school some years – I told the prisoner that Johnson's employed a great many clever writers in hopes that he should go and ask for some business there – I knew him to be clever and out of employment, and it occurred to me to say so – Johnson & Son printed the catalogue of the last International Exhibition – it occurred to me, as a matter of kindness, to mention it to him, he being out of employment. I suppose he had no idea that I meant the information for him – Mrs Watson did not say anything about that, she was very silent – the prisoner did not shake hands with me, but he thanked me for my words, for what I said – I have been always in the habit of calling on the families I lived with, and seeing how they were getting on. I had not been there for a year and four months.

Charlotte Jane Hall. I live at 87, London Road – the house 28, St Martin's Road, Stockwell, belongs to me – Mr Watson had occupied it six years last Midsummer – the rent was sixty guineas –I did not know Mr Watson personally – I never saw him till I saw him here. In October 1870, I received this letter, I know it to be his writing – I have corresponded with him, and received rent from him – (*Read:* "October 27th, 1870. Dear Madam – I have received Mr Duett's note, and shall be prepared to receive him according to his notice, on Saturday next. It will be convenient if he calls before half-past twelve. Circumstances have occurred which render it necessary for me to give you notice that you must be prepared for my quitting this house at Midsummer next. It may be possible, if you should find a desirable tenant before that time, I may be able to leave it sooner, but I shall be able to speak more confidently on the subject in January next, and I shall be obliged if you will acknowledge this notice.") Mr Duett is my agent – I sent an answer, and on 19th May, 1871, I received this letter, which is in the prisoner's writing – "May 19th, 1871. Mrs. Hall. Madam. I did not say anything to your agent when he last called about the rent, my movements being uncertain, and expecting to remove at or about Midsummer next. Still, not being decided as to leaving at Midsummer, I should ask, if I could stay beyond that time, would you allow me to go on another quarter? Please understand that I may leave at Midsummer or not, but it will be a convenience to know that I can stay another quarter if I have occasion to." – I answered that letter, and gave my consent to his leaving at any time at a quarter's notice – on 23rd May, I received this letter – "May 23rd, 1871. Mr Watson presents his compliments to Mrs Hall, and begs to thank her for her note of yesterday, giving him permission to either leave at Midsummer or to remain until the following Michaelmas, as may suit his convenience." – On Monday morning, 25th September, I received this letter from him, the 23rd was on Saturday – 'September 25th, 1871. Dear Madam. I called at your place today to speak about our continuance in this house, but had not the good fortune to find you at home. I had fully expected to leave it before this time, but uncertainty as to our movements has still detained us. I have been looking out for several weeks for a suitable place to which I may remove, but I have not been able to fix upon one. I have something in view in one or two directions, but, whatever we decide, I think it will be impossible we can clear the house before quarter-day. Under these circumstances I was going to ask of you to show us an indulgence for a time. It has occurred to me that, as the house must be unoccupied for a quarter to be done up, you would not be particular as to our staying a little beyond the stated time. Of course, I don't want to put you to inconvenience, or to be encroaching. An early answer will oblige." On Wednesday morning, 11th October, I received this letter by the first post – it is written by the prisoner – it enclosed his own cheque for 15L.15s – 'October 10th. Mr Watson has the pleasure of enclosing to Mrs Hall the amount of the quarter's rent, ending at Michaelmas last." I paid away the cheque to Mr Duett, my agent, and afterwards gave the receipt to Mr Fraser, the prisoner's solicitor. The day after I received that letter, I heard of this melancholy transaction.

William Longman. I am a member of the firm of Messrs Longman, publishers, of Paternoster Row. I have known the prisoner about sixteen or seventeen years – I received this letter from the prisoner, at least,my firm did, when I was out of town. It is in Mr Watson's writing – (This was dated 22nd August,1871, and was a request to Messrs. Longman to look at a MS, entitled *A History of the Papacy* in two octavo volumes.) I afterwards received this other letter dated August 24th, 1871 – (This stated that the prisoner had forwarded his *History of the Papacy* to Messrs Longman) – the manuscript of that is in our possession still – there is no other work of that nature that I am aware of – this (produced) is the manuscript – unquestionably it is a work of very great labour. I have no exact means of knowing within what time that work was accomplished, but I rather think he had been engaged on it for some time – it was completed probably about the time he wrote to me – I entertained the idea of publishing it – we told him we had taken it into consideration. We had not come to any decision as to publishing it – no such decision was conveyed to him, either for or against it; it stood over. We have published three works for him – one was the *Life of Porson*, the other was the *Life of Warburton*, and the other, I think, was a book called *The Sons of Strength*, which were essays on Samson, Solomon and Job. He was undoubtedly a man of considerable learning and attainments – I am not aware of a publication in 1844 – I am only aware of those three – I am acquainted with other publications besides my own – I don't recollect that Mr Pickering published for him. I don't know of a poem in seven books on the subject of geology. I am aware that he translated a great number of classical works for Mr Bohn. I believe those books are on sale – they are a kind of school book, Sallust, Xenophon, and so on, Florus, three vols. of Xenophon, Cornelius Nepos, Cicero's *Brutus*, Pope's *Iliad*, with notes, and other rhetorical works. The *Life of Porson* was published in 1861 and the *Life of Warburton* in 1863 – I don't know that he also published through Mr Tegg. He was a very methodical man, rather one of the old school – I have no other manuscript works of his in my possession – he has not offered me any others recently, or spoken to me about any others. This (produced) is a biographical history of the Papacy from the beginning – I am not aware that he also published the lives of Cobbett and Wilkes for Blackwood, or the life of Sir William Wallace, or a book entitled *The Reasoning Power of Animals*.

Re-examined. I think the last work we published for him was Warburton's Life – that was in 1863. It was tolerably successful – a book showing a great deal of research and learning, and a knowledge of the times of which it speaks. I have not myself studied the manuscript of the Popes. It would not have been a work, supposing we had undertaken to publish it, for which we would have given much money, on the grounds that his other works had only a moderate success.

Court. Q. Did he realise much by them? A. No. There was only one book on which he realised anything and that was quite a trifle – I think that was the *Life of Warburton*. I believe his share of the profits was something under 5L. The other books were not successful.

Dr Edgar Shepherd. I am a member of the Royal College of Physicians, and a fellow of the Royal College of Surgeons, and professor of tracheological medicine at King's College. I am medical superintendent of the Colney Hatch Lunatic Asylum, and have been so upwards of ten years – that is one of the lunatic asylums for the county of Middlesex – there are 2050 patients there, male and female. I have seen the prisoner since he has been in custody – I have had four interviews with him in Newgate; I think the first was on 17th November, the second on 20th November, then I saw him again on the 29th, and again on 11th December – from those interviews, and the conversations which took place, I think he was of sound mind.

Cross-examined. I was requested by the Government to examine him, with Dr Begley, the resident physician at Hanwell – we examined him together, but I saw him on one occasion myself, without Dr Begley. Insanity is a disease of the brain – it is recognised by me as a disease, just as any other disease to which humanity is liable – I hope that the great object of my life is to cure it if I can. I know Dr Blandford, by name, as a gentleman of reputation in the profession. I know Dr Maudsley, by name, and personally also; he is also a gentleman well known in the profession, who has devoted a great deal of his life to studying the disease of insanity, and writing upon it – there is a recognised form of insanity called melancholia – it is a disease that has been brought about by some sudden calamity, such as loss of fortune or status. A person labouring under melancholia is liable to outbursts of madness, during which crimes are committed – in such an

178

outburst of madness, under certain forms of intense melancholia, the reasoning powers are entirely gone. It would very much depend upon the intensity of the disease, whether such a person would be a fit subject for confinement; it is a disease that varies very much in intensity. I am not by any means prepared to say that persons labouring under melancholia are liable, upon provocation, however slight, to an outburst of maniacal fury; I am prepared to deny it as a positive fact – provocation would certainly act with more force on a person who might be liable to an outburst of this kind than upon an ordinary and rational man – a person labouring under melancholia might be liable to an outburst of madness, and after that outburst was over recover comparative sanity; that is very common. As to suicide being an indication of insanity, it would depend very much on the form of suicide – suicide is unquestionably a very common accompaniment of melancholia; homicide also, but less common – such a patient has homicidal and suicidal tendencies. The meaning of melancholia is extreme despondency and depression – repeated attempts at suicide would be an element that I should take into consideration in judging whether a person was insane or not, particularly a certain form of committing suicide. I will explain what I mean by that; the forms of suicide committed by the insane are intensely clever and crafty, and contain, as a rule, no element of clumsiness about them; for instance, no insane person attempting to commit suicide would, in my judgment, tell another that he might be ill at a certain time. Madness by no means signifies an utter want of design – madmen sometimes, both before and after the commission of a great crime, have exhibited considerable craft and cunning – that has been within my observation; in fact, it is very often what we have to guard against in patients we are entrusted with. I don't think that absence of remorse for a crime is a sign of insanity at all – I am sure it is consistent with sanity; it is also consistent with insanity – it is common in the insane to exhibit an absolute indifference to a great crime, although it is consistent with sanity; it is consistent with both. I would go so far as to say this; I do not think there is any case on record of an impulsive act of insanity involving homicide, in a person who has never given any evidences of insanity before – there are always very striking premonitory symptoms – a person might be liable to such an outburst and afterwards recover sanity – it is a matter of great uncertainty what time ought to be allowed for that, depending very much on individual temperament – some

179

persons would subside rapidly and very quickly, and other persons would take some time to recover. I think a person might commit a homicidal act under the influence of melancholia, and be conversing and conducting himself as a rational person, in all respects, as a sane person would do, within an hour or two after the act – indications before the act are more important than indications after the act – I don't think that an act of this kind could be committed without very manifest symptoms beforehand, but it might be committed without any manifested symptoms after – the acting and behaving rationally after the act would not form any indication to my mind as to whether it was an act of madness or of sanity. I can conceive of nothing more improbable than that an insane person should give notice that a doctor would be required, shortly before intending to commit a suicidal act – it is entirely at variance with my experience and judgment of insane persons.

Dr William Chaplin Begley. I am M.D. of Dublin University – I am also a member of the Royal College of Physicians, and of the Royal College of Surgeons – I am the medical attendant at the Hanwell Lunatic Sylum – I have seen the prisoner on four occasions – I don't remember the dates – the first was in November last – I conversed with him freely. On the first and second interviews he was very coherent, but very reticent and reserved, somewhat sullen – on the third he was much less so, and on the fourth he was actually garrulous, and wandering from subject to subject, and there was a degree of mirth about him, which I could not explain. He was talkative, and went on from subject to subject with a degree of levity that I thought inconsistent with his position, and could only be accounted for by some mental infirmity – I can't recollect the date of that interview – I don't recollect the dates of any of them – I think the first and second were in November, but I am not positive – I saw him in Newgate – he talked about a great number of subjects connected with classical literature, and about various other matters; but there was an inconsistency and incoherency – I can't remember an instance, but he went from one subject to another with great rapidity and great volubility – I encouraged him to talk – I wished him to talk – he generally spoke on the subject of classical literature – I don't think he talked about anything else – he mixed the subjects up together – he began a new subject before he had finished an old one – sometimes he finished his sentences, and sometimes he left off in the middle of them.

John Rowland Gibson. I have been surgeon of the gaol of Newgate sixteen or seventeen years – I am a Fellow of the Royal College of Surgeons and a Licentiate of the Apothecaries' Company. The prisoner was brought there on 14th November last, I have had him under my charge, medically from that time to this – from the time I first saw him I have paid particular attention to the state of his mind in order that I might be able to form a judgment of it – I have seen him every day, and sometimes more frequently, and conversed with him at every interview – I am not quite sure whether Dr Begley did not see him for a short time alone; but I was present at all the interviews spoken of, and heard the conversations – I was present long enough to hear a good deal of the conversation that passed between the prisoner and Dr Begley, and I also conversed with him on that occasion. I have always found him rational; and I should say remarkably self-possessed – I did not at any time observe any incoherence or inconsistency in the answers that he gave – sometimes he was more depressed than at others, and I may say at times his conversation has almost approached cheerfulness – there was nothing in my treatment of him, or in the medicines that I gave him, that would have accounted for a greater amount of cheerfulness at one time than another. I did not medically treat him, except an occasional dose of opening medicine. I did not give him tonics – I saw nothing between one visit and another to indicate anything like insanity; I think the depression from which he suffered was nothing more than one would expect from a person placed in the position in which he was – it was a sort of depression which from my experience I have found in the case of sane persons as well as insane.

The following Witnesses were called for the Defence:

William Joseph Fraser. I am solicitor to Mr Watson – I produce a certificate of his baptism showing that he was baptised in Crayford Church, in the year 1804 – I produce also his marriage certificate, at St Mark's Church, Dublin, on 2nd January, 1845 to Annie Armstrong. I also produce a gold medal – he was gold medallist of the Dublin University. I also produce certain letters written by Mr Watson to Miss Armstrong before the marriage – the first letter is December 4th, 1844 – there are five or six. I found the letters in Mrs Watson's bedroom, tied up in her satin gown. I was a pupil of Mr Watson, at Stockwell School. I am his attorney, but have not been so in any business before this – I occasionally wrote to him, but only visited them at their house this time last year, when the school was under consideration – he did not consult me professionally. I was a proprietor of the school. I also found some letters written to Mrs Watson, at different periods during their married life – I have not gone through them all.

Revd Collett Baugh. I am a clergyman of the Church of England, and rector of Chelsfield, Kent. In September last my curate was absent temporarily, and I communicated with Mr Ingram, who keeps a register of clergymen to do temporary duty, to get a clergyman to take my curate's place – I was not in very good health then, and not equal to duty at all; certainly not to doing whole duty, two full services – Mr Watson was recommended to me and I communicated with him, and received a letter from him, stating that he would come and take part of my duty. The letter is lost – it was in September, 1871, just one month before the murder was committed – I had not known or heard of Mr Watson before – the duty I intended him to perform was very likely none at all; it would depend upon how I felt on Sunday morning. He came down on Sunday morning, and I had not then made up my mind what part of the service I would ask him to take – he was rather nervous when I met him in the vestry, but nothing to remark particularly. Nothing occurred in church which would throw any light upon his state of mind – he said one prayer in the morning-service which is not generally used; a prayer for all sorts of conditions of men, but it was a mistake, which might occur to any man – he was very weak and weary, and listless – I should have asked him to take part in the Communion service, but his voice was so dreary and listless that I preferred taking the whole myself, though it was Sacrament Sunday. At the conclusion of the service I walked home with him – my house is about a quarter of a mile from the church – I soon found that he was labouring from extreme depression of mind or body, or both, which showed itself in a gloomy silence, which continued throughout the day, and a total want of interest in any subject whatever, or in anything which was going on about him. I endeavoured during lunch to interest him in conversation; both I and my wife endeavoured to try to get him to talk, but I do not think he originated a single observation himself, and in answer to any remark or question of mine he replied wholly in monosyllables. "Yes," or "No." This depression of manner continued during the day – it seemed to me that it was an effort for him to speak – there was no afternoon service; an evening service at 6.30, I think, or 6 o'clock – in consequence of what I observed in Mr Watson, his depression and listlessness, I told him, after luncheon, that I thought that I was quite as equal as he was to preaching, and therefore I would take the sermon myself, and I did. He read the prayers – I observed the same weakness of voice. After the evening service he returned to the rectory and dined with us – there was no change at all in his manner during dinner – I endeavoured to try and enliven him by asking him to drink a glass or two more wine than I might generally do; it did not have the least effect upon him, his manner still continued dejected and depressed to the greatest degree – he seemed very feeble, and in consequence I ordered my carriage to take him down to the station, which, on Sunday, I should not generally have done – it is a mile from my house to the station – I did not remark any access of cheerfulness at any time during the day – the only time at which I saw the slightest approach to a smile was when I paid him his fee. I thought he was worn out with old age. That was the opinion that I formed at that time, and I expressed it at that time.

Ann Wall Baugh. I am the wife of the last witness – I remember Mr Watson coming to my husband's rectory on 3rd September – he read prayers at the morning service – his manner was exceedingly feeble and weak. I was at luncheon with him and my husband – his manner was perfectly quiet; he scarcely uttered anything during the whole time – I tried in every way to induce him to talk, quite without success – I remember taking him upstairs before lunch – I remarked that he was exceedingly feeble, so feeble that I feared he would fall. He scarcely raised his head during luncheon, and his eyes were closed nearly the whole day also. There was a discussion about how the evening service should be conducted. I said I was sorry there was no one who could read the lessons for him, and he said that I could read them myself – he seemed in earnest. He had great difficulty in getting to church in the evening. His conduct and manner made a considerable impression on my mind, and my husband and I communicated with Mr Fraser, Mr Watson's solicitor.

Cross-examined. He seemed completely crushed, simply unable to take interest in anything – he was very reserved, generally answering "Yes," and "No," to every question that was asked – I tried all I could to get him to converse – I was going to have a school treat, and I endeavoured to interest him in that school treat, not to get him to come, but to get him to talk. I asked if he had any experience of treats for children, and he replied that he had run a Grammar School, not a Kindergarten.

Henry Rogers. I reside at Beulah House, South Lambeth Road – I am manager of the Beulah Laundry – I have resided there twenty years. For about ten years of that time, Mr Watson lived next door but one to me. I knew Mr Watson by general reputation and by sight – he bore the reputation of being a very great classical scholar, and being a very excellent master of the Proprietary Grammar School, and a great writer. His ordinary walk and manner were quite familiar to me for twenty years. On Saturday, 7th October, last year, I was walking in the Clapham Road and I met Mr Watson. He was walking towards Kennington, and I was walking the contrary way – it was about 11 o'clock, or a little before. When I was about seven or eight yards distant from him, I happened to cast my eye upon him, and his eyes were staring. They appeared fixed on me in a very staring manner. I kept my eye on him, and when he came within about a yard or a yard and a half from me, he threw his umbrella under his arm, and made a noise in his throat, like groaning, or growling rather; a deep heavy noise in his throat; at the same time he made a gesture with his arm three or four times. He must have known me, because we lived very near together for years. He was not in the habit of speaking when he met me – I never spoke to him but once, about seventeen years ago. After he passed me – I turned round – he repeated his growling. I remarked his manner for the first time about three months before the unfortunate occurrence; that would be about July – I met him twice in one day in Stockwell, and his eyes were then cast upwards, and his lips were moving rapidly; of course I thought at the time that he was making devout ejaculations to the Almighty. When I saw him cast his eyes upwards and his lips moving I naturally thought that, but a week or two after that I met him again, and his eyes were very different, they stared so, stared very much. He had a vacant look in his eyes. I met him eight or nine times before the murder, in about as many weeks, and I noticed the same staring manner in his eyes – I had never seen anything like that before 1871. I have seen him about every week for twenty years. When I saw those expressions which I have spoken of, I thought that his mind was going.

184

The house, No.28, St Martin's Road, Stockwell, made so notorious by the murder of Mrs Anne Watson by her husband the Revd John Selby Watson, M.A., M.R.S.L., etc., has been the scene of much excitement. An application for the property and effects of the reverend gentleman to be delivered over to Mr Fraser, his solicitor, was acceded to. A notice was issued that the household furniture and effects of the reverend gentleman would be sold, and Mr Murrell, auctioneer, of Walbrook, was entrusted with the task of disposing of the property. In order to prevent as far as possible the entrance of a large crowd, one shilling was charged for a catalogue. Despite this, a large number paid the entrance fee, in order to satisfy their curiosity by looking at the various rooms and articles within the dwelling which had all been associated with the murder. Many went even so far as to take away leaves and little branches of trees and shrubs in the front garden as mementos. The sale commenced about one o'clock in the afternoon, but long before that time a large number of persons, chiefly composed of the usual brokers and buyers at sales, were present. The room in which the unfortunate lady was found was, as far as possible, kept closed. The catalogue comprised 228 lots. The usual household effects were knocked down to about average price. One lot, comprising a photograph in a gilt frame, two small pictures, and five pictures framed and glazed, fetched £1.14s including the portrait, as announced by the auctioneer, of the reverend gentleman. Some pistols fetched a few shillings, and two silk gowns, cassock and girdle, Trinity M.A. hood and Oxford ditto, realised about £1.10s. A Trinity College medal, gold masonic medals, and other articles of jewelry, fetched fair prices. It will be remembered that, according to the evidence, the reverend gentleman ordered a large, iron-bound chest to be made, in which it is supposed, he intended to conceal the body of his victim. This cost £1.5s, but was sold for 7s. The utmost interest was manifested when the stuffed leather armchair, in which it is supposed the deceased lady was seated when the first blow was struck by her murderer, was brought forward. It had a piece of the leather cut out on which bloodstains had been found. There was much anxiety to catch sight of the chair, but it fell to a purchaser for 16s, the remarks of several about being that they would sooner have it burned than take it home. The valuable books, papers, etc., of which the reverend gentleman was author, were disposed of privately.

Revd Joseph Wallace. I am vicar of St Andrew's Stockwell – the prisoner and his wife have had sittings at my church for about the three last years. I have known the prisoner more than ten years, and saw him very frequently to speak to – no man could have a higher character for kindness and humanity. On 3rd November I visited him in Horsemonger Jail – he asked me to go – I had been before – I did not communicate with his advisers – I was with him about three-quarters of an hour. I first of all observed that he had quite forgotten that he had sent for me, and when he did begin to talk it seemed that his conversation was in intelligence very unlike what I had heard from him before; as, for instance, at the beginning he said he thought that if he had opened his mind to me before, perhaps he might have taken a different course. He did not continue long talking on one subject, which was very unlike what had been usual with him; he passed rapidly from one subject to another without much connection – that was not his habit at all, formerly. As an illustration, he spoke about the inquest, "that horrible inquest," and in the middle of the conversation about it he said "They won't let me shave here'. I observed also what struck me as a singular absence of remorse for his fault, for his crime, which was strange in a man of religious habits; he was full of anxiety and trouble, but it was all about the dismantling of his house and the sale of his library. He said that he was very hardly dealt with. I mentioned that the Bishop had highly commended a Latin letter which he had written to him, and he said "Here is a man whom the Bishop of Winchester can highly commend, and they have shut him up in a place like this." He was laying out a plan for writing an essay on the union of Church and State, and he did not know how he should do it without his books, and he hoped the authorities of the gaol would help him in the matter – it was for a competition prize essay which somebody proposed. He did not seem conscious of any peril that he was in; he always spoke of it as a thing which would soon pass away. I wrote a letter to Mr Fraser immediately after that interview.

Cross-examined. I have assisted at the examination of his school and he came to my house – we did not discuss matters of business, but ordinary conversation. Since he ceased to be master of the Grammar School, he came to me on two or three occasions to ask me to help him to obtain an appointment – he came last at the end of July. I cannot recollect how lately, before July, I had seen him, but, I should say, more or less once a fortnight. I went three times to Horsemonger Lane Gaol. The first time I only saw him through a grating in the door, and we had not an opportunity of conversing – I do not know that I lay more stress on the second time but it was after that I communicated with the lawyer. All the facts I have spoken of took place on the second occasion – on the third occasion I had a conversation with him but nothing occurred to throw any additional light on the state of his mind. He still repeated his complaints as to the sale of his library and his house, but it was a shorter interview – I am not sure whether he talked about his trial, but he used language and expressions which led me to know that he contemplated being tried for the offence. He did not speak to me of the probability of his being acquitted, beyond what I have said, but he seemed to assume it. I went to him voluntarily the first time, and the second time in consequence of a letter – I do not know what I have done with that letter, it was two lines – I put it in the waste paper basket, most likely. He was in a large cell, with plain walls – there was a bed and a chair – two other prisoners were there. After a while I asked him what he asked me to come for – I said "Why did you send for me, Mr Watson?" Each of his sentences was complete – besides the horrible inquest and the Latin letter, and about taking a different course, and not letting him shave, and the essay – he conversed about his library. There were also detached sentences, there must have been, to fill up the time. He asked where Broadmoor was, that is the asylum where criminal lunatics are confined. He did not tell me why they had not permitted him to shave. I understood that the prize-essay had been advertised before this offence, but I do not think he had been at work on it before.

Re-examined. I forget who began the conversation about Broadmoor, but it was in reference, of course, to his prospects – that was on 3rd November, at Horsemonger Lane – I did not write or give any further information to Mr Fraser after the third interview – I did not observe anything on the third occasion beyond what I did on the second.

Robert Colman Hall. I am a tea-dealer and live at Pembroke Lodge, Brixton – I had a boy in the school under Mr Watson, and in the beginning of 1871 I had occasion to call on him respecting my son. I had known him seven years, and I noticed a very great difference

187

in his demeanour and manner on that occasion, to what I had noticed before – he seemed depressed and lost. The interview lasted perhaps ten minutes or a quarter of an hour, and I had ample opportunity of forming a judgment as to whether he was depressed or not.

Cross-examined. I went to him because the gentleman whom my son was going to, in Mark Lane, said that he should like to have a letter from a clergyman.

Court. Q. What do you mean by "lost?" *A* He seemed low, and he hardly knew what he was speaking about at times. He said he had been treated badly – that is all the explanation I can give of the word "lost".

Henry Maudsley. I am M.D. of the University of London – I have paid great attention to the disease of insanity, and have written a work on the physiology and pathology of mind. I was lecturer at St Mary's Hospital, on the subject of insanity. I was at one time resident physician of a lunatic asylum at Manchester, where there were usually 100 patients of the middle classes. I visited the prisoner first on 27th November, for the purpose of ascertaining, if I could, the state of his mind – I was with him for an hour, and conversed with him during that time, and at the end of the interview formed the opinion that he was not of sound mind – that was the conclusion I came to. I believe he is suffering from melancholia. The symptoms I observed in him were such as in my opinion would follow an attack of melancholia. I found that his age was sixty-seven or sixty-eight, and in a person of that age melancholia would have greater effect and force than in a younger person. I heard Dr Shepherd examined, and I agree with him in the main in the description he gives of melancholia. A person suffering from melancholia is liable to outbursts of mad violence, and while those outbursts prevail his mind is diseased; gone; his reason is in abeyance, and he is nearly unconscious of what he is doing; his mind decidedly deranged – after such an attack of disease the mind sometimes regains comparatively its tone; that is a matter in which I agree with Dr Shepherd entirely – the mind may be restored within an hour after such an attack, decidedly in some cases, and before the very act itself he might appear calm and comparatively rational. I mean by comparatively, that his conversation would be coherent and rational. In the course of my experience I have known patients suffering from this disease, and

188

who have exhibited violence under it – it is essential that I should form a regular diagnosis of the disease, as I should in any other, and enquire into the history of the patient, the circumstances under which he had lived, and so on. If he had never exhibited any symptoms of violence, unkindness, and inhumanity before, that would be an element of consideration. I remember the questions you put to Dr Shepherd with reference to suicidal acts on the part of patients labouring under melancholia. I don't agree with him in the answers which he gave. Suicide by an insane person may be entirely impulsive, as well as crafty – I understood Dr Shepherd to say it was not so in such cases. Persons suffering from melancholia are sometimes aware that they are liable to homicidal and suicidal propensities. I had a patient of my own who told me that he would do it unless we took care of him, and it ended by his doing it – he was under certificate as an insane person, and under the charge of attendants. The case of Charles Lamb and his sister is a well-known instance – that was homicidal madness. Miss Lamb killed her father. Method and design is very commonly exhibited by the insane, and the concealment of an act is very frequent; I mean of an act committed whilst in a state of insanity. I was very much impressed, at my interview with the prisoner, at the entire indifference which he displayed with regard to the crime, and the position in which he was placed.

Cross-examined by Mr Denman. I asked him about the events that had immediately preceded the crime, and he said very much as he said in that letter that was read yesterday, that she was rather of a hasty temper, she said something angrily to him, and he was provoked – he did not tell me what she had said to him. He said that he had struck her on the head with a pistol. I asked him about it, and he said it was one that he had inherited from his grandfather, that he had always had by him. He did not say whether it was in his hand at the time, or whether he fetched it – he said that he had had in the course of his life quarrels of that kind.

Dr George Fielding Blandford. I am a Fellow of the Royal College of Physicians – I have, for about sixteen or seventeen years, entirely devoted my time and attention to the study of insanity – I have written a book upon "insanity and its treatment" – I am lecturer on psychological medicine at the school of St George's Hospital, I am also visiting physician at Blackland's and Otto House lunatic asylums, private asylums of the late Dr Sutherland.

One is for ladies the other for gentlemen – I have, in company with Dr Maudsley, examined Mr Watson – I agree with Dr Maudsley that there is a well known form of insanity called melancholia – when a person of advanced age becomes insane, that is, very often, the form of insanity which attacks him, more often perhaps than any other form. When a very self-absorbed and reserved man becomes insane, that may be the form of madness which it takes. I saw Mr Watson on 27th November, I was with him about an hour in the gaol of Newgate – I came to the conclusion that he was of unsound mind then – I should say it was certainly not an affair of a few days or even weeks, but I could not state any limited time. I was in Court yesterday – I heard the evidence of Mr and Mrs Baugh and Mr Henry Rogers – the symptoms described by them were such as in my experience I have observed in some patients suffering under melancholia.

Dr Joseph Rogers. I am a physician of Scotland, a member of the College of Surgeons, and of the Apothecaries' Company – I have been in the profession thirty years – I was for twelve years in charge of the infirmary of the Strand Union. In the course of my practice I have made insanity a study, and made myself acquainted with it – I have seen a great many cases, and certified a great many insane persons before the Magistrate – that was a part of my duty; they have been persons who came into the hands of the police for some criminal offence. I have had the opportunity of seeing the prisoner five times; once in Horsemonger Lane Gaol, and four times in Newgate – I agree with what Dr Maudsley and Dr Blandford have stated – from my observation of the prisoner at those five visits I believe him to be of unsound mind.

Cross-examined by Mr Poland. The form of insanity he is suffering under is melancholia – I first saw him on 11th November – Mr Fraser, the prisoner's solicitor, requested me to go and see him – I have known Mr Fraser since he was a child – I practice in Dean Street, Soho, and Mr Fraser lives opposite to me – he asked me to go and see Mr Watson, knowing from my previous position that I had seen a great deal of insanity. He was suffering from melancholia – that is very different to low spirits – a person may be low-spirited and yet in sound health – a person who has melancholia has something the matter with his brain. The prisoner had not any delusions that I noticed. It would be a difficult thing to describe the difference between extreme low spirits and melancholia, because in melancholia you have an exaggeration of extreme low spirits. A man who is low-spirited may pass on into melancholia, and he may pass out of it. The difference between melancholia and low spirits is as I tell you; low spirits may arise from a transient affection of the mind, perhaps arising from a disordered state of body, or a transient trouble, which the mind is strong enough to resist; but melancholia is a disease where the mind has given way; there is some defect of the brain structure, or something of that kind. The first thing that I noticed about the prisoner was this – I put him in a good light in the cell at Horsemonger Lane Gaol, and I watched his countenance while talking to him, and I noticed that he had a dazed appearance of the eye when his countenance was at rest – he was lost – there was an expressionless appearance about his countenance, a lost look about the face when the countenance was at rest – he showed, as the other witnesses have said, great indifference to the condition of things, a singular indifference – I don't mean that he was hopeless as to the result of the trial – I will give you an instance of what I mean – I was talking to him about the affair generally, with a view to leading him on to make some remarks, and in the midst of it he saw a piece of fluff on his trousers, or something, and he put down his hand and picked it off, and jumped up and gave himself a shake down in a manner that struck me as very singular in a man I was talking to – I should have looked at it as a piece of rudeness in an ordinary individual, but in his particular case I looked at it as real evidence of a want of mind – he was guilty of what I considered irrational conduct in that one act that I have spoken of – then there was another thing, he told me he thought he was entitled to consideration for what he had done in the past, which certainly appeared to me to be a very irrational thing, seeing that he had only kept a school. He talked of the labours of Hercules. I referred to the crime itself – he said that something was said to him and he became angry, and did what he did – he did not say what it was that was said to him; something was said to him by his wife which made him angry, and then he did the deed. I did not ask him where he got the pistol from, but it was asked in my presence, and the remark was made that it had belonged to his grandfather – he did not say where he had fetched it from, or how he had got it – I saw him four times in Newgate – Mr Gibson, the surgeon, was present each time, and the third time I saw him Dr Shepherd drew my particular attention to the difficulty he had in collecting his thoughts – he did not tell me anything of the circumstances that occurred after he had committed the deed. In a light and frivolous manner he told me, at Newgate, how he attempted to commit suicide in Horsemonger Lane Gaol; and it so struck me, the light and frivolous way in which he told me the story, as if it in no way referred to himself, that I put to him what appeared to me this crucial question: "How could you, as a Christian minister, dare to rush into the presence of your God, unprepared," and he said, "There is no prohibition against suicide, the law only applies to murder" – I thought that, coming from a clergyman, was not an evidence of sanity, quite the reverse – I did not ask him what it was his wife had done or said that made him angry; it was asked in my presence, and he made no answer – I believe he shook his head; I am not certain – he may have said "I can't say" – I think he said something of this kind, that she had provoked him on previous occasions, and that they had had quarrels – he stated that in his paper – I am in a difficulty about whether he said it then or not, because I saw him so many times; whether he said it to me, or in my hearing, I can't say. I did ask him a question about the box – I think I said "What did you want the box for?" or "How did you come to order the box?" and he shrugged his shoulders and said something to the effect that it was not for the purpose that was assumed – I did not speak to him about his trial – I said nothing to him individually as to whether he was to be defended on the ground of insanity. My treatment for melancholia would be to send the patient away from the place where he had become the subject of it; to make a radical change in his habits; to give him an opportunity of amusement. If it were a lady I should encourage her to dance, if a gentleman I should try to give him some intellectual interest.

Mr Serjeant Parry, in briefly summing up the case for the defence, which then closed, remarked that the letters which had been addressed by the prisoner to the lady whom he afterwards married, were important, as showing the natural state of his mind when his prospects were fair and his position likely to be comfortable. That state was, he urged, entirely antagonistic to the idea of his committing such a deed of violence. The letters exhibited also the then excellent qualities of both the prisoner's mind and heart. The next piece of evidence went to prove conclusively that immediately before the commission of the murder the prisoner showed undeniable evidences of insanity, or approaching madness. He appeared, in the words of the witness, Mrs Baugh, to have been completely crushed down by some great sorrow, and so utterly prostrated by depression as to be unable to perform his usual duties as a clergyman. At that time, a month before the murder, there was some lurking and gradually developing insanity. The evidence of Mr Henry Rogers on that point was very remarkable, for he proved that the day preceding the commission of the crime the prisoner, whom he had known for 20 years, was walking along the Clapham Road, his eyes glaring in a most unusual manner, making a gurgling in his throat and throwing about his hands in a very strange way. That conduct, itself most singular, had been preceded by other circumstances, just as notable as indications of the unsound state of his mind, which the various witnesses had detailed. The great depression from which he suffered proved the form the disease was taking, and it was during a sudden outburst consequent upon that disease that he killed his unfortunate wife, with whom he had never been known to quarrel previously. He was invariably a kind and humane man, and it was very possible that his own statement as to previous quarrels was a mere delusion

Commenting upon the medical evidence and the prisoner's strange conduct in gaol, Mr Serjeant Parry argued that it had been proved conclusively, or as far as any such matter could possible be proved, that at the time of the murder he was neither a reasoning nor a responsible being; and that he was then ignorant of both the nature and quality of the act. On those grounds he appealed to the jury to return a verdict of acquittal

Mr Denman, replying on behalf of the Crown, said the trial, though having occupied a considerable time had not been for a single moment prolonged beyond the limits which its great importance demanded. Most important testimony had been given on both sides, and that testimony did, to a certain extent, arraign the established law of this country as laid down by the Judges, upon which, more than anything else, the safety of each member of the community depended. The facts in this case were terribly plain and simple, and nothing had been elicited during the investigation tending to impugn the theory that the crime was the wilful and deliberate act of the prisoner. He admitted that from his previous habits the prisoner was in the last degree unlikely to have been guilty of such a crime, but that he had committed it was fully proved, as far as human testimony was concerned, and proved, moreover, most conclusively by his own statements. He had had the advantage of being defended by the most eloquent member of the bar of England, who had pleaded everything on his behalf that could possibly suggest itself as appropriate to his mind, and his observations were worthy of the most careful attention by the jury

Turning to the evidence of the defence, Mr Denman remarked that the letters written by the prisoner 28 years ago to his wife could have no possible value in furnishing an indication of his mental condition at the time of the murder. It was perfectly clear that the prisoner had experienced considerable disappointment in life, and that it had caused him great depression of mind, but the same might, perhaps, be said of every person in that court. It would be most unsafe to lay down the doctrine that any amount of such depression could be tolerated as a defence to the crime of murder, for if such a defence was once permitted there would be a terrible increase in the risk to human life. The jury should in this case not rely blindly on the evidence of the medical men, but should themselves judge from the admitted facts the probably condition of the prisoner at the period in question. Was he capable of distinguishing between right and wrong, and of judging the nature of the act he was committing? If he had not that capacity then it would be their duty to say that he was 'not guilty'. It was not impossible that even a man whose mind was in a diseased state could be perfectly competent to distinguish between right and wrong. Terrible was the evidence of the servant Pyne. She observed that Mrs Watson was sometimes a person of hasty temper, and it was not, therefore, improbably that some provocation was given. The heavy weapon, the horse-pistol, must have been brought from the drawer in which it was usually kept for the purpose of committing the murder. His learned friend had said that there had been unnecessary violence, but how could they possibly tell? Repeated blows might have been necessary to accomplish his object. Then the remark as to the absence of deliberation could hardly be well-founded if the pistol was fetched for the purpose of murder. As to the prisoner being afflicted with melancholia it was not for him to deny that medical men recognised such a disease as one of the forms of madness. Where was the difference between melancholia and low spirits? That was one of the most difficult questions to which the human mind could easily be directed, to decide when it was that a man labouring under extreme depression ceased to be responsible for his actions. None of the medical witnesses had been able to draw that line. The letters the prisoner last wrote, including those to his landlady, Mrs Hall, were of a businesslike character, showing that he was a man of sound mind. Mr Serjeant Parry had said that there was more secretiveness in cases where crime had been committed by sane persons than there was in this case. What became of the cuffs of the shirt? The shirt itself too had apparently been imperfectly washed; and the blood stain on the stairs was stated by the prisoner to be port wine, which the deceased had spilt. Was that not evidence of secretiveness or of his knowing how to distinguish between right and wrong, and the nature and quality of the act? Then, when he ordered the box he had no doubt entertained the idea of stowing away the corpse in order to get rid of the traces of murder; and the sponge was a very important article in the case, it having been washed to free it of blood. Nothing could be fairer than the observation, when they were enquiring into the sanity of a man at the time a homicide has been committed, that an act of suicide after homicide was far less important evidence of insanity than an act of suicide committed by a man who had never done anything at all like homicide. The prisoner had, no doubt, been a hard-working man, and his works were always of an intelligent description. But, after his dismissal from the school, his acts showed that he was capable of writing and reasoning soundly and judiciously, and considering and making proposals which did not seem wild or irrational. It was not his duty, on the part of the prosecution, to press for verdicts, but to ask the jury to do their duty in the case, to apply their minds honestly, conscientiously, and truthfully to a solution of the case, and not to care or think of the mere result of the verdict they might give. If they found the prisoner not guilty, it must be because they were firmly satisfied that he was not of sound mind, and if they found him guilty they must do so because the law constrained them to do so, and because it had not been made out in the defence of the prisoner that he was not responsible for his acts, and did not know the difference between right and wrong and the nature and quality of his acts.

Mr Justice Byles then proceeded to sum up. After stating the charge against the prisoner, he said there was one matter which was often the question in such cases, but which did not arise in the present enquiry – viz. whether the prisoner did kill the deceased. This was admitted by the prisoner's counsel. It was also clear that there was no provocation which would reduce the crime from murder to manslaughter. The real and only question in the case to which the counsel had directed their attention was the true question, and it was this: Was the prisoner at the time he committed the act legally responsible for it and was he a responsible agent? That depended upon a question, on which the counsel also agreed, did he at the time he committed this act know what he was doing? If not, of course he was not criminally responsible. Did he also know that what he was doing was wrong? He was perfectly aware that doubts on the universal applicability of this rule had been expressed by many eminent persons for whose opinion he had the greatest respect. But if it was to be altered at all, it must be altered by Act of Parliament. It was the rule laid down by the Judges, and was that which guided the House of Lords in a well-known case, when a learned Judge, perhaps the most learned and the most cautious he could remember, Mr Justice Maule, expressed a doubt upon some parts of the rule not now before the jury, but upon this part of the rule he was of the same opinion as the other Judges. Therefore, the jury must take it from him, and upon the authority of counsel upon both sides. The question then was did the prisoner know what he was doing? The jury must look at the act itself, and say whether they believed upon the evidence that the prisoner was or was not in a condition to know what he was doing, and the nature of the act at the time he committed it. Mr Denman was perfectly right when he said that the burden of proving that lay upon the prisoner. Prima facie, this was a case of murder. They had had a large body of evidence to show that the presumption was rebutted by the circumstances of the case, and that the person who committed it was not of sound mind in this respect, and that he did not know what he was doing and the nature and consequences of his act. There was abundant evidence that after the offence he was conscious that the act was wrong; but the question was, was he conscious that he was wrong not after, but at the time? Something had been said about suicide. He did not think that the attempt to commit suicide was so very material either one way or the other. The learned counsel for the prosecution, who was himself a distinguished scholar, knew perfectly well that in the ancient heathen philosophy, in the times of Zeno and Epicurus, after all the duties and trials of life had gone, and nothing but suffering remained to be endured, it was taught that a man might go quietly out of the world. But one of the wisest men had written that the human frame should be taken to pieces, and was best taken to pieces, by the Power that compacted it and put it together. The doctrine of the Christian Church was plain. They would be doing the prisoner no more than justice by supposing that he believed the doctrines he taught; and, therefore, suicide in a clergyman, who believed in the doctrine of repentance and forgiveness, was a more formidable sin than in ordinary cases, in which persons committing it rushed into the presence of their Maker in the commission of the actual sin. It might be that this act of suicide should be looked at in that light, and not as though it was precisely the case of an ordinary individual. He had endeavoured to state the evidence to the jury on both sides. If they fancied they discovered any leaning in him, he begged them to disregard it altogether. The responsibility was not with him, and he did not mean to assume it. It was entirely with them. Prima facie, it was a case of murder, but if they thought upon this evidence either that the prisoner did not know what he was doing or did not know he was doing wrong, in that case they should acquit him, but they must state the reason why.

*   *   *

The jury retired at five minutes past 5 o'clock to consider their verdict, and returned into court at 25 minutes to 7. Their names having been called over, and the prisoner having been brought to the dock, the Clerk of Arraigns (Mr Avory) asked them if they had agreed upon a verdict. The foreman replied that they had.

Mr Avory: Do you find the prisoner Guilty or Not guilty?

The Foreman: We find him Guilty, but we wish strongly to recommend him to the mercy and clemency of the Crown on account of his advanced age and previous good character.

Mr Avory, amid profound silence, asked the prisoner if he had anything to say for himself why the Court should not give him judgment to die according to law.

The prisoner in a low voice answered – I only wish to say that the defence which has been maintained in my favour is a just and honest one.

Mr Justice Byles, assuming the black cap, said – Prisoner at the bar: Nobody who has heard this trial can regard your case otherwise than with the deepest compassion. My duty is simply to pronounce the sentence of the law – that you be taken to the place whence you came, and then be delivered to the custody of the Sheriff of Surrey; that you then be taken to a place of execution, be hanged by the neck until you be dead, and that your body be buried within the precincts of the prison. May the Lord have mercy on your soul.

*   *   *

He was taken down to the condemned cell and searched to the skin. He was convinced that some mistake had been made and that it would be remedied. His own clothes were taken away and he was handed a pair of moleskin trousers and a loose-fitting blouse. They shaved his beard and examined the hair on his head for lice. Then he was given a plug of tobacco, which he declined and, later, his dinner. He had read that Calcraft, the hangman, charged half a crown for administering a flogging, and ten shillings for dropping a man into eternity, and it seemed to him that both sums were inadequate. He ate everything on his plate and wiped it clean with a piece of bread. Then he lay down and instantly fell asleep

He slept almost continuously for several days, only waking at meal times when he sat at a rickety table and devoured his food as though in the hours between he had been employed at building roads.

At intervals Fraser visited him; he talked of appeals and petitions. A woman named Gattie was indefatigable at getting signatures. Two more former pupils of the Grammar School had come forward with offers of help. Did he remember H.H. Hudson, and Caldwell who was now a Fellow and Bursar of Corpus Christi College, Cambridge? A lady had written to the Home Secretary confiding that many years before, on holiday at some resort or other, she had met the prisoner and been told by him of a murderous attack by sailors. She understood that his mouth had been stuffed with sand like an hour-glass, and his skull cracked. Such an injury, she felt, might have a bearing on what had transpired at St Martin's Road. Was there any truth in the story, asked Fraser? If so, was it likely that there would be any medical records to substantiate it? Watson replied that he had never had a holiday in his life.

The prison chaplin came often. He mumbled about contrition and God's abiding love. Watson sat slumped on his bed; it was all he could do to keep his eyes open. Besides, what had either contrition or the love of God to do with him? The one was inappropriate and the other inaccessible.

Sometimes while he munched his food he considered the evidence which had brought him to such a place, in particular the remarks made by Longman, the publisher. To have told the court that his author's works were 'moderately successful' was bad enough, but then to have judged them 'not successful' at all was criminal. It seemed to him that it was Longman and not Anne Armstrong who had pushed him into the condemned cell.

When he thought of that other evidence, that detailed and bloody analysis of his clothing, he looked down at the mess on his plate and waited, as he had waited in court, for some sensation of nausea to take hold of him, and, as before, he felt nothing. On that fateful, now distant Sunday afternoon he supposed he had suffered such a cataclysmic surge of passion that he had emptied himself of feelings forever. I have waded in blood, he thought, and it was not of my doing.

Then one night his own voice, crying out, woke him up. The warders, who had been dozing at the table, swivelled on their chairs to look at him. He frowned and turned his face to the wall. He had to bite on his lip to stop from whimpering. In imagination he took that walk towards the dreadful dark. Calcraft, that one time shoemaker, butler and pidgeon fancier, was waiting in the shadows of the yard, his sweet, grey eyes searching for him. They were both old men, but on different ends of the rope. The last thing I shall see in the whole world, thought Watson, before the hood is slipped over my head, will be the little white flower that the hangman wears in his buttonhole.

Mr Watson, as was announced yesterday, is not to be hanged for
the murder of his wife. Against the equity of this decision it is not
our intention to protest. There was so much that was painful and
piteous connected with the story of the wretched old man, that it is
hardly possibly to feel righteous indignation, even if justice had
erred somewhat on the side of mercy. In all that we have written on
the case, we have carefully avoided saying anything which might
seem to be an argument against Mr Watson's being deemed an
object for Royal clemency. However, now that Mr Bruce, with the
concurrence of the presiding Judge, has taken upon himself to
decide that Watson's crime is not one which should be visited with
the extreme penalty of the law, we are able to speak more plainly
about the character of the offence than we felt justified in doing
while his life hung in the balance. We gather from the terms of the
respite that the verdict given by the jury is not to be reversed; and
that therefore the plea of insanity submitted on Watson's behalf
has been discarded by the Home Secretary. Indeed, upon the
evidence adduced at the Trial, the plea was palpably and almost
absurdly untenable; and there is no reason to suppose that any
more satisfactory testimony on the point was forthcoming. We are,
therefore, to understand that Mr Bruce agreed with the jury in
their recommendation to mercy, and held that the prisoner's age
and previous good character were extenuating circumstances
which removed his crime from the category of wilful murder. It is,
of course, possible that facts may have been brought to Mr Bruce's
notice, which, had they been disclosed to the jury, might have
influenced their verdict. If so, it is a matter for grave regret that
those facts should not be made public. As things are, we know that
Mr Watson beat his wife to death under circumstances which
showed deliberation and vindictive violence. Putting aside the plea
of insanity, the only excuses alleged on his behalf were that he was
in straitened circumstances, and that his wife had a bad temper.
Opinions may differ on how far incompatibility of temper, distaste
for a wife's society, and insufficiency of income are adequate
excuses for beating the wife's brains out with a horse pistol. A

good deal has been said about Mr Watson's high character and blameless life, but it must have struck everybody that there was an ominous absence of all testimony with respect to his domestic relations, though we are aware that this lack of testimony may be accounted for by the peculiar circumstances of the unhappy man's existence. Still, for any proof to the contrary, it may have been Mrs Watson and not her husband who was the sufferer in this wretched household. In a great city like ours there must be thousands of homes made miserable by a woman's ill temper, and by narrow means. It must be a comfort to all respectable elderly gentlemen in Mr Watson's position, who are tired of their wives, and find some difficulty in making both ends meet, to reflect that, if they think fit to murder their wives with singular brutality, they cannot, after the reprieve of the Stockwell murderer, be sentenced to any worse punishment than imprisonment for life. It is, no doubt, unfortunate for poor SHEWARD – who was hanged, on his own confession, for murdering his wife, in spite of having led a blameless life for twenty years after instead of before the deed – that Mr Bruce had not yet made up his mind as to the fact of general respectability being an apology for this description of crime. Possibly WRIGHT, the man who was hanged for cutting, in a fit of drunken passion, the throat of the woman with whom he lived, might regret, if he could hear of Mr Watson's case, that he had not lived respectably and taken holy orders before he yielded to the dire temptation of committing murder. Our criminal law is in a curious state. Watson was found guilty, and as everybody agrees, properly according to the law as it exists. One of the Judges is said to have expressed the opinion that he ought not to be executed. This seems odd, but then it is an odd case in all respects. Watson is the 'Revd Mr Watson', Mr Watson 'the clergyman', the 'venerable looking prisoner'. Would the same sympathy have been felt if a Mr Mick Connor had knocked his wife's brains out with a pick-axe? There are cases which make one wonder if an unconscious feeling for respectable people has not influenced exertions to save such persons. While on this subject, attention may be called to a strange state of the law. Some years ago a commission recommended that unpremeditated murder should not be punished capitally. The report was of such a character (to say no worse of it) that legislation did not follow on it, but the Home Office acts on that recommendation, so that, pro tanto, it has repealed the law to murder. The present state of things is most unsatisfactory. If the Home Secretary is not strong enough to deal with these questions (and none is more capable than the present) let some tribunal be constituted which can. At present it is chaos.

To the Editor of The Times

Surrey County Gaol, Jan.23, 1872
Sir, The following statement was drawn up yesterday by the Revd Mr Watson, for the purpose of transmission to the Secretary of State. Before, however, it had left the gaol the respite arrived.

Your obedient servant, The Chaplain.

Surrey County Gaol, Jan.22, 1872
Sir, I beg leave respectfully to submit to you the following statement, with a view to remove from your mind a possible misapprehension of the purpose for which I ordered the packing-case, concerning which I have reason to believe that an entirely erroneous impression exists with the public.

My desire is, if the sentence of the law is carried into execution, to relieve my memory from the undeserved and terrible imputation which would otherwise rest upon it, and, if my life is spared, that I may, at least, have had the satisfaction of clearing whatever seems ambiguous in regard to this matter.

When his Lordship asked me after the verdict of the jury whether I had anything to say why sentence should not be pronounced, it did not occur to me, as it ought to have occurred, that that was the time at which I should ask to be allowed to make some observations on the evidence such as I had wished to make previously, but was precluded from making through being defended by counsel.

It did not strike me, as it ought to have struck me, that that was the only opportunity which I should have of contradicting or qualifying any misrepresentations which I considered to have been made concerning my case.

I said merely, to his Lordship, that the defence maintained for me had been fair and honest, meaning as to its general character; but I ought to have added that there was one great particular as to which it was quite erroneous. I had suffered all observations regarding the box or packing-case which I ordered from Mr Robert Turner to pass without remark, except privately to my solicitor, to whom I gave a written paper on Wednesday, the first day of the trial, telling him, as I had constantly told him at other times, that the packing-case was intended only for the reception of books, manuscripts, and letters, but that finding myself on Tuesday afternoon, the 10th of October, not in a condition of mind to sort and arrange my manuscripts, and to make such selection from my letters as I had purposed, I told Turner, when I called to pay him between 2 and 3 o'clock on that day, that he need not be in any hurry to send the case, as I should not want it at that time, and that indeed he might wait to send it till he should hear from me again; a permission which I gave him merely for his own convenience. I then did not suppose that anything more would be heard of the case by myself, or that it would ever give rise to any public remarks. You will please to understand that the case was never brought to the house at all.

My solicitor tells me that he communicated my observations, stated on the written paper which I gave him on the Wednesday, to Serjeant Parry, but that the learned serjeant was not influenced by them to alter the nature of the defence which he had premeditated on this point.

By a reference to the report of the proceedings at Kennington Police-court, it will be seen that Turner gave his evidence there much more fully than he gave it at the Old Bailey. He stated at Kennington that when I ordered the packing-case, I told him that it was for holding papers; and he stated truly. He asked me when I ordered it whether it was to go abroad, or on shipboard, and I told him that it was not. He asked me also whether he should bind the corners with iron, and I answered that in that respect he might do as he pleased, provided that he made it strong. I assert now, as I have invariably asserted to my solicitor, that it was intended for no other purpose than for holding a few printed books, a large quantity of manuscripts, and a great number of letters, and that there is not, and has not been, the least foundation for representing that it was intended for any other object. There was nothing in the size of the packing-case to excite astonishment. A case 2ft.6in. long, 2ft.3in. wide, and 1ft.9in. in depth is not one of extraordinary dimensions. If compared with such packing-cases as may be seen by hundreds, of a far greater size, on wharves or in warehouses, it will appear but small. I had it made of such capacity because I had, as I have said, a great number of manuscripts and letters to put together, and I thought it better to have them in one receptacle than in more than one, as when several boxes are used for such a purpose they may possibly get separated, and one or more of them be lost.

Let me add that there was neither word nor act of mine to connect the ordering of the packing-case on one day with anything that I had done on the preceding day. Such connexion as has been made has arisen only in the imaginations of those who have concerned themselves with the affair. As it seems to me it was not known either to the judge or the jury that the packing-case was not in the house with me. What I had said to Turner about the case being intended for papers was, if known to the prosecuting counsel, studiously kept in the background by them.

I do not suppose that anything I could have said in court would have altered the final determination. But it has caused me much sorrow and many anxious and sleepless nights to reflect that I so unhappily failed to avail myself of that opportunity of saying what (as I did not then consider) it would not afterwards be permissible for anyone to say for me.

My desire in troubling you with this letter is, as I said at first, to free myself from hearing more to my disadvantage than I justly ought to hear.

I have the honour to be, Sir, your obedient humble servant, John Selby Watson

To the Editor of the Daily Telegraph

Sir, Amidst the general feelings of sympathy and pity for the unfortunate victim of this crime, and of commiseration for the unhappy murderer, one person who played a prominent and painful, yet unavoidable, part in this domestic tragedy has been entirely overlooked, although deserving of much consideration.

I refer to the Revd Mr Watson's servant, Ellen Pyne, whose evidence established the nature of the crime, and was so important in the interests of both justice and the criminal, that she was complimented in court upon the manner in which her valuable testimony was given.

While the case is so recent in the minds of your readers, it will be unnecessary to dwell upon the horrors and mental sufferings which she must have endured for months past.

With her mistress found cruelly murdered, her master charged,

204

tried, and convicted of the murder, and herself obliged day after day and week after week, to appear as one of the principal witnesses against Mr Watson, can it be wondered at that her health has become completely broken down, and her nervous system shattered, by the continuous concentration of her thoughts upon the circumstances surrounding this fearful crime? A long period must elapse before she will be able to resume – if, indeed, she will ever be able to resume – her original means of livelihood, and her friends, who formerly occupied a better position, can render her no assistance. She came under my care shortly after the murder, so that I have had ample opportunities of ascertaining how little amenable her case is to mere medical treatment. She urgently stands in need of absolute repose of mind and body, change of scene, and a general regimen wholly out of her reach without help.

Will you kindly allow these few words of appeal on her behalf to appear in your journal? The Revd Mr Henry Thompson, of Stockwell Park-road, S.W., who knew the young woman during her faithful service of the Watsons, will take charge of any subscriptions, which will be duly acknowledged, or contributions can be sent to yours obediently

Abbotts Smith, M.D. 7, Princes-street, Hanover-square W., Jan.27.

To the Editor of the Dublin Evening Mail

Sir, May I direct the attention of the public to the case of an aged lady, who has been left absolutely destitute, owing to the death of Mrs Watson, her only sister and from whom, for the last 26 years, she obtained her sole support – a pension of £17 per annum. The lady for whom I make this appeal is Miss Olivia Emily Armstrong, who resides at 80 Great Britain Street, and whose destitute circumstances are known to the Revd Mr Stamford, Rector of St Thomas's, and Mr Tiverton, soda-water manufacturer, 57 Upper Sackville Street, who have kindly consented to receive subscriptions on her behalf. I have already received towards the fund 10s from Mr John Moore Abbott, solicitor, Lower Gardener street; anonymous 10s6d; and from kind friends in Charlemont House, £2.

I am, Sir, your obedient servant
Joseph Bridgeman, 80 Great Britain Street.

PART 5

He was taken with eleven other convicts to Parkhurst prison on the Isle of Wight. They travelled to Portsmouth in a railway carriage whose blinds were drawn in case the sight of the occupants should give offence. He wore a handcuff on his wrist with a length of chain linking him to the next man in the line. When he sat down he held the slack like a woman gathering up her skirts. He stumbled climbing the gang-plank of the ferry and that daisy-chain of wicked men jerked him upright.

At Ryde, a covered cart, circled by screaming gulls, waited to drive them westward. After some miles the wind tore open the rotten flaps of the wagon and he glimpsed a stretch of puddled sand and the white crested sea. Turning a corner close by an orchard the cart entered a lane sprayed with blossom. In that whirling drift he watched his old life, that life of books and papers, ripped into a thousand pieces and scattered to the winds.

* * *

For six years Fraser petitioned the Home Office to review the old man's case. He was driven as much by guilt as pity; how could he ever forget that he had been a member of the Proprietary Board which had dismissed him from the school?

For over two years he corresponded with a man named Dempsey, a relation of Watson's living in Williamsburg, USA. Dempsey was a son-in-law of Abraham Watson who had emigrated thirty years before and was now dead. Dempsey had been willing, if the authorities had agreed to Watson's parole, to take responsibility for him and bring him to America. Fraser had written to the American Embassy in London, offering, should Watson be released, to put up money against his good conduct. In an attempt to show the Home Office that they were in earnest, he had even persuaded Dempsey to come to England.

He had written a long report in which he dwelt on Watson's

206

extreme age and declining health – prisoner Y 1395 was down to 133 lbs in weight and had asked for brown bread.

He had badgered Maudsley – head of the Mad Doctors brigade – and five other medical men, into signing a certificate stating that in their opinion Watson had been of unsound mind when he killed his wife. One of the signatories, Gibson, had said at the trial that he thought Watson sane. Gibson had once let a man out of an asylum as cured who had afterwards gone round saying that he was Jesus Christ and who had ended up trying to crucify himself on his mother's gatepost. Fraser had sent the certificate to the Home Secretary, and a copy to *The Times*.

None of his efforts had come to anything, except that for a time convict Y 1395 was allowed brown bread. Dempsey's approach had been turned down. No reason was given, but a friend of a friend who knew someone in the Penal Settlement Division had heard that it was on account of the murder having been 'a very bad one', and, advanced years or not, the prisoner's sentence must stand.

He believed that Watson still had moments of insanity. Only recently he had received the following letter:

Y.1395, John Watson
17th October, 1879

Dear Fraser,
He who is about to write a letter on this sheet of paper has nothing more to say of himself than that his 'condition' is much the same as when he last wrote on a similar sheet, and has little to say to him whom he addresses beyond an expression of hope and trust that he continues healthy and flourishing. He will therefore resume the subject of which he was previously treating – I read lately, in a scientific treatise, that light, which travels at the rate of 192,000 miles in a second in air, travels in the same time *in vacuo* 192, 500 miles. By what experiment this slight difference is supposed to be demonstrated, I cannot conceive. Indeed, from no theory regarding light is it apparent that light can exist in a vacuum. The old theory of solar emission, which considers light as oceans of luminous particles, makes the presence of such particles necessary whenever light appears; and the more modern theory, which represents light as the effect of motions in an ether, motions which in the notion of most men of science are undulatory or wave-like, but which I would fain believe to be mere impulses among the ethereal particles unproductive of waves, assumes that light can exist only when that

207

ether also exists. Under either hypothesis there can be no light in an absolute vacuity. We must suppose that the luminous ethereal particles are of so subtle a nature as to permeate the particles of glass, and, more or less, the particles of other transparent or partially transparent bodies, and that a receiver, though it be exhausted of air, may yet retain 'within' it the ether, its particles being of so fine an essence as to defy the power of operations that act on glass or material. The scientific experience of the present day seems to substantiate the old saying that 'nature abhors a vacuum', and experiments on light *in vacuo* may apparently be deferred *sine die*. We observed above that the sun's solar influence, or, in common phrase, the sun's beams, act in a straight line. But they are also to be regarded as having a lateral action. When the sun rises, his rays appear to shoot in a rectilinear course through the atmosphere from east to west. But how is it that rooms having windows looking towards the south or north, and plains and vales that lie beneath the path of the solar radiance, are partially enlightened by his influence even before he ascends the horizon? It would appear that his more direct influence, which, by agitating, in a greater degree, the particles of ether in its rectilinear course, produces the more brilliant light, causes, at the same time, in a less degree, an agitation among the particles around it, which, propagated to a certain extent, generates the first light which we call the dawn. So in the evening the twilight will be the result of the agitation left by the radiance of day; an agitation which gradually decreases till all the particles of the ether sink into tranquillity, and total darkness ensues. Such effect may be compared to that of the flight of an arrow, or of a bird through the sky, which will disturb not only the particles in its direct course, but also those bordering on it; a disturbance which will spread and continue till the resistance of ether particles near enough to act upon it forces it to subside. But a thousand questions may be asked concerning the causes of the most ordinary phenomena of light, to which no satisfactory answers can be given. How is it, for instance, when I stand before the mirror, I see my features and figure exactly depicted on its surface? I am not ignorant of what books on optics tell us, that rays fall from every part of my face and person upon the mirror, and that certain of these rays are sent back or reflected to the eye, the angle of incidence and reflection of such rays as reach the eye being equal, as is shown by the perpendicular raised on the surface of the mirror at the point of contact. But how am I to really know all this? How am I to know that rays of light perpetually proceed from every part of my face and person, falling upon every surface within a certain distance, and that, if the surface on which they fall happens to be what is called a reflecting one, a certain proportion of them are directed back at my organ of vision? They may, indeed, if they proceed from my person at all, be so directed back to me from every surface on which they alight, though I do not perceive them, and though the science of optics speaks only of their return from surfaces that show by reflection, as it is termed, the figures or objects before them or within their scope. There must certainly be some medium of communication between me and the mirror, or my figure, which I see more exactly as I move, would not be represented in it at all. There must also be a medium of communication between the mirror and every object animate or inanimate, whose figure is reflected on its surface. What he is asking is, what is the cause, the mode, the nature of communication? How is he to feel certain that the communication is effected by rays, and not by the simple impulses of the particles of ether surrounding his person and around any other reflected object? Obliged to break off. Titcombe, Bishop of Rangoon!! Sounding brass – but anything for a 'Colonial'. Sincerely Yours, J.S. Watson.

As far as Fraser was concerned such a letter spoke for itself and he had sent it to the Home Secretary, though he doubted it would be read, let alone have any effect.

He felt there was nothing more he could do for Watson, except to get books sent to him, and to keep in touch by letter. He had visited him twice. They had both been locked into cages separated by a narrow corridor patrolled by warders. He would have gone regularly – prisoners were allowed a twenty-minute visit every six months – but Watson had told him not to bother. No one else had ever been to see him.

On that first occasion Watson had complained of cracked spectacles – they had been trodden on in a fight – and on the second, and last, of his teeth. Fraser had been appalled at the thought of his former head master involved in a brawl, but Watson had explained it was an accident. He had merely got in the way and his glasses had fallen off. The springs in his teeth had broken through age.

Neither visit had been a success. Apart from the business of his teeth, Watson had spoken offensively of a book entitled *Classics for the Million*, written by Henry Grey and sent to the prison library at Grey's request. The prison chaplain had recommended it.

'And did you look at it?' asked Fraser uncomfortably.

'Certainly not,' replied Watson. 'The man was incapable of constructing a worthwhile paragraph. It's obviously unreadable.'

Fraser had felt relief; a glance inside the cover would have shown Watson how wrong he was. The book had already sold sixteen thousand copies. Fraser then told Watson of the sudden death of the Bishop of Winchester, Samuel Wilberforce, who had fallen from his horse. Fraser thought Watson would be upset, but all he said was, 'Poor old Soapy Sam, slippery to the last.'

Fraser remembered other news he had planned to impart. Henry Bohn had sold his business for a fortune and was growing roses and collecting pictures in Twickenham. William Longman had reached his peak and passed away as President of the Alpine Club. George Denman, who had been unable to translate a simple piece of Latin, was now a High Court Judge. Serjeant Parry still hadn't won a case ... None of it seemed worth the telling.

They said good-bye to each other through the bars. When the warder led Watson away Fraser was distressed to see that the old man was without stockings. Later he sent a letter of complaint to the prison, and money to pay for the mending of both spectacles and teeth.

*   *   *

He had been too old for the treadmill, and too slow at picking oakum. Besides, his hands were soft and bled easily. They had tried him in the kitchens, washing pots, but he caused trouble. He was always in a bad humour, tetchy and glum, and it had upset the other men to have someone so morose among them. He didn't think the work too menial, but he argued about how it should be done. He was very dogmatic, and irritatingly precise. What set him apart from the rest was not that he was an educated man and had consequently fallen further than most, but his refusal to accept that the standards of a previous life no longer applied.

The chaplain had thought that the library might be the most suitable place for him, though it was unusual for a man to gain this privilege so soon after beginning his sentence. Having looked through the books on the shelves Watson said they were all the work of third-rate authors, and that it would be a waste of anybody's time to read them. It was discovered that he had crossed out words and scribbled comments in the margins, and he was put on bread and water for it. He was brought low, though not in the manner expected, for he remarked that such a diet, for a short while at least, could actually be beneficial.

Finally they settled him in the tailor's shop,chalking out armholes for prison uniforms. They hadn't felt he could be trusted with scissors. Surprisingly he had taken to the work. Like father, like son, he thought, remembering the baptismal entry in the church register at Crayford, and the occupation of his unknown father.

He was convinced that finally he would be released. It was not a hope, but a belief; it was not his destiny to die in such a place.

But the years passed, and though his body remained alive he began to be afraid for his mind. He was never required to use it and he felt it withering like some dried-up plant. He knew that he must think of some intellectual exercise, some system of nourishment, if it was not to crumble away altogether. But what exercise, what system? He was without companionship and he had neither books nor writing materials, save for that one sheet of blue paper handed to him every six months when he was allowed to write a letter. He saw nothing but the tailor's shop, the yard and the walls of his cell. Those convicts who worked out of doors, in the vegetable gardens or in the quarry, were the best off. They soon stopped complaining of aches and blisters, and grew hardy. Exposed to the sea breezes, they slept like children. For them, time raced. For the rest, each day was a century and each night another one, and each man crawled across the terrible years like a snail along a highway.

Then one morning – he had been in Parkhurst for seven years – as he was walking from the prison to the chapel, the answer came to him. It was winter and still dark. The procession of yawning men was led by a prisoner who had been blind from birth. Only the day before, a small fir tree had been planted in a little plot of earth in the centre of the yard and, scarcely altering his step, the blind man skirted it and marched confidently to the chapel doors. This same man distributed the hymn books, walking in darkness as sure-footed as a cat. If a man who had lost his sight, Watson reasoned, could develop, by way of compensation, heightened sensitivity of hearing and touch, then surely a man physically restricted should have a greater capacity for mental expansion.

That night, lying in his hammock, he began to construct in his head a corner of the front room in his grandfather's house at Dartford. To some extent he had always lived in the mind, and he hadn't expected to have so little authority over his thoughts. He leapt like a frog from one figment to another. No sooner had he built the fireplace – he remembered there was an iron hook set in the stone – than he found himself going up the stairs to the room above, and before he had reached the landing he was suddenly transported to a cobbled forecourt which instantly changed into a platform at Euston railway station. He forced himself back into the house, only to find that he was in another room altogether, one of a later date, in a street in Dublin. And then he fell asleep as abruptly as if he had stepped off a cliff.

It was the same for months, this uncontrollable jumping from one image to another, followed by that quick fall into sleep. It puzzled him. In the past he had never had any difficulty in concentrating, and he had never felt tired by reading his books.

Then, one afternoon in the tailor's shop, he was caught in a broad beam of sunshine which shone through the fanlight of the roof. He remembered his preoccupation, some years before, with the causes of light. He had even written to Fraser about it, though he had never considered Fraser very bright and had certainly not expected a sensible reply. If anything, he had written the letter to irritate the prison authorities; it amused him to think of the prison censor racking his brains in an effort to understand its meaning. Now, blinking under that slanted and dazzling pillar of light, he thought his problem might be solved if he pursued again the relation of surfaces to reflection.

As soon as he was taken back to his cell he looked into the cracked oval of mirror on the wall and studied his face. He saw his features, the glass and a patch of the wall behind him. The mirror hung crookedly and he reached out to straighten it. No sooner had he done so than he realised that he had never seen, would never see, and in fact could not *ever* see the mirror he had just touched, any more than he could touch or would ever touch the mirror that he saw. To say that he both 'touched' and 'saw' the extension of the mirror, or of any other object in his cell, was merely to play with words. What he 'saw' and what he 'touched' had nothing but the name in common. He certainly couldn't touch the light all around him, and wasn't even sure that he was 'seeing' it, for when he shut his eyes he retained, if only for a brief moment, an image of his face and that patch of wall behind his head. If 'seeing' was independent of either eye or glass, then 'unseen' light must be the conductor of visual shapes whether internal or external. If he was to 'see' he must fill his head with light. But how was he to trap the light for longer than a fraction of a second?

He began by imagining that his mind was a black box with the merest pin-prick of light showing at the top right-hand corner. The difficulty was to rid himself of the image of the box and to focus on the light. When he had succeeded in doing so he enlarged the aperture, and now he had a prism of light into which he put a straight-backed chair. Having mastered the shape of the chair and held on to its image for perhaps half a minute, he placed the chair on a rug and the rug on a floor. The concentration required was enormous.

Sometimes he almost gave up in despair. He was surrounded by so many ruffians, so much meanness of spirit and ugliness of expression, that it was a Herculean task to lift himself out of the darkness. Often, when he had just managed to break free, and was standing in a sunlit field or swimming on the surface of a bright river, some groan or curse from the adjoining cell distracted him and he was dropped into blackness again. At such times, peering up at the barred window he would tell himself that it was always there, that shining, illuminated world, whether he could see it or not.

Gradually he became more successful. He was able to retain the light and to prolong his stay in the place he had put himself. He furnished a room in Dublin and filled the shelves with books. He arranged them first so that the authors were in alphabetical order – Seneca, Sismondi, Skelton – and then took them all down and replaced them in order of subject – Beekeeping, Binary Arithmetic, Biology, Birds etc. The pleasure it gave him was immense. His appetite improved and once or twice he was seen to be smiling as he bent over his bench in the tailor's shop.

He went back to Guernsey, where he had once been an assistant, and tried to conjure up the French master with whom he had been friendly and whose name he had forgotten; but he couldn't remember his face. Then one summer afternoon, when he was walking along the beach below the college, he noticed a shell lying at the water's edge. He bent down to pick it up and was instantly in the dark, in his hammock, the sweat running into his eyes though the cell was bitterly cold. He felt afraid, as if he had been exposed to some frightful danger.

After that he was careful to remain in his room in Dublin, although he couldn't avoid going to the window. He was drawn there, and spent hours watching the people in the street below. There was a particular woman wearing a blue dress who came out of the house opposite at the same time each day and loitered on the corner as if waiting for someone. She stood with one gloved hand tapping the column of the street lamp. He tried to keep away from the window, resolutely sitting down at his desk to read, but after no more than a minute he found himself back at the window, his book forgotten.

He decided he would go out and speak to her. He changed his clothes and brushed his hair. On the stairs he passed a cat licking its paws in a pool of sunlight. Even before he had crossed the street the woman turned to look at him; it was as though she already knew him.

He began to court her. She was taller than him and blushed easily, and when he looked up at her rosy profile, in particular at the chaste curve of her mouth, he thought he had never been so happy. Every day they walked to the cathedral and strolled about the square. With her at his side he noticed everything – the green fruit on the apple woman's barrow, a lame pigeon strutting lopsided in the shadows of the lime trees, the drunken man snoring beside the fountain. In the evenings they walked to the river. Nothing altered, not even the position of the sun. The crippled pigeon hopped in a circle round a rotten plum, and the same drunken man, a bottle between his knees, sat with his back to the water.

She was always silent, and he believed she was thinking intensely about him. He made up his mind to invite her to his room. If she had refused he would have taken her anyway, but she came of her own free will. When he leant forward to kiss her she blushed more than ever. He had imagined a delicious continuance of time during which he would gradually bring her to accept more intimate embraces, but no sooner had he taken her in his arms than she clung to him, trembling violently. Her lips burned. The room melted away and he lay on a headland with the sound of the sea in his ears, that fiercely burning mouth pressed to his heart.

He tried to begin again, banishing her into the street and going out to meet her for the first time, but it was of no use. She had always known him. He was love-sick and he tried to tell her what she meant to him, but at the simplest endearment, the slightest contact, her body prepared itself for surrender, and afterwards, in that drowsy state following on physical pleasure, she lay beside him as if dead.

Outside the circle of his arms she was restless and uneasy. She was incapable of reading a book. He introduced a friend into the

214

room, a student from Trinity College, but she behaved as though he wasn't there, and pushing between them perched herself on his knee and wrapped her arms so tightly about his neck that he could scarcely breathe. He attempted to play draughts with her; she laid her hand suggestively on his arm and sighed, and when he pretended not to notice she swept the pieces to the floor. She never spoke to him of her own accord, never said she cared for him, not unless he put the words into her mouth.

And now he looked oddly, critically at her. Her nose was too big and her eyes not light enough. Often there was a sour smell in the creases of her skin. She knew he had changed towards her. He watched her eyes fill with tears which spilled down her crimson cheeks. He tried to comfort her, holding her close and caressing her, but her lips sucked at his neck and her body trembled so much that he actually heard her teeth rattling. He pushed her down on all fours and entered her from behind, and he thought, I am an animal, an animal, I am mating a bitch, and he looked down at the speckled marks on her back and flung himself off her in revulsion.

Then they both cried, she no doubt because he had hurt her, and he because it had all gone, all that enchantment and forgetfulness of self, and there was nothing of love left in him. He despised her. She had never cried before.

Rather than meet her again he took to walking all night about his cell, and if she slipped into his mind, rather than abuse her he would push her out of the window or down the stairs.

* * *

He asked to see the Governor and said that he needed intellectual stimulation. He would like to translate some work of a scholarly nature. His arrogance had left him now, and he said he would take it as a privilege if permission could be given. The Governor replied that a decision was not up to him but to the Directors of Convict Prisons.

Watson wrote to Fraser and asked him to visit. He knew that nothing would be done unless he had someone on his side. When he was first put in prison he had wanted a Greek Testament and it had taken two years to get it, and even then it was not given to him directly but placed in the library. He had thought that unfair. The prison was full of Jews, all of whom were supplied with Hebrew Bibles, though most of them could scarcely read their own names, let alone Hebrew. Fraser had paid for the Greek Testament.

As soon as he was locked into the cage in the visitors' room, he called out to Fraser, 'I must have books.'

'What sort of books?' asked Fraser.

Watson told him that he was anxious to do some translating. He seemed very excited and beat on the bars of the cage. 'I have been thinking of it for some time,' he said.

'What books in particular?' asked Fraser.

'I should like to begin with Seneca. No doubt you have forgotten, but his letters and essays are eminently suitable to a man in my position.'

'I haven't altogether forgotten,' Fraser said. He had to shout to make himself heard. There was a woman sitting next to him with a child at her feet. It was bawling and drumming its heels on the floor.

'Then you'll remember he believed that if a man was to develop that gift of reason which separates him from the animals, he should learn to go without everything save the necessities of life.'

'Yes,' said Fraser. He was shocked by Watson's vigour, by his almost indecent will to survive. The man was approaching his eightieth year and was practically a skeleton. Recently he had suffered an attack of nettle-rash which had put him in hospital; the backs of his hands were rubbed raw. Even now he was scratching.

'Of course, at the time of writing,' said Watson, 'Seneca was a very wealthy man.' He lectured Fraser for ten minutes on Stoicism, and concluded by saying that he didn't think Seneca had slept with the Emperor's mother. It was a lie put about by Publius Suilius Rufus.

From the end of the corridor came the clanging of a hand-bell. The warders rushed forward to unlock the cages.

'I can't promise anything,' said Fraser. 'But I will try.'

Above the rattling of the keys he heard Watson shout, 'I must have them. Otherwise I shall go mad.'

Fraser wrote to the Directors of Convict Prisons. He said he didn't see what harm it would do to give an elderly man reading matter which could only uplift and sustain him in what was an otherwise miserable existence. It wasn't as if John Watson was asking for extra rations of food or a supply of tobacco. He himself would provide the cost of books and writing materials.

Six months passed. He wrote again, and after a considerable

delay received an answer to the effect that permission had been withheld. It was a question of censorship. Anything written down on paper had to be rigorously studied by the prison staff, in case it contained any coded references to escape or other breaches of security. It should be realised that it would require special abilities, notably a knowledge of classical languages, to keep pace with any literary work undertaken by prisoner Y 1395.

The notion that Watson was thought capable of plotting an escape from Parkhurst struck Fraser as so absurd that he nearly informed the newspapers. His wife stopped him. She said he had done enough – the old man would surely die soon.

He wrote to Watson, telling him as gently as possible that it might be some time before the books arrived. He must be patient.

Watson never replied.

*   *   *

Shortly after dawn Watson climbed on to a three-legged stool and looking out of the window saw a rabbit crouched in the yard, sniffing at a tuft of grass that sprouted between the flag-stones.

Just then the sun topped the wall and poured directly into the courtyard. A moment before, the rabbit had been a grey lump on a grey slab – now, fur tipped with light, it shimmered like a jewel. The transformation seemed to him miraculous, and he craned forward. The stool jerked from under him and fell over, and he was left hanging from the bars, his forehead pressed to the wall. He grimaced, afraid to let go, though he was only a foot or so above the floor. Then the strength went out of his arms and he dropped safely enough.

At his bench in the tailor's shop he couldn't help mentioning the rabbit to the convict next to him. Generally he kept to himself and had hardly addressed a dozen words to him in as many years. He used the word 'beautiful'. The man looked at him dully and licked his lips. 'I'd sell my grandmother for a nice bit of rabbit,' he said.

Later that morning Watson felt ill. He slumped forward and his piece of chalk rolled across the floor. He was allowed back to his cell. When they brought him his dinner at midday he couldn't eat it. It wasn't like him to leave his food and the warder said he would fetch the doctor.

He dozed a little, lying in his hammock. Then the chair appeared. He opened his eyes immediately – he had done with living in his head – but he was tired and his eyes closed again. The chair came back, and now there was a woman sitting in it. A man stood beside her, looking down at his hands with an expression of disgust.

The woman's chin was sunk on to her breast so that her face was hidden. The top of her head was spangled with fiery specks of light, and for a moment he thought of the rabbit. Then he was in the room with her and he saw the blood bubbling from her head.

The man said, 'Take her into the next room. I'm afraid of someone coming back and seeing her.' He protested that it was none of his business, but the man insisted.

He bent over the back of the chair, his arm round the woman's chest to stop her from toppling forwards. There was so much blood gone from her that he couldn't think why she was so heavy. He had to drag the chair to the door, tilting it like a wheel-barrow; her head fell backwards and her slippers dangled above the carpet. When he got her out on to the landing a dog bounded upstairs, barking and leaping. He kicked out and caught it on the shoulder with his boot, and it squealed and skittered away down the stairs. He left the woman on the chair in the next room and went halfway downstairs to look for the dog – it was a cruel thing to have kicked it. He held out his hands in front of him and saw that the cuffs of his shirt were stuck to his wrists. And yet his hands were quite steady. He called up to the man, though he knew in his bones there wouldn't be any answer – while he had been dragging the chair into the next room the man had slipped from the house.

He realised that he was in a dreadful situation. If the body was discovered he would be suspected of a crime. Someone was coming back, and he had to be prepared. He must behave as though nothing had happened.

He returned to that room, hoping it was a dream, but she was still there on the chair, one bloody fist clenched on her knee. Squatting, he looked up into her face and was astonished at her disgruntled expression. She wore her brains on the top of her head like a squashed flower, like a bunch of crimson ribbon.

He noticed that the furniture was dusty and the bed-sheets discoloured. There was a papier-mâché box on the bedside table with nothing inside but cheap jewelry – a bracelet, a beetle brooch, an enamelled pin with the Crystal Palace stamped on it. On the mantel-shelf – the fire was out – was a collection of combs, a curious shell, and a miniature of an old man wearing a black wig and a hunting coat.

Suddenly he sensed danger. He picked up the shell and took it into another room. It was a precautionary measure. He was worried in case some sound, some last lascivious cry, had lodged within its crusted ear. He would get rid of it when he had the opportunity.

And now he had to work quickly. He found a sponge and rubbed at the carpet where the chair had stood. Then he wiped the paint work. His boots were covered in some sticky substance and he found another pair under a bed and changed into them. He went downstairs to the basement and washed his hands under the tap. He took off his coat and was about to remove his shirt when he was seized with a fit of shivering. There were some scissors on a nail beside the window, and, pulling down his sleeves, he cut off first one cuff and then, with difficulty, the other. The material was as stiff as a board. He put the pieces in his pocket, and throwing the sponge under the sink went upstairs again.

On the floor in the library, half hidden under the folds of the window curtains, he discovered an old pistol. He supposed the man had shot the woman with it. He hid it in a chest of drawers, under the man's shirts.

Somebody knocked at the front door. He called out, 'Wait, wait,' and ran up and down the passage, not knowing what to do. The knocking was repeated. He was sure they would be able to tell by his face that there was something terribly wrong in the house, and he extinguished the light in the hall before opening the door. He let in a friend; he had nothing to fear from her.

When the girl had gone to bed he waited several hours before going in to attend to the woman. She seemed to have shrunk; all her bright blood had turned black. He tipped her out of the chair and she fell sideways. He propped her upright in a corner and threw an old blanket over her and carried the chair back into the library. He cursed the man who had run away.

Afterwards – it was daylight – he went out into the streets and looked for a chemist's shop. He was not sure any more that he wanted to live. He was in a state of such frightful anxiety that he didn't know how much longer he could endure it.

He remembered that the man had a great many books, and he called on someone and asked if there was any space in the attic, but apparently there were women up there. Whatever the man had done, his books had to be looked after, so he went into a trunk-maker's shop and ordered a packing-case.

When he got back to the house he told the girl that he might be unwell at a later date. He was thinking of her; it was unacceptable that someone so young and so kind should find him dead without warning. She said, 'I have been upstairs and tidied your boots away.'

'Thank you,' he replied.

'I have put them in the wardrobe.'

'The proper place,' he said.

'I saw her coat, her bonnet and her outdoor shoes,' she said. Then she gave a loud cry and immediately clapped her hand over her mouth.

'You're a good girl,' he said. 'I know what I'm doing.'

He went up to the bedroom and removed the stopper from the medicine bottle, intending to do away with himself there and then – but he couldn't bring the bottle to his lips. He had no idea how long it would take for the poison to act, and he shrank from the thought of a lingering death.

He walked to the railway station and stood on the platform waiting for a train to come. It was night time and there was no one about: he could hear the rumble of traffic and, far off, the frantic barking of a dog. He believed that when the train came he would throw himself under its wheels, but as the hours passed and still the train did not come, he began to feel relief. It struck him as absurd that he should die in place of someone else. Besides, what harm would it do to wait one more day? He went to the edge of the platform and taking the rags from his pocket threw them on to the rails. Then he returned to the house.

As soon as he let himself into the hall he heard them arguing upstairs. Her voice was louder than his. He stood on the landing, listening to them.

'My mother made my father happy,' the woman said. I remember a particular smile.'

'You won't remember mine,' the man said, 'particular or otherwise. You've not caused me to smile in twenty years.'

He was glad that they had come back, and entered the room with the intention of averting a tragedy. Neither of them took any notice of him. The woman was holding a pistol on her lap. She said, 'Unlike you, I was dismissed years ago. Now you know how it feels.'

'You're drunk,' the man said.

'You've never given me anything,' she said. 'Not love, not friendship, not hope. Never, never, never.'

'You're drunk,' the man repeated.

She lurched to her feet then and stabbed at his chest with the pistol; the barrel was so rusty and full of dirt that it left a grey smear on his coat. They stood there, swaying. The man wrenched the gun from her and raising his arm struck her on the head with it. She fell to the floor. Throwing down the pistol, the man went out of the room.

'Help me,' the woman said. She struggled to her knees and reaching out clutched the gun to her breast. The blood ran in stripes down her face.

He took her in his arms and held her upright. He wept for her. At that moment the love he felt was so complete that he thought his heart must break. But she pushed him away from her. 'It's too late,' she said. 'You've never given me anything.'

'You're drunk,' he said. 'And your breath stinks.'

She ran at him, jabbing at his chest with the pistol. He raised his arm to fend her off. She was gobbling like a turkey, working her jaws up and down, gathering saliva to hawk at him. Revolted, he punched her on the shoulder, and a gob of spittle dripped from her mouth on to his manuscript. She was winded, and he was ashamed of himself. He thought the contest was over, but she lunged at him again, eyes dilated, that wretched pistol still stabbing at him, catching him in the ribs, the stomach. I can sink no lower, he thought, listening to the dog raking its paws against the panel of the door.

They were standing between the window and his desk. In front of the window was set an armchair covered in moroccan leather: one of its castors was missing and it stood lopsided, jammed against the skirting board for support. Just then the coals in the grate settled and there was a sudden leap of light across the blinds.

'You had nothing to give,' she said. 'You're a cold fish.'

A curious thing – she had a brown mole on her cheek, with a hair sprouting from it. It was the shortest hair imaginable, and yet, when the pistol swung up and caught him on the ear, it seemed to him, looking at her face through tears of agony, that it had grown immeasurably. He took the gun from her and hit her repeatedly on the head. She clung to him, slithering down his chest, his stomach. A strand of her hair caught on his waistcoat buttons. She was moaning. He was horrified at the sound, and he hit her again and again to finish her off. Her hand clutched at his leg and he jerked her away with his knee and continued to strike at her, and still she held on to him. He pushed her down into the chair and struck her across the knuckles. At last she let him go.

It was done now and he was glad. He had not harmed her, merely rid her of the bad things that had kept them apart.

There was nothing in his head but light. He wondered if he was in the presence of God. He had never known anything so dazzling, so infinitely bright.

*   *   *

July 5th, 1884
Medical certificate sent from Parkhurst Prison to Directors of Convict Prisons: Re Prisoner Y 1395. Further imprisonment will probably not affect the life of the above, who is not likely to survive the next few days. Medical certificate enclosed.

July 6th, 1884
The Home Office, London, to Directors of Convict Prisons: Is this the clergyman and schoolmaster who killed his wife in Stockwell in 1871 and was very nearly hanged for it?

July 7th, 1884
Directors of Convict Prisons to the Home Office, London: Yes. Prisoner Y 1395. John Watson. He is in the prison hospital.

July 8th, 1884
The Home Office, London, to Directors of Convict Prisons: As his disease is said to be erysipelas from a cut on the ear it might be as well to ask the Governor of prison how it occurred, whether by accident or self-inflicted.

July 9th, 1884
Parkhurst Prison to Directors of Convict Prisons: He is dead now — there is no reason to suppose it was self-inflicted — he cut his ear when falling accidentally out of his hammock — on his tin pot.